A DOUBLE BLAST OF HOT SHOOTIN'
AND EVEN HOTTER LOVIN'
IN ONE GIANT SPECIAL EDITION!

FIRE!

Spur and Abby crept around the burning house, staying back in the shadows away from the firelight. On the far side, Spur spotted a man near a tree in the yard. He held a six-gun. Spur threw a rock at the nearest window. It broke and the man by the tree fired five rounds through the broken window.

Spur pulled the trigger on his .45 once. The man near the tree screamed and went down, slammed backward by the force of the heavy slug. Spur surged up to the arsonist and kicked the gun out of his hand, then dragged the man forward so he could tell for sure who he was.

"Rawlins, you slimy bastard." Spur punched him in the jaw.

Abby ran up and kicked him twice in the stomach. "You burned down my house. Nothing can save it now."

"I'm shot," Rawlins howled. "You've got to stop the bleeding. You shot me."

"Lucky I didn't aim for your heart," Spur said. "You got a slug through your shoulder. It won't kill you. But I might before I get you to the jail."

Other *Spur Giants* from *Leisure Books:*
KLONDIKE CUTIE
HIGH PLAINS PRINCESS
DENVER DARLIN'
MINT-PERFECT MADAM
TALL TIMBER TROLLOP
PHOENIX FILLY

SPUR

WILDERNESS WANTON

DIRK FLETCHER

LEISURE BOOKS   NEW YORK CITY

A LEISURE BOOK®

June 1994

Published by

Dorchester Publishing Co., Inc.
276 Fifth Avenue
New York, NY 10001

SPUR

WILDERNESS
WANTON

Chapter One

A rifle shot shattered the Montana mountain stillness just as the lumbering Concord stagecoach rounded the bend at Waterman's draw and straightened for the stiff uphill pull. The heavy .50 caliber Sharps slug caught shotgun-guard Big Ed Johnson in the chest, bored through his heart and tore out his back, taking blood, bone and tissue with it. He jolted to the rear over the driver's seat, sprawled for a moment on top of the stage, then slid off the side of the bouncing coach, and tumbled in death to the dusty Montana road.

Driver Ben Whitmore ducked and swore as Big Ed died; then he saw three armed men ride into the road ahead with their rifles aimed at him. A quick look to each side confirmed that there were no more holdup men. Ben spat a

Dirk Fletcher

stream of tobacco juice between the first team of horses and pretended to pull back on the twelve leather reins in his gloved hands, as if he were stopping the coach. At the last moment, as the team swept toward the gunmen, he yelled at the lead team and whacked the reins on their backs. The stage careened to the side of the narrow trail and missed two of the surprised robbers, but the lead horse on the right slammed into the third bandit's mount and jolted him to the ground. The other two were too surprised to react at once, but within seconds they got their horses under control and rode up the rise after the stage.

The riflemen were now behind the coach and tried to aim for the driver, but Ben hunkered down below the seat near the footboard and sat on the tool sack, whipping his team of six.

Inside the Concord, the four passengers reacted differently. A burly man in his forties promptly jerked a Remington New Line revolver from his gunbelt, pushed aside the canvas curtain over the window, and fired at the robbers behind them.

The only woman in the rig, a pretty girl in her early twenties, gripped the seat tightly and frowned. The man beside her had fear clawing at his face, and his hands shook.

The third man, Spur McCoy, caught the canvas at his window, pulled it inside, then snapped a shot from his Colt .45 six-gun at the nearest bandit. The heavy slug hit the rider just under his shirt pocket, glanced off a rib upward, tore into his heart, shredded the pulmonary artery

8

and the large aorta, continued through his vertebra, shattered a pair of tightly muscled bones, and exploded out his back. Bone fragments and blood sprayed the ground as the man slammed out of his saddle, fell off the running mount and rolled into the weeds and seedling Douglas fir trees along the side of the road.

Spur fired at another rider, who swerved just as the hammer fell. A dozen rifle rounds pounded into the stage. One shattered the doorframe just over Spur's head. He quickly pushed the woman passenger to the floor between the seats, and shoved her helpless male companion on top of her for protection. Then Spur ducked low and shot twice out the window as the volume of fire increased and the coach careened half off the trail.

The rig tilted, slowed and tilted more to the right until it was nearly at a 45-degree angle. It came to a stop with two wheels mired in a soft spot at the side of the trail.

Spur looked over the door of the slanted coach. His side was high and he could find no target. He looked at the shooter near the other window and saw him sprawled on the forward-facing seat, a small bluish-black hole over his right eye. His face showed dubious surprise at such a sudden death.

The firing outside stopped.

"You in the coach with the guns. Throw them out now, or the driver gets a round in the head. You hear me, heroes?" The voice came heavy, hoarse, demanding. Spur peered over the edge of the window again. All he could see were the fringes of fir trees near the mountainous track and the upslope of the road ahead. He had no target. A rifle cracked and he heard the slug hit the coach above him.

"Fer Christ's sakes, men. We've got no chance. Throw out your damned guns or I'm a dead man." The voice came from just above Spur's head. It had to be from the driver. Spur lifted his brows, swore softly, and threw his favorite Colt six-gun out the window.

"Now the other handgun," the gravel voice demanded. "They was another shooter in there."

Spur found the dead man's Remington five-shot, forced it from a death-grip, and threw it out. He heard horses moving up. One whinnied in the still, crisp mountain air.

"Everybody out!" a younger voice snapped.

Spur slid past the couple on the floor and unlatched the low side door. It swung open by itself. He levered over the dead body and stepped to the ground. Then he helped out the young woman. She was slender, with a strong, pretty face and lots of blonde curly hair draped around her shoulders. Her features were grim now, but curiously unafraid.

Behind her, the young man crawled out of the tilted coach and staggered, shaking so hard he could barely stand. A mounted, masked man herded them to the other side of the stage in the dust of the trail. Ben, the driver, waited there, his eyes glazed with frustration and fury.

"Where's the other owlhoot?" a masked rider asked.

"Dead," Spur answered. "Check for yourself."

"Yahoo!" a young robber whooped. "Knew I nailed that bastard on my side. Just knew it."

Spur McCoy stood with the rest, watching the outlaws. He was a tall man, just over six-two, a little lean at 185 pounds and in excellent physical condition. He had the reflexes of a cat and a quick mind, and he wore a black broadcloth suit, string tie, white ruffled shirt, and a fancy silver-and-black vest. Spur watched the stage bandits with a keen interest.

Three more men rode around the front of the coach with six-guns trained on the stage passengers standing in the heat of Montana's June sun.

All five bandits wore masks, kerchiefs pulled up so only their eyes showed. Automatically Spur memorized what he could see of each face, the clothes worn and the size and color of the horses. He would write it down later.

The leader was a large man, over six-four and heavy, with a dirty gray, high-crowned Texas hat and a denim jacket. He sat a sturdy black that could carry his weight with ease.

"Get that damn strongbox down," he ordered. Two men jumped off their mounts onto the driver's seat and drove the rig back on the trail. They knew exactly where to look. A moment later they pulled the tool sack away; behind it lay a metal box the size of a carpet bag. It was chained in place. Three revolver shots sounded and the men cheered, pulled the box off the stage, and handed it to the ground.

"Now we see if this all was worth it," the

gravel-voiced leader said. He flipped open the box and grinned. Spur could see the green printed bundles of bills. The heavy man chuckled and told one of his men to put the loot into the saddlebags on three horses. Then he looked at the passengers.

"Well, well, what the hell do we have here?" He stared at the woman. "What's your name, pretty girl?"

"I'm Mrs. Leroy Davis."

The bear of a man slid off his horse and stood in front of her, then reached forward and put one hand roughly on her firm, full breast.

She gasped and looked at his hand. Then her face relaxed, but at the same time it took on a new hardness that matched her inner resolve.

"If you're a gentleman, you'll remove your hand."

"I ain't no gent. Now what the hell is your girl name, pretty little one?"

"Opal. It's obvious that you're not a gentleman and not much of a real man either because you have to use force to get what you want."

He snorted and shook his unkempt head at her. "Little sweet tit, a real man takes what he wants, from banks, from stages, from cash boxes like this one, and from women. Maybe you'd like to show me how brave you are and make me move my hand."

Her foot slashed out under her gingham dress and cracked him sharply on the leg just above his boot-top. He jumped back, his face red as the setting sun. His hand moved to the butt of his six-gun.

The others watched him as he obviously struggled with his temper, which he finally controlled.

"You fucking little bitch!" he roared in his gravelly voice. He slapped her hard. Opal swayed to one side, took a step away from the force of the blow, then moved her foot back when she had her balance. She didn't move again. Two of the men came up behind him, their weapons ready.

He looked at them. "Keep everybody else covered. I got to take me some time out and teach this little bitch a lesson she won't never forget. Never kick a man, slut!" he shouted in her face. "Never!" He roared the last word, his mouth an inch from her nose.

Then he moved so quickly she couldn't stop him. He grabbed her around the waist, boosted her over his shoulder like a sack of flour, and carried her off the road 20 feet to a patch of grass under some tall fir trees. He bent and dumped her on her back in the shade.

"Don't move, you stay right there." He knelt beside her. "You know what we're gonna do, don't you little Opal, little sweet tit?"

Opal stared at him, her arms folded across her breasts and her legs locked firmly together. Now her flashing green eyes were angry, sparking off energy, but she tightened her mouth and said nothing.

"Hell yes, you know. I'm gonna tear off your clothes, every stitch until you're naked as a skinnydipping girl. Then I'm gonna eat up your bare tits, chew them beauties half off, and when

I spread your legs, you're gonna get done by the best, so you'll know who the goddamned boss is around here."

"No, please don't."

"Don't what, fancy bitch? Don't fuck you?"

"That too, but please don't tear off my clothes. I don't have that many. I'll . . . I'll take them off if you want me to."

"Well, I'll be damned!" He sat back and pulled off his hat, wiping sweat off his forehead with his sleeve. His mask was still in place. "You'll take your clothes off, all of them? You a fucking whore or something?"

"Certainly not! I'm simply not frightened of you, nor am I awed by or fearful of sexual intercourse. It's a natural bodily function. Neither am I a silly young virgin."

The bearish man rocked back on his heels and laughed. He leaned up and petted her breasts. "You sure as hell ain't no prissy virgin, so strip, Opal sweet tits. Take it all off right now and let's see what's inside the package."

She sat up, her shoulders squared proudly, her head erect as a queen's, dignified and aloof. "You might take me, violate my body, but you won't get any pleasure from it." She looked toward the coach. "You'll make the other men go down the road a ways, won't you?"

The leader laughed. "Hell yes, good idea. Almost forgot about the boys. Hey, all of you men," he shouted. "Everybody come over here. The stage guys, too. Come on over, we got us a free tit show coming up. All you guys get to watch. Then if you like what you see, you can

14

stay and learn how a real man puts his meat to this little woman here. No extra charge, hurry for best viewing."

His masked men prodded the three captives off the road to the patch of grass and told them to sit.

Opal had just unfastened the first few buttons on the top of her traveling dress. She watched them come, then looked away, but she didn't hesitate, opening the bodice all the way to her waist. She lifted the skirt from under her legs where she sat and pulled the brown-and-white dress over her head. Under it she had on two white petticoats and a wrapper.

"Every damn stitch!" the leader roared in his rumbling, heavy voice. "I take all my women bare-assed."

She knelt, looked away from the men, and lifted off the two petticoats both at once. That left the wrapper around her breasts and her waist-to-knee white drawers. He motioned to her to stop. The leader moved up close, loosened the wrapper, pushed his hands under it, and grinned.

"Can't let her show everything all at once. This part is all right. She's only got two tits up there. Didn't want to scare any of you boys if she had three!"

Some of the masked men laughed.

Slowly he took the wrapper off her and let her breasts swing out unrestrained. There were murmurs of approval from the men, who watched from a dozen feet away.

Opal kept looking at the woods. She had felt

his hands on her breasts and shivered slightly, then sensed him taking off the wrapper. It didn't matter. None of this mattered. She stared at one tree and tried to see every minute detail of the bark.

She wouldn't think about this, she would not feel his hands on her tender breasts. It was as if no one were watching. She wouldn't feel a thing.

Spur McCoy frowned as he looked at the man who had been beside Opal on the stage. He must be her husband. What the hell kind of man was he who would let these outlaws rape his wife without a single protest?

Spur looked at the husband again. The man's face was set in an expressionless pose. Something was wrong here. Maybe they weren't married after all.

He frowned and watched the men around him through keen green eyes. Spur had black hair, was clean-shaven and wore a black, low-crowned Stetson with silver Mexican pesos strung around the headband. At 32 years of age, he was in peak form and had an open, friendly face that women usually described as ruggedly handsome.

Ever since he had stepped down from the stage, Spur had been looking for a slip-up, any relaxation or mistake by the masked men who guarded them. None of them had worried about their dead comrade. They didn't even check on him, and he lay where he had fallen. Now they crowded around the pair on the grass, offering ribald comments and giving unneeded advice.

Wilderness Wanton

The one masked man designated as the guard for the three prisoners had put away his six-gun and held a Remington repeating rifle loosely in one hand.

Possible, Spur thought.

Spur lifted cautiously to his knees, staring at the pair on the grass. The leader spread across the half-naked girl, chewing on a breast. The guard nearby watched the sex show, too.

It could work.

Casually, Spur looked around for cover. Down the incline from the road ten yards stood a thicket of brush and four Douglas fir trees about two feet thick. Between him and safety there was no cover, not a rock, a ditch or a tree. It was a long, slim chance. It was a gamble with his life as the stakes.

Then he thought about the strongbox. For $10,000 or whatever was in that chest, this band of cutthroats just might decide to do the job cleanly and leave no witnesses. One was already dead. That left only five more to kill. Spur watched the leader.

He had no idea who the man was. He was not a wanted bandit Spur had seen. Spur decided the gamble must be taken, that he had no real choice. If he waited, they all would die.

The big man dropped between Opal's spread legs on the green grass. He had loosened his pants and pulled them down.

"Now, little girl, you gonna feel what a real man is like slamming into you. First, we get off them damn drawers." He untied the strings at her waist and began to pull the cotton garment

17

down over her hips. He grinned as the lowering
fabric exposed her crotch and the triangle of soft
brown pubic hair.

"Hey, that's the spot I've been hunting!" he
screeched. "Look at that, men, ain't that a
glorious sight?"

Opal closed her eyes. "If you're talking about
me, I can't hear you. I've shut off all my senses.
I breathe, my heart beats, but I can neither see
nor hear nor smell, nor do I have any sense of
touch."

He grabbed one of her breasts and twisted it
until she screamed.

"Good with the words, ain't ya?" the outlaw
leader shouted. "Sit up, woman. Your tits are all
spread out, all flat. Sit up, I want to suck me a
good sugar tit again."

He pulled Opal up and pushed her forward
until her breasts hung down. The outlaw
groaned and bent under her, sucking on them.
Three of the bandits cheered.

The guard beside Spur laughed and tried
to clap as well. His rifle rested loosely on
one wrist.

Spur moved so quickly the robber hardly saw
him before he smashed into his chest with a
hard shoulder block, jerked the rifle from the
guard's limp hand and bowled him over into the
grass and weeds. It took the outlaw five seconds
to catch his breath before he could scream a
warning. By then Spur had charged halfway to
the cover of the trees.

He knew precisely where he wanted to go.
Spur darted five yards down the slight slope,

then charged six more yards across to the edge
of the timber, where he dove into the brush and
trees. Only two bullets whizzed past him as he
ran. Three more thudded into the fir tree above
him as he rolled over in the cover. He scrambled
to his knees behind the firs and checked the rifle.
He aimed it around the first big Douglas fir.

One of the outlaws was still in plain sight. The
leader hopped around on one foot, desperately
trying to get his pants up from his ankles. Spur
fired a .45-70 round through the big man's chest
and saw him jolt backwards to a sitting position.
The outlaw struggled with his handgun and tried
to bring it up to point at Opal. Spur aimed
and fired quickly. The second heavy lead slug
bored into the outlaw's left eye, shattered into
20 pieces as it churned into the criminal's brain,
pulping dozens of vital, life-sustaining centers.
The gun fell from his suddenly-dead fingers and
the outlaw slammed backwards, his bloody head
rolling onto the startled girl's bare stomach.

Spur had recognized the rifle he used, a
Remington-Keene. It carried eight cartridges
when the magazine was full. He hoped the
outlaw had refilled the long spring-loaded
tube under the barrel after they had stopped
the stage.

As soon as he fired the second time and
levered in a new round, Spur rolled to his
left behind another tree and looked around
it. No one moved. Someone whispered and the
sound carried, but Spur couldn't understand the
words. He spotted a man's shoulder behind a
tree near the road, but there wasn't enough of

him for a practical target. Spur guessed the bandits were getting ready to cross the open road. The horses were all on the other side.

It was still four against one. Spur positioned the front blade-sight of the rifle midway in the area where he guessed the shoulder man would run to cross the road. He waited. Spur heard some noise ahead and across the road, but he waited. His stare never left the target's estimated future position. After two minutes, the outlaw came out of the brush in a rush and pounded hard onto the stage road. Spur had guessed correctly. He followed the bandit only for a second with the sights of the rifle before he pulled the trigger.

The lead slug hit the robber under his churning left arm, splattered through his lung, nicked his heart, turned upward and to the rear, where it shattered the third dorsal vertebra. The man wearing the blue shirt and crushed black hat spun to his left and died before he flopped into the Montana stage-road's red dust.

Two shots answered Spur's deadly slug, but they were both wide and high. He levered in a fresh round and waited.

There came only silence. Spur lay in the foliage, watching and listening. He heard the girl talking quietly; then from beyond the stage and out of his line of sight he heard someone moving around. A man was behind the stagecoach with the horses. Spur heard the horses again, and then leather creaking as men mounted. There was nothing he could do. The stage and its six-horse team masked the outlaws completely.

20

A mount whickered. Spur heard three or four horses moving away through the brush and tall trees on the other side of the road. There was enough cover for them to get away, and Spur couldn't see them.

Spur lay there and didn't move for another five minutes. Then he lowered his rifle.

"Mrs. Davis," he called. "Mrs. Davis, are you all right?"

"Yes. My husband and I are on the road. The driver went into the woods."

"Yahoo!" Spur bellowed. "Stage driver. Ole, ole, out's in free."

"Don't got to holler, boy. Been right behind you for five minutes. Nice bit of work with that Remington."

"You all in one piece, driver?"

"Ben's the name. 'Peers as how I'm good. They missed you, too, I reckon."

"True. How are the other passengers?"

"All dressed again, worse the luck. She's a real looker."

"The big jasper with his pants down?"

"Deader than a used horseshoe nail. You right smart with that long iron."

"Tolerable. You suppose we can get the stage underway?"

"Reckon. Want to look at them other three mounts first. Hoping the killers missed one of them money-filled saddlebags."

"You round up the stock, I'll get the passengers."

Spur walked carefully to the spot where the attempted rape had taken place. Only the dead outlaw lay there. Spur took the six-gun from beside the dead man, pushed it in his own belt, then marked the spot on the road with three rocks piled on top of one another. The girl and her husband were at the side of the stage. He found the three other bodies. The driver came up and motioned toward the stageline's shotgun guard.

"Want to take Big Ed back with us. The bandits' bodies we'll leave for the sheriff."

It took them ten minutes to roll the guard's body in a tarp and tie him onto the Concord's rear boot. They put the dead passenger there as well and covered both with canvas, then roped them down securely. Together they found two more rifles, the company shotgun and Spur's favorite six-gun. He fastened the three saddle horses on a long lead line to the rear of the stage.

"The bastards took the right horses," Ben said. "Money's all gone. Gonna be holy hell to pay when we hit town. Old man Rawlins is gonna burn butts for a week over this."

"Who is Rawlins?"

"Who? The jasper who owned that box of bank notes they got away with. Some bunch of money in there. Nobody'd tell me how much. Gonna be one whole passel of trouble."

"Wasn't your fault, Ben."

"Sure it was. I ain't dead. That's what Rawlins will say. If I was a corpse he'd excuse me."

"Want me to ride up top with the shotgun?" Spur asked.

"Son, you done enough. You sit comfortable

Wilderness Wanton

inside. We should be at South Junction inside of a couple of hours. Them three who got away have what they want, the money. They won't bother us none."

Spur swung into the coach and sat down. Opal Davis looked at him squarely, with no embarrassment or sign of strain from her ordeal.

"Sir, I want to thank you for the outstanding way you outwitted those six outlaws. Remarkable. You saved our lives today. There is no real way for us to thank you."

"No thanks needed, ma'am."

Her husband sat beside her. He looked like a wall-eyed wild stallion ready to bolt at the first quick movement. He kept shooting worried glances out the windows and had to fight back tears. At last he held out his hand to Spur.

"You did save our lives today, mister. Those miscreants would have killed us all for half that much money."

"They certainly were thinking about that, Mr. Davis. Glad they were in no rush." As he talked, Spur reloaded his Colt .45 with rounds from his gun belt.

"Sir?" the girl asked.

Spur looked up.

"You know our names. I'm Opal and this is Leroy Davis. But we don't know your name."

"Spur McCoy, ma'am. I'm on my way to South Junction."

"We, too, get off there," she said. "We've purchased the closed-down newspaper, the *Clarion*, and will start publishing it soon. I'm the editor and Leroy handles the composition

23

and back-shop printing. The first edition will have a big story about you and what happened here today. Oh, did they get away with all of the money?"

Spur settled back in the seat, let the $20 low-crowned black Stetson slide most of the way over his eyes.

"Yes, ma'am, they did. Picked out the right mounts. They had protection behind the stage. Nothing I could do about it."

She frowned, and the first hint of worry that he had seen there all day crossed her face. She glanced at him quickly and for just a moment her guard dropped and he saw how vulnerable and frightened she really was. Her defenses snapped back in place at once.

"Oh, I didn't mean to insinuate that it was your fault."

"No, ma'am. No offense taken." A touch of a smile lit Spur's face and the hat slid lower. The view of the pretty woman with nerves of steel and a will that must be ten times stronger faded from his sight.

Chapter Two

E. B. Guthrie lay dead still in a clutch of brush near a creek that meandered down a still green valley in central Montana Territory. He watched the small ranch a half mile up the way. Smoke came from the chimney of a modest log cabin. A man left a barn near a pole corral and went into the cabin.

E.B. waited another half hour and saw no one else. He grinned and nodded. "Yep, we won't have no damn trouble here. Quick and easy."

He slid away from the edge of the brush so he would be concealed from sight and worked along behind the green shield until he could see his covered wagon, parked another quarter mile down where the larger valley was joined by the small one that held the ranch.

E.B. walked quickly toward the wagon. He

was forty, but it was impossible to tell that through the layers of dirt and grime he had built up on his body and his clothes. Dirty strings of hair sprouted from his sunburned scalp. He scratched his chest, then his crotch as he came up to the wagon with two mules still hitched in the traces.

An old woman looked out the front opening, saw who it was and lowered the rifle.

"So what you find?" she asked, stepping through the opening to the wagon seat.

"No problems." He scratched the ears of one of the mules.

The woman was work-worn and had seen her sixtieth birthday pass some years ago. Only half of her front teeth were in place. She wore a man's hat to cover her hair and had blue, watering eyes. She spat from a chaw of tobacco and didn't bother to wipe the drip off her lip that trailed down to her chin and darkened a brown stain already there.

"Meaning what, no problems? We going in or not?"

"We go. It's like picking feathers off a brown hen just out of the scalding water. Damn right we go in."

Another face poked out the front canvas of the covered wagon. It belonged to a fifteen-year old girl with long blonde hair now stringy and dirty. Her pert young face was not quite as smudged and dirt-stained as the others, but nearly so. She was slender, wore a soiled yellow blouse and did not look like either of the other two.

"We gonna get a sister here for me to play

with?" the girl asked. "You promised me a sister."

"Shut your mouth, girl," E.B. said. "I seed a grown woman down there. If she's got big tits I'll do her first and then we'll worry about the rest of what to do."

"How many of them, E.B.?" the older woman asked.

"Just four, near as I could tell. All I seen. A couple and two kids, maybe ten and twelve."

"We going in sick again?" the old woman asked.

"Works, why change it?" E.B. snapped.

"I want to be sick this time," the girl blurted.

"Shut up, Melody," E.B. said. "Ma will do it this time if we need a sick one. She's good at it."

Melody pouted. "Why you want old big tits down there? Ain't I been doing you right?"

E.B. looked at her, stepped closer and rubbed her breasts through the dirty yellow blouse. Melody jumped away and pulled up her blouse and held it high to show her breasts. They were small and round and pink tipped.

"Ain't my titties good enough for you no more? You sure liked them last night."

E.B. fondled her breasts, then pushed her back into the covered wagon.

"Girl, you keep your mouth closed and do what I tell you to. Don't worry, you'll get your share of the poking. Now let's get moving. We want to be there just before dark so we'll get an invite to stay over."

"After this one, we set up and sell in Harding?" Ma asked.

"Closest place. No sense carting things over half the territory. We still in Montana, ain't we?"

"Bet your brisket, E.B. Your old Ma didn't raise no idiots. Harding is near where we meet up with Josh and Frank. We still on the way. Wonder if they're there yet?"

"We'll all get there in due time, Ma," E.B. said, grinning. "Hope this one has big tits. Might want to spend a week or so down there just chewing." He whacked the two mules, and the wagon moved ahead.

"Giddap, you worthless critters. Hiiiiiiyah. Let's move."

The tattered covered wagon rolled down the valley and into the opening of the smaller valley, then turned north toward the log cabin and pole corral. It was only a quarter of a mile away now.

E.B. walked alongside the mules when they were closer to the cabin. He stumbled now and then, putting on a good act to make anyone think he was on his last legs. E.B. grinned under his four weeks of beard and grime. He hated shaving almost as much as washing. He almost never took a bath.

When the wagon came within 50 yards of the cabin, a man stepped out and the screen door slammed. He held a shotgun benignly in the crook of his arm. E.B. knew how quickly the double barreled scatter gun could come up and go into action. His own weapon, a New Model

Army Revolver made in 1872, had been fired plenty. It hung low on his thigh in well-worn leather.

E.B. staggered and had to hold on to the harness now to keep from falling. The mules stopped. He urged them on again. The rancher walked toward him.

"Evening, stranger. You having some troubles?"

E.B. stopped the mules. "Evening, sir. Me, I'm in good shape, just a little tired. It's my Ma inside who's really sick. Wondered if we could park here for the night. I heard there was some Indian trouble and figured they wouldn't hit a wagon and a cabin both together. Renegades, I figure they are."

The man frowned and stepped forward, his hand out.

"Of course you can stay. My wife is good with sick ones. Maybe she can help your Ma. Oh, my name is Charles Eagleton."

E.B. walked forward and took the offered hand. "Pleased to meet you. I'm E.B. Guthrie. Sorry I'm such a mess. We've had a tough time last few weeks. Got plumb lost more'n I care to tell."

"You're not lost now. Come up to the house and we'll get some good venison stew, coffee and big slabs of bread inside you. That always helps."

"Don't want to put you out any. You got a big family, hired hands around?"

Eagleton laughed. "No hired hands on a spread like this. Barely enough here to keep

29

the wife and our two kids eating. But we have plenty to share with strangers. You all come down now and we'll take a look at your Ma and get you fed full."

Just as Eagleton finished talking, a rifle snarled one shot from inside the covered wagon. The round hit Eagleton in the jaw, shattered the bone, drove upward through the top of his mouth, and took off half his skull as it exploded through his scalp.

E.B. lost his lethargic pose, drew his six-gun in one swift, practiced move and raced toward the cabin. A young boy ran out and stared at him, then at his father on the ground. E.B. clubbed the boy with the six-gun, knocked him down, then charged on to the cabin door.

A woman stood in the doorway wiping her hands on a towel.

"Was that a shot?" she asked. Then she saw her husband on the ground and her son trying to get up. She saw E.B. bearing down on her.

"No!" she screamed, and turned to get back in the cabin. E.B. caught her by one arm, holstered his gun and grabbed the front of her calico dress. He jerked hard until it ripped down seams and fell to her waist, exposing her white binder. E.B. worked at the binder covering her breasts until he freed it, then tore it off. He gaped at her large breasts as they swayed and jiggled with the movement of the cloth.

"Yeah, now there is one pair of fine big knockers," he said. "Let's see what we can do with them."

A young girl, maybe ten, ran out of the

back room and stared at her mother and the stranger.

E.B. watched the girl for just a moment and shook his head. He drew his six-gun, and before the girl or her mother could move, he shot the girl in the heart. She jolted backwards and died with a look of surprise and curiosity on her face. She had never seen her mother's bare breasts before.

Ma White ran up to the cabin, screaming at her son. She came in the door, saw the woman, then the dead girl and scowled.

"Now what the hell you do that for? I wanted to play with the girl. Now all I got left is the little boy."

Jane Eagleton screamed when her daughter died. Now she clawed at E.B.'s face with her broken fingernails, drawing blood from one cheek. She jerked away from E.B. and bolted to the door. By the look on her face she must have known who these people were, but by then it was too late. She rushed to the door just as E.B. caught her again. She saw her son cowering on the ground outside.

"Run, Willy! Run for the woods and don't come back!"

Willy's eyes widened for a second; then he looked at the six-gun still in the killer's hand, and he jumped up and ran away, zig-zagging from side to side like a rabbit trying to escape from a hunting dog.

E.B. swore, shot twice at the boy, then fired once more before the target scurried out of range.

He shrugged, holstered the weapon, and used both his hands to catch the woman's clawing fingers. She screamed at him and kicked and cried, but he grabbed her around the waist from behind and brought one arm across her breasts. The pain stopped her shouting.

Her sobs came clearly.

Ma White looked at the woman, who stood half a foot taller than she did, and shook her head.

"No female except a milk cow should have tits that big," she said. "Just ain't right. E.B., you have your fun. Girl and me will do the work this time. On the next one you promise to save the man for me, you hear?"

"Me? You shot him, old woman, not me."

"Oh, yeah."

E.B. wasn't listening. He propelled the woman back into the cabin, saw a bed built against the far wall, and shoved his find down on it and stripped off her skirt and under-drawers.

For a moment the woman lay quietly, but just as E.B. began to open the buttons on his fly, she sat up, whirled and stabbed at him with a pair of scissors. The sharp blades plunged into his left forearm, and E.B. bellowed in pain. He knocked the scissors away and slapped her face twice and threw her back on the bed.

"For that, bitch, you get it fast and hard, and I'm gonna chew your tits until they're raw. You hear me?"

Ma White and Melody came into the cabin but paid no attention to the bed. They expertly and systematically looted the room of everything of value.

"Cookie jar," Melody said. "How can they be so stupid?" She took out a roll of federal bank notes, mostly one dollar greenbacks. Ma grabbed the roll and counted.

"Twenty-eight dollars, not bad. Check the man's body. He might have a purse on him."

An hour later, the two women had carted small pieces of furniture, silverware, some dishes and clothes, as well as three guns out to the wagon and loaded them. By then it was dark.

E.B. sat on the edge of the bed naked, staring at the woman he had tied to a chair. She was still nude. Melody looked at her bare breasts and shook her head.

"It just ain't fair! Look at all them tits. It just ain't fair she got so much and me so little."

E. B. laughed. "Hell, girl, you're young. Yours gonna grow some more. Meantime they need lots of rubbing and chewing."

Melody darted back from him. "Not by you, old man. I want me a young hot man."

Ma looked out the front door and screeched. "Fire! Our wagon's on fire!"

They all rushed out. E.B. caught up a bucket of water at the well and threw it on the flames. The fire had started on the backside of the canvas. Melody ran and pumped another bucket of water, and with the third one E.B. had the fire put out. The flames and smoke and water had ruined some of the things from the cabin.

E.B. scowled at them. "Damn kid must have done it."

Before anyone could answer, the roar of a shotgun shattered the stillness of the mountains. Ma White screamed as the buckshot tore into her chest and stomach. The force of the pellets knocked her backward three feet, and she sprawled in the Montana dirt.

E.B. pulled out his six-gun and fired four times toward the flash he had seen when the weapon went off. He was flat on the ground and rolled to the side after each shot. Melody ran to Ma White and held her head in her lap. By the time E.B. got there, his mother was dead.

E.B. kissed the old cheek, then stood and stormed into the night, firing his six-gun at any sound he heard. It was two hours before he came back. Then he ordered Melody out of the cabin and turned to the woman still tied to the chair.

"Your son done killed my Ma with that shotgun, so now you gonna pay for it."

"You killed my husband and my daughter. You're the one who should be doing the paying."

"Ain't the way it is, woman. Ain't the way." E.B. took out his skinning knife with its razor-sharp blade, and made a shallow cut across her right breast. The blade went deep enough to draw blood.

Jane Eagleton screamed. It was as if she knew there was no use holding back or being brave. He must intend to kill her, and he would do it slowly, sexually, and she would suffer more than she had ever thought possible.

She kicked at him. He laughed.

A shotgun blast tore through the one window in the cabin, the birdshot barely missing E.B. He dove for the coal oil lamp and blew it out, then scurried out the door. Melody sat by the well.

"He shot, then ran into the woods," she said. "Left the shotgun. Must be out of rounds."

"You supposed to be on guard duty, girl! I near got my head blown off."

"I can't fight a shotgun with a bucket. Give me your six-gun."

E.B. laughed. "And let you kill me? Not a chance in hell. Now watch for him. If he comes back, you scream your head off."

E.B. went inside, found the woman in the dark, and cut her loose from the chair. He slapped her four times, until she cringed back in the half-light of the moon that filtered in through the broken window.

He threw her on the bunk and fell on top of her. The idea grew in his mind as he began raping her. Yeah, why not. He'd never done that. He put the skinning knife where he could reach it easily.

When E.B. climaxed a few minutes later, Jane Eagleton died at the same time when his knife slashed her throat from one carotid artery to the other.

E.B. set the house on fire, made sure it was burning well, then burned down the small barn and scattered the half dozen horses in the corral. He couldn't sell them, because they were too easy to identify and trace.

He hustled Melody into the wagon, and they drove two miles away into some deep brush to hide until daylight.

"That damn twelve-year-old kid might know where there's a rifle or a six-gun. Yeah, yeah, I know. I should have killed the kid when I first saw him. A twelve-year-old can pull a trigger and do as much damage as a grown man." He would be on the lookout for the kid with the straw yellow hair and big blue eyes, standing about chest high.

He figured he'd done right letting his mother's body burn up in the fire. Cremation. They did that lots of places around the world.

E.B. lay on the bed in the wagon, thinking. He'd have to be careful the next few days around the little town of Harding. He would camp a day out of town and clean up and shave, repaint the damage on the wagon, and get his medicine-man banners and displays ready. He'd be all slicked up and waiting for the suckers within two days.

"Then rich widows and man-starved matrons of Harding, watch out. E.B. the slicker is coming to town."

Melody rolled over where she lay naked beside him, and he caught her breasts.

"Again?" she asked as he began fondling her.

"Hell yes."

"We already done it twice tonight. Don't you ever get enough?"

"Not lately, little darling. Doing in that ranch woman gave me a big hunger. Before morning I intend to burn it all out on

36

you. Unless you don't think you can handle it."

Melody sat up and shook her breasts at him. "Try to get it up again, old man. I can outlast you any day or night. Bet you five dollars I'll be asking for more when you're too pooped out to do a poking."

"Bet," E.B. said. He lost and he paid her.

Chapter Three

Stewart Rawlins was slender, fifty, rich, carefully dressed, easily angered, owned most of the town, and was deadly when crossed. He stood five-feet five-inches tall, and right now he was gut-ripping furious.

"What the hell you mean, they got away? You killed three of them and they still ran off with all my goddamned money?" Rawlins caught Ben Whitmore's brown shirt and vest in one hand, and now twisted them so tightly Ben had trouble breathing.

"You just sat up there and let them outlaws steal *ten thousand dollars* of my money?" Rawlins bellowed, his face turning purple with the effort.

Ben's face twisted, and he gagged trying to

suck in air. He choked; his arms flopped uselessly at his sides.

Into a small silence came the ominous sound of a six-gun cocking. Rawlins looked up, startled.

"Let him go right now," Spur McCoy's voice commanded. It was soft, yet had the taste of death about it.

Rawlins glared at Spur, then looked at the black hole of the deadly .45 not six feet from him. He relaxed his grip on Ben, adjusted his wire-rimmed spectacles to see Spur better, and pushed the stage driver aside.

"Who the hell are you?" Rawlins demanded.

"A friend of Ben's, and I don't like the way you're treating him. If Ben doesn't breathe, little man, then you don't breathe either. Understand the logic here? If you want to talk with Ben, I'd suggest two shots of whiskey. You'll find out more that way and you owe him that much. Ben damn near got killed today because of you and your blasted ten thousand dollars."

A crowd had gathered around the stage when they found out about the robbery. They had listened to Ben's quick recital. Now gasps went up when the people heard how Spur talked so rough to the town's richest man.

Rawlins turned from Ben, stepped close to Spur, and whispered so no one but Spur could hear him.

"I don't know who the hell you are, mister, but you're a dead man. You hear me? You're nothing but vulture bait." Rawlins' voice spewed out venom befitting a rattlesnake.

Spur stepped back and dropped his six-gun into leather.

"Folks, I want all of you to witness that this man, Rawlins, just threatened to kill me. I'm giving public notice that one Stewart Rawlins did now, knowingly and willfully, threaten my life. If anything happens to me, he's your prime suspect."

Far in back two men laughed. Rawlins growled and tried to see who they were. The crowd rumbled with excitement.

From his mild, easygoing manner, Spur suddenly changed. He grabbed Rawlins by the shirt front, twisted it the way the banker had done to Ben, and pulled Rawlins to the back of the Concord stage.

"Untie those ropes, Rawlins, and you'll see part of what your ten thousand dollars bought you today. Go ahead, open up the boot, damn it!"

Rawlins straightened his shirt and wide black tie, then looked at Spur's angry face for just a moment before he undid the ropes. The dead passenger rolled off the rear boot. The canvas fell away and the corpse sprawled in the dusty street next to some horse droppings. His lifeless eyes stared at the crowd. One woman in front fainted, others gasped and shuddered. Then people pushed up closer to see.

"We don't even know his name, Rawlins. He was one of the passengers on the stage and he died trying to defend himself and your precious ten thousand dollars. How much is his life worth, Rawlins? A damn sight more than your ten thousand. Now, open the other canvas."

The small banker almost gagged as he undid the ropes. He must have known it was a second body, but he couldn't have known whose. When he pulled back the flap of the tarp and exposed the bloody head of Big Ed Johnson, the shotgun guard, there were angry shouts from the people pressing around. They knew Johnson.

"That's the second man your cash box got killed today, Rawlins, and there are three more out on the trail. You must be proud of your day's slaughter."

Spur scowled at the banker. "You can at least take care of the expense of burying them." Spur grabbed his carpet bag from the stack on the boardwalk beside the stage and walked down the uneven planks toward the hotel.

Rawlins' voice stabbed after him. "Sheriff Halverson, arrest that man. I'm charging him with robbing the stage of ten thousand dollars and the death of these two fine citizens. I want him locked up in our jail this very instant."

Spur turned and stared hard at Rawlins, who stepped behind a medium-sized man in a black suit wearing a badge on his doeskin vest.

"Sir, I'm Sheriff Halverson. I'd like to ask your name."

"I'm Spur McCoy from Denver."

"Mr. McCoy, just a moment, please." He turned and talked with the banker. They argued quietly for two minutes.

"Mr. McCoy, I have a citizen's complaint charging you with armed robbery and the death

41

of the stage guard. I'm afraid I'll have to ask you a few questions down at the jail."

"Sheriff, I'll be glad to talk to you tomorrow. I'm not going anywhere. You get a formal arrest report ready with the charges and Mr. Rawlins' signature as the complainant, then I'll be glad to come in and talk. At the same time I'll file my own suit charging false arrest against you, the county and Mr. Rawlins. I'll be seeking punitive damages of three hundred thousand dollars. You think it over. I'll be at the hotel right down the street."

"I'm not sure what to do, Mr. McCoy."

A tall, gray-headed man in a long-sleeved white shirt, no coat, and a spread poker hand still in his fist, strode quickly through the crowd to the sheriff and talked to him. Soon he was arguing with the lawman and the banker. After two or three minutes the tall, gray-haired man nodded to the two and walked to where Spur waited.

He held out his hand. "I say, it's good to meet you at last, Mr. McCoy. I'm Penley Northcliff, your erstwhile employer."

Spur nodded and took the hand. It was a firm but unenthusiastic handshake.

"So you're the man I'm working for. Sorry about the small problem here, but I hate to see people stepped all over by self-important, stupid little martinets like Rawlins."

Northcliff chuckled. "I say, that's rather well put," he said smiling. His strong English accent gave his voice an interesting sound so foreign to the Montana country twang. "Shall we go

42

on to the hotel and get you settled in? I've arranged a room. Then later on tonight we can get started on what your duties will be. I don't think you should worry about being charged with anything. Our sheriff is easily swayed but basically an honest sort of fellow. I convinced them that they would lose to you in a lawsuit and bankrupt both them and the county. They backed off."

At the hotel, Spur registered, was led to his room, and stood looking out the second-story window at the three-block-long business section. Northcliff revised his schedule and said he would meet Spur in the lobby at nine the next morning.

"Now, go over again what you told me in your wire, Mr. Northcliff."

"As you know, I'm a rancher, the Bar-B. I have ten thousand acres to the north and I utilize another forty thousand or so. I bought a going spread here two years ago and I'm expanding it. Some of the local ranchers don't like that. Lately I've had a serious loss of cattle to the rustlers. My foreman figures we're missing more than a thousand head of steers. With beef worth forty dollars each at the railhead, that's forty thousand dollars worth. I want this rustling stopped. I don't care how you do it, and I'll pay your fee of five thousand dollars after you've done your job."

Spur nodded. "I'll need that five hundred dollars advance we talked about, to match the five hundred you wired me in Denver. Then I can get to work. You have the maps of the whole area I asked for with each ranch's boundaries marked?"

"Yes, the maps are waiting for you at the hotel desk, along with the other items you wanted, Mr. McCoy."

"I hope you've drawn in any fences that are involved in the district, and remote areas that are hard to get to."

"You should find everything you need. We've already had our spring roundup, but still I'm losing cattle. I can't afford to have any more of my breeding stock rustled." He paused. "I might as well tell you. The other big ranchers don't like me. They refused to let me join their cattleman's association. They say they are looking for the rustlers, too."

"Right. Always good to know where I stand. I'd say it shouldn't take me more than two weeks, Mr. Northcliff. By then I should have this case solved. But, right now, what I really want is a bath. The clerk said he would get me some hot water in that first bathroom, so if there's nothing else, I better get down there and scrub off a five-day accumulation of travel dirt."

Northcliff looked pensive, then frowned. "Just for the record, McCoy. Did you have anything to do with that robbery? I have to go back and talk to the sheriff again, and I want your word on it that you aren't involved."

"For the past five days I've been on the road coming here from Denver. Dickens of a place to try to find. How could I possibly know there was going to be money on that stage, or recruit six outlaws to do the job? My guess is that it was an inside job, perhaps by one of Rawlins' own men."

"Right, quite right. I'll square it with Sheriff Halverson. I never have trusted that little banker, Rawlins. Trouble is he's the only banker in town. Now, first thing tomorrow when the bank opens, we'll get your money. Then you can talk to the sheriff, and after that we'll ride out to my ranch, and you can start getting acquainted with the lay of the land. That about does it, old boy." He clicked his heels in the best British army tradition, popped a hand salute, and walked out the door.

Spur looked around his room. It was a standard cheap Montana hotel: an iron frame bed, dresser with three drawers and a small wavy mirror, one straight-backed chair, a white chamber pot under the bed, a washstand with china pitcher full of water, and a china wash bowl. He checked the bed. At least it had white sheets. Spur unpacked his carpet bag, adjusted the Colt .45 on his hip, and went down to the desk, where he picked up the packet of maps and two large brown envelopes.

"Mr. McCoy, bathroom one is ready for you, sir," the eager young clerk said. "There should be plenty of hot water and two big towels. If there's anything else you need, just call out."

He thanked the clerk, deposited the envelopes in his room, and went down to the bath on the first floor. He knocked, then cautiously opened the unlocked door. No one was in the small bathroom. He went in, locked the door and saw the iron-footed steel bathtub painted inside with glistening white enamel, half full of steaming hot water.

Spur tested the temperature, poured in another bucket of hot water and stripped, putting his clothes on a chair. He stepped into the tub and winced at the scalding water. Two new bars of white soap lay in a soap dish. He inched downward gradually in the water as he grew accustomed to its heat, then sat down carefully, sighed, and leaned back on the slanted end of the tub. He folded his legs at the knee so he would fit and relaxed.

Spur had just closed his eyes, ready for a glorious half hour soak, when he heard a key in the bathroom lock. He looked over quickly and saw the door swing inward. A woman in a red dress backed into the room, closed the door and relocked it.

"Miss, I beg your pardon, but this bathroom is being used," Spur said.

"Uh-huh, I know," she replied, her back still toward him. She was slim and trim and had long dark hair.

"Well, it would seem natural for you to leave."

"No, I'd rather not leave. I know who you are. Spur McCoy—a special agent for the United States Secret Service."

His brows lifted, and Spur sat up in the tub. "You know me?"

"I used to, Spur. I hope that I still do."

As he watched, she loosened the dress in back and did something at the front, then pulled the dress up and over her head. She tossed it on the chair over his clothes. Under the dress she wore only a fancy corset with lace around the back and wide ruffled bands. Below the corset he saw only one half of a petticoat.

"You are beginning to get me interested," he said. Spur could see mostly her back, part of it fetchingly bare, and her slender, delightful legs.

"I'm glad you're at least a little bit interested." The words purred from her. Her dark hair was curled at the ends and fell well below her shoulders. From his partial view she had a good figure. Spur tried to remember anyone he knew who was about this size with dark hair. He couldn't remember any woman like her.

The girl's hands reached around her back and undid five hooks that let the corset come loose. She pulled it from her back and started to turn slowly.

She had just made the first move with her shoulders when he knew her name.

"Abigail Buchanan," he said softly.

She turned the rest of the way, her pretty face smiling. She still held the corset over her chest. "Well, I am pleased that you didn't forget me entirely. Kansas City, Denver and that wonderful week in San Francisco. I certainly never will forget that month-long fantasy with you."

She let the corset slip a little until it revealed a thin line of cleavage. Abigail grinned.

"When I saw that grand entrance you made into town this afternoon, and the devastating way you ridiculed poor Mr. Stewart Rawlins in front of half the citizens, I knew I better make my move fast. Rawlins is bound to have you killed before sunup. After all, Spur, sweetheart, you made him grovel in his own dung, and he'll never forgive you for that."

"Rawlins? Is he that important around here? I never would have guessed. We can talk about him later. Are you going to just stand there with your clothes on, or come down here and give me a kiss?"

She knelt by the tub, and her lips were hot even before they met his. Her arms went around him and he murmured his approval. The corset pressed against the tub, staying in place until he edged her back from the metal; then the hellish device dropped to the floor. One of his hands came out of the water and caught a breast.

"Now, this is more like the Abby I know. Don't be so shy. Get out of that silly petticoat and come on in and share my bath."

"There isn't room."

"We'll make room."

She smiled, then giggled. "I've been waiting for you to ask me. I mean, a girl shouldn't be too forward, you know."

She stood, and he lay there enjoying the way her breasts bounced and jiggled as she finished undressing. She slid out of the half-petticoat and wore nothing else. Abigail posed for a minute, one bent leg a little in front of the other, her breasts thrust out proudly, shoulders back.

"Yes, Abby, lover. I see you. You are just as gorgeous as you were three years ago. You haven't put on a single pound, and you're ravishing. Now get your pretty little ass into my tub before I come out and rape you right there on the bathroom floor."

Abigail grinned and stepped into the water.

"Ouch. It's scalding. How do you stand it?"

"You started the water boiling with your strip tease. You sure you locked the door?"

"I did, and I left my key in it so no one else with a key can get in."

"Hussy."

She nodded. "Yes, I admit it, and you love it."

"True."

She edged into the steaming water a little at a time, and at last sat down beside him, then with a grimace lay in the water half on top of him.

"Oh, my, but this is nice." She looked at him. "The hot water is fun, too."

They both laughed. His hands came around her and covered both her breasts.

Abigail moaned in delight, then wiggled, turning around in his arms to face him. Her mouth came at him like a swarm of hungry hornets, buzzing at his eyes, nose, chin, neck, lips. Her hips and the wet swatch of fur at her crotch writhed against his loins in the ancient dance, a demanding ritual that no man could long ignore. Suddenly an all-consuming heat burst into flames within her that she had to put out.

She chewed on his ear lobe, and between panting gasps crooned to him.

"Darling, Spur. I want you. I need you right now. It's been so long for us, so terribly long."

Her hands worked over his body in and out of the water, exploring his flesh, touching him so softly yet insistently that within a few moments he knew he could deny her nothing that she wanted.

Her saucy breasts peeked out of the water and his hands caught them, washing them, fondling them, bringing the soft pinkness of her large areolas to a brighter shade and turning the small brown buds of her nipples into erect pillars twice as long as they had been. They now were gently throbbing.

Abigail's body, slender as a sleek panther's and hotter than the Montana plains in August, writhed against him in and out of the water. Her light blue eyes turned to him, and she bent back a little for a better view of his face.

"I don't know why the hell I ever let go of you, Spur McCoy. This time I'm going to tell everyone that I'm pregnant by you and then you'll have to marry me. Oh, it'll work. I've got a lot of good friends in this town. I usually let Penley Northcliff win at my poker table, but win just a little. I make sure that no matter how poorly Stewart Rawlins plays, he never loses more than five dollars. I have friends, the right kind of friends with power and money."

"Shut up Abigail," Spur said huskily, grinning as he did. Then he kissed her and his hands worked around and around her tempting breasts. He sat up with her out of the water, their wet bodies pasted together, her tongue darting into his mouth, lacing into the hotness of him, detonating her potent desire. Their mouths slid apart, returned, welded together as their tongues explored, dueled, then made a joyful truce.

She left his lips and pulled his head lower to her breasts. He was surprised that they weren't dry already from their hotness. They stung his lips as he kissed them, and her fire seeped into him as his kisses circled around and around her glorious mounds, to arrive at last at the tops, where he rewarded her with a gentle chewing of the pulsating nipples.

"Oh, yes, darling Spur."

His hand worked down across her flat belly, into the water over the small rise, and entered the waving forest of her furry heartland.

"Yes, sweetness, oh, yes, please."

She tried to spread her legs. There wasn't room. Abigail lifted one foot from the tub and draped it over the side. His fingers smoothed her, sped over the treasure spot and then came back. Her hand inched toward the hardness at his crotch.

"Darling Spur, please take me, right now."

His finger found her tiny nub, the glory trigger, and he rubbed it back and forth. Abigail moaned, her teeth chattered, and when he hit the tiny node the third time, her whole body stiffened. She let out a small cry and her flanks trembled as if she were being shaken to pieces by a large dog. She rattled and gasped for each precious bit of breath. Her hand flattened against his belly and her head nuzzled his shoulder. At last she whimpered, shook once more, and he saw the glowing blush on her chest. She opened her eyes slowly.

"Delicious, delicious, delightful." She closed her eyes and snuggled against him. Suddenly she came alert. "That's a fine start, a good beginning. Now let's get a little wild."

"It can't be done under water," he said.

"You ever try it?"

He nodded.

"Ever try it with me?"

He shook his head and gently turned her until she lay on her back in the hot water, one foot on the top edge of each side of the tub. He kneeled between her spread legs and she helped guide him as he pushed forward. Her hips floated up to meet him. He probed and punched and at last she moved slightly and then yelped as he drove into her.

Abigail's cry was a sudden shout of surprise, wonder and joy all mixed together. A glorious gift, a sexual serendipity. She tried to kiss his lips but couldn't reach that high and settled for kissing his chest. Then she brought her legs around his back and locked them together as they surged against each other. He felt the shock waves quivering through him, lighting fires in him that hadn't been touched so deeply for years, fires in the deepest center of his being.

"So beautiful," she whispered. "Sweet, gentle, different somehow. It's never been quite this way for me before."

Their passions heated more, boiled, over-flowed in the moment. She kissed his chest. "I've always loved you, Spur McCoy, you must know that. Loved you and wanted to keep you, always. But every time you slip away."

He said words then of love, because right then, in the heat of their union, he did love her, wanted her, needed her, and he said the words as simply as he could and meant them, every one, for that time and place.

Water sloshed in the tub. One wavelet splashed over the side. They didn't notice. She rose to meet each of his potent hip thrusts, her face glowing with a madonna smile. Then she stiffened below him, tried to cut him in half with her legs as the darting explosions ripped through her slender body again, stinging her eyes with tears, ripping through her svelte form like a tornado through a Kansas cornfield, slamming everything aside, driving forward to its dark destiny far across her landscape.

Then Spur couldn't contain his own surging desire any longer. He knew the floodgates had opened, some small valve had dumped the species-perpetuating fluid into his system, and that primitive urge was driving it through his tubes. The wonder and the glory of it built and built until he knew his whole body was going to explode. He countered it by pumping faster and faster. Water cascaded out of the tub again and wet the round braided rug on the floor. Neither of them noticed.

"Yes, darling, yes," she shouted. She knew he was close as she detonated herself into another rolling climax that she thought would never end. It rumbled again and again. She panted for breath, then held it all and tightened every muscle in her body, and at that moment she knew she was dying. Her body and mind erupted into a volcanic flow of pure molten lava, burning, searing, vaporizing everything in its path, and she willingly fell into the fiery stream.

He felt her soaring into her climax and met her thrust-for-thrust, until some unseen force tore him apart, blasted him into outer space, zoomed him around the stars in a soaring and gliding comet with a fire tail a million light-years long, and at last his hips pumped in the final ecstasy-filled surge, and he fell softly against her. She pushed up to him and then relaxed, and her face sank under the water. She surfaced and smiled, but her eyes were still shut.

They clung to each other in the still-hot water, a womb for two. For five minutes they panted and fought for fresh breath to revitalize their spent bodies. Gradually they drifted back to reality. He found the drain-plug chain and pulled it out with his foot, and they lay there as the water gushed down the drainpipe into the sump somewhere below.

Abigail opened her blue eyes and watched Spur, then stretched up and kissed his lips.

"That was a fine re-introduction, Spur, darling. Now let's get our clothes on so we can go up to your room and talk about old times."

"I won't be able to talk coherently for hours."

"Then you can just hold me and I'll talk. We can order dinner sent in and get a bottle of champagne. Darling Spur, I plan on this being a long and a fabulous night where neither of us will get a single wink of sleep."

Chapter Four

Abigail sat naked on the rumpled sheets in the darkness of room 302, smoking a hand-rolled cigarette. Her frown had grown over the past half hour, and now she slid off the bed and padded to the window where Spur McCoy straddled a turned-around, straight-backed chair.

She draped herself over his shoulders, pushed her breasts hard against him, then reached around and kissed his cheek.

"Nothing yet?" she asked in a whisper. "It's almost two A.M. You'd think they would have come by now."

"Patience, pretty lady. When you're trying to kill somebody every detail must be exactly right. A stray dog, a sudden wind, a spooked black cat, somebody walking past on the street, almost anything will scare off a serious bushwhacker. I figure when he comes it will be just one man with a shotgun loaded with double aught buck rounds."

Abigail shivered. "It wasn't this scary when we were in Kansas City."

"But there I didn't boil into town and challenge the biggest banker in the country, who also is probably as crooked as a rattlesnake tied in six bow-knots."

"What if nothing happens tonight?"

"Then I lose some sleep. Better that than losing my head." He smiled at her, reached around and kissed her soft lips warmly. "Now, get back to bed. I think it will happen soon."

"But. . . ."

He kissed her quivering, excited lips again, quieting her protest. She caught his hand and pressed it against her bare breast.

"Later," he said.

"Oh yes. Four or five more times. Promise?"

"Promise. You'll have to kick me out of your bed to get rid of me. The hotel clerk didn't think it was unusual when you rented a room for yourself?"

"No. I know him. He understands that once in a while I need to vanish for some privacy, a time all to myself."

"Good. And nobody connected you to me, so they could try to gun us down here in your room?"

"No. Impossible. I own the First Class Saloon and gambling hall down the street. Won it in a poker game. That's how they know me."

"Good." Spur looked back at the half-open

window of room 206, one floor below and two rooms over. The lamp had been turned down low inside the room. It was the spot he had rented. Most of the occupied rooms in the hotel had the windows open on this warm, humid night. Someone would come, Spur was sure now. He could sense it. From what Abigail had told him, he had blundered in and insulted the most powerful man in this end of Montana. He was a small person physically, but with a giant pride, and rich enough to back up his threats with fast guns.

Spur had tried to make it easy for the killer: The open window, a second-floor room on the alley, two pillows and a blanket in the bed under the sheet, and the room lamp turned on low but still giving off plenty of light so the killer could see the "body" in the bed.

It was a perfect set-up for a bushwhacking. If not, Spur would have to be doubly careful the next day.

Spur didn't want the shooter dead, but chances were slim that he would say who hired him even if he lived. Spur made up his mind. Better to have the killer dead at the scene than have any questions about the man's intentions. Yes, Spur would take him out in the window, dumping him into the room if possible.

Spur had put on black pants and a black long-sleeved shirt in case he had to go out the window after the bushwhacker. A coil of half inch rope lay at his feet, one end of it tied tightly around the heavy iron bedstead. His favorite .45

Colt tapped the back of the wooden chair as he waited.

This whole assignment was a strange one. When his boss in the United States Secret Service, General Halleck, had first wired him about the problem, he was in Denver cleaning up a nasty counterfeiting case. The first wire and mailed envelopes contained background material on Big Sky County and the rustling problem there that several large ranchers had written the Secretary of the Interior about. The Secretary, Columbus Delano, was a man who made things happen.

The basic problem was rustling, with the large herds being hit time and time again for 50 to 100 head that were driven away in small groups, so none could be tracked and located.

Rather than send in Spur in his official capacity, it was suggested that he go in undercover, with no one on-site knowing about him. He had printed a letter about his exploits in gun-for-hire work, especially in cattle-rustling problems. This along with his fee he enclosed in letters to four of the large cattle ranchers in the area, including Penley Northcliff.

The stated $5,000 fee was designed to weed out the small-timers, and perhaps interest the men who could afford him. Northcliff had answered with a telegram the day after he got the message. He accepted the fee, and the man had urged him to come at once.

This problem Spur had kicked up with Rawlins was unfortunate, but it might make his cover story look more authentic to Northcliff.

Wilderness Wanton

Spur scanned the dark alley again. The nearly full moon had come out from behind a cloud and now cast sharp shadows on the alley floor, outlining the tops of buildings. He saw no movement. Spur sighed and kept up his vigil.

He had never been sorry he joined the Secret Service. It had been created by President Lincoln with the sole purpose of protecting the currency from counterfeiting. In those early days, the Secret Service was one of the few federal law forces that had the authority to handle law-breakers in any of the states and territories. It began to be assigned many new duties besides the currency.

Spur had joined the service shortly after the Big War; he was the only agent west of the Mississippi. It was a huge territory. Out here his bachelor's degree in arts from Harvard University, near Boston, did him little good. But at least he was not corralled in one of his father's businesses in New York.

He stretched and then quartered his field, checking every part of it for movement.

A few minutes later one of the shadows near the far end of the alley moved. A blob detached itself from the fence and drifted closer to the hotel. The figure worked cautiously and slowly through the alley, checked cardboard boxes behind the hardware, looked in a barrel near a saloon, examined every spot where someone could hide. He vanished into the heavy shadows again and came back with a lightly built ladder. A long weapon hung over his right shoulder.

The man moved rapidly now with no wasted

time or motion. He put the ladder against the hotel, below and slightly to the side of the open window of room 206, swung a shotgun off his shoulder, and climbed soundlessly up the rungs. The man stayed at the side of the window when he reached the right height. Then he slid to the side so he could see into room 206, which still had a light on.

Spur moved the chair soundlessly, knelt at the low window sill, sighted in on the assassin and waited. The man looked into room 206 again, then pushed the shotgun inside and leaned partway through the window.

Spur's finger tensed on the trigger as he refined his sights on the broad back of the man for the down-slanting shot. The blast of the shotgun came as a muffled roar from inside the room. Spur squeezed off a round at once, saw it slam into the killer midway in his back. Spur fired three more times rapidly, each slug jolting into the bushwhacker, driving him farther into the room.

The killer's leg twitched and pushed at the ladder; then he lay still. He had been jolted far enough into the room that he now hung half in and half out the window, balanced there, his body not moving. He was dead.

Spur pulled his six-gun inside the window, checked the silent, darkly empty alley, and closed the window and the sash. He sat on the floor, ejected the spent shells, and filled the cylinders with four new ones.

Abigail dropped beside him, tears flowing down her cheeks. She pushed past his hands and put her arms tightly around him.

"My God, Spur. We both would have been killed down there. That was a shotgun, wasn't it? Right now we both could be. . . ."

"Dead, is the word. You have a tough little town here, Abby. I don't think they like me."

"But this has happened to you before, right?"

"Someone trying to kill me? Yes. But I never get used to it, especially this kind of a cowardly attack. It would be damn helpful if this killer has a letter in his pocket signed by Rawlins ordering him to murder me. Afraid that's just a wishful dream."

Spur held her as Abby shivered, then he kissed her lips.

"Hey. Hey, pretty lady. Are you all right? You were sure right about your hunch I'd have a visitor. I owe you one."

She kissed him hard on the mouth, nestling against him. "You would have figured it out before long, but you did say you owed me one, right? Then I'd like to collect it right now. You don't want to go down to your old room, do you?"

"Nothing I can learn down there."

"Good, then I'm collecting, so get rid of those clothes just as fast as you can. That damn shotgun, it was wild. That set my juices running. I was instantly hot and ready. Every time after this when I hear a shotgun, I'm going to feel so damn sexy I won't be able to stand it."

Spur stood, picked her up and carried her to the bed. How did he thank someone for saving his life? He tried to think of a response, but couldn't. He wasn't sure of the answer, but at least now he would give her exactly what she wanted.

When they awoke, it was nearly 8 A.M. He had brought his carpet bag and everything he owned from the room below when they moved upstairs late last night. Now he dressed in his usual working clothes: a fine black suit, white shirt with cufflinks, and a quarter-inch-wide string tie knotted in a bow at his throat. His boots were Cavaliers, the best riding boots made. They were from the best quality cowhide leather, with range-slanted heels. This pair showed fancy leather tooling of a bucking bronc unseating a cowboy. They were polished a deep shade of brown and glistened as if they were wet. He eased his low-crowned black Stetson on his head and buttoned his black vest.

"Don't worry, Spur. I won't let on to anyone that I even know you, let alone that you're staying up here with me."

He smiled. "Good, we'll both live a lot longer that way. I have some business to attend to. But I'll be back tonight. You'll be here?"

"You bet. Like I told you, I learned my lesson. I ain't never gonna let go of you again."

He bent and kissed her inviting lips, then went to the door and outside without looking back. No one was in the hall. He walked down the nearest stairs and out the hotel's back door.

A medium-sized man sitting in a straight wooden chair tipped back against the hotel wall waved at Spur.

"Morning, Mr. McCoy. A fine day, isn't it? I'm Sheriff Halverson. We met briefly yesterday."

"You're up early, Sheriff."

"True, and I just won fifty cents from my deputy. He said you'd come out the front door. Guess you know what happened here in the hotel last night?"

"Can't say as I do, Sheriff. Last night I slept so well a runaway freight train wouldn't have roused me."

"Some drifter got himself killed trying to bushwhack you in your bed in room 206."

"You better tell him that he seems to have missed, Sheriff. You and your men must have meted out quick justice for the county. I hope you arrested Stewart Rawlins for my attempted murder."

"Nope, not that easy, Mr. McCoy. The aldermen are getting worried. They say since you came to town six dead men have littered our fair city. All of them dead by gunshot."

"Happens in the best of towns, Sheriff. The three I shot yesterday were outlaws, you know that. Now I want to swear out a complaint against Stewart Rawlins, since he threatened to kill me and then someone tried, you say, last night."

"Wouldn't be a good plan, Mr. McCoy."

They walked around the end of the hotel. Across the street Spur saw a storefront sign: "The *Clarion*, South Junction's own newspaper."

"Why wouldn't it be wise to file a complaint against Rawlins?"

The sheriff waved one hand. "You can't prove

it was him who tried, or even that he said what you claim he said. He owns about two-thirds of the town, including the Montana hotel where you slept last night. What do you think a jury would say?"

"Yeah, Sheriff. I been considering all that. I'm here on another job. Guess I should keep my nose down one trail at a time. What about the stage? Can he prove I held up the coach?"

"Nope. Ben Whitmore and me had a long talk. He told me what happened, what you did. Damn good work. The stage driver figured them outlaws was gonna use the girl for a couple of hours and then kill all four of you. Nice and clean for them, no witnesses left and them ten thousand dollars richer."

"The problem of staying alive out there yesterday did occur to me, Sheriff."

"What I figured. No charges against you. Stewart will be sore as blue blazes in July. I'd watch out for him. He'll try to get back at you somehow. But what the hell, he's only got one vote."

"Right, Sheriff. But he also owns the bank and all of the election campaign funds for the county, I'd wager. Thanks for the good words. You never did say how that bushwhacker met his maker last night."

"Somebody pumped four slugs into him from outside and above. We figure a third-floor room window. You wouldn't know anything about that, would you, Mr. McCoy?"

"Like I said, Sheriff. Last night I slept like the

living dead. Well, I've got to see our new lady editor on business."

The lawman nodded. "Northcliff tells me you're working for the Bar-B on that rustler problem. Good luck. I really wouldn't mind burying a few more rustlers myself." The sheriff waved and walked down the street toward his office.

Spur adjusted the Colt on his right hip, looked both ways along the street, and then moved across the dusty expanse with long, sure strides. He stopped at the boardwalk in front of the newspaper office. The boardwalks were put up by each business in front of its store. They varied not only in height, but in width and evenness as well. Where there was an empty lot, there was no boardwalk at all.

Spur went through the door into the newspaper office and heard a small bell ring. At once he caught the characteristic smell of every small town newspaper—a combination of newsprint and ink that was unmistakable.

A head lifted from behind a waist-high counter across the width of the room, six feet in from the front door. It was Opal Davis. Her pretty blonde hair was captured in a bandanna. A dark smudge showed on one side of her nose, and a black streak on her forehead.

"Oh, Mr. McCoy. You're just the person I want to see. I need a story about the attempt on your life last night in the hotel."

"You'll have to talk to the sheriff about that, Mrs. Davis. I don't know what happened. What I came in for was to talk about your printing some calling cards for me."

"But didn't someone try to kill you last night?"

"That's what the sheriff says. I was thinking of some regular-sized business cards. A man in Denver said I should have some. You do print business cards?"

She smiled and nodded, a dimple breaking out in her right cheek. "Oh yes, of course. That is, we will be able to soon. But about the man killed in the hotel. I heard that he fired a shotgun into your room at a dummy in your bed, and that the man in the window was then shot from the outside and killed."

"That's what the sheriff told me this morning."

She frowned at Spur and pushed a pad of paper and a pencil toward him. As he reached for the pencil her hand covered his. There was a startling tingle that caused them both to react. He smiled, and she looked at him steadily with serious green eyes.

"Oh, I didn't mean to touch . . . what I mean is that . . ." She sighed. "Mr. McCoy. I never did get to thank you for saving all of our lives yesterday. The holdup men were going to have their way with me and then kill all of us, weren't they?"

He nodded. "I decided that was the plan, so I had to take a chance of breaking free."

"That's something else I owe you for. I would have survived his . . . his having his way with me, but I'm grateful it didn't go that far."

Her green eyes turned up to watch him. They

were strong, sure, not at all embarrassed, not asking for help. Instead they evaluated his reaction.

"No thanks are needed, ma'am." He wrote on the paper in a good hand what he wanted printed on the card. It said simply:

"GUN FOR HIRE"
Wire Spur McCoy
New Princess Hotel, Denver, Colorado

She looked at what he had written, then up at him. "Now about the style and size of type. I think we should. . . ."

"You pick out something that looks good, Mrs. Davis. You'll do a good job. The usual business size. Two hundred will be enough."

"It's going to take us a week," she said. "Things are still a real jumble around here. Lots of things broken, many of the type fonts pied, the big press is down. . . ." She stopped and brushed back a strand of long blonde hair. "I'm sure, Mr. McCoy, that you don't want to hear about our problems. You're in town to work for Mr. Northcliff, I understand, to stop the rustlers."

"Right. That is, I am if I meet him at the bank. I'm almost late." He paused and smiled. "You've taken on a big job here, Mrs. Davis. I wish you luck."

"Thank you. I know I can do it. I worked on my father's newspaper for six years in Ohio."

Spur smiled. "Then I'm sure you can handle this one." He tipped his hat and went out the front door. As he left, he saw a curtain leading into the rear shop part and the sullen face of the lady's husband, Leroy Davis, staring at him.

Spur found the bank by looking down the three-block long main street. Most of the businesses were those of any small Western town: general store, hardware, blacksmith, hotel, livery stable, sheriff's office, stage lines office, millinery, saloons, gambling halls, and at the end of the street a house that must be a brothel.

A meeting hall had a banner on it proclaiming that the Chicago Traveling Troupe would be on hand April 13, last April.

The bank was a well built, two-story brick structure, with offices upstairs. Spur was sure a sturdy safe was inside. A row of heavy wooden chairs sat on the covered walkway in front of the establishment. Penley Northcliff rose from one of the chairs and knocked ashes from his pipe.

"I say, McCoy, you're here right on time. Bank opens in two minutes. I hear you had a bit of a close call last night at the hotel."

"No, Mr. Northcliff, not close at all. But if I'd stayed in my old room, I'd be so much undertaker's meat today. I don't suppose we could link the shotgunner to our friend Rawlins, could we?"

Northcliff shook his head. "Unfortunately no, old chap. The dead man was a drifter. He arrived in town only yesterday afternoon and was seduced by someone into doing the deed. Obviously he was not working on his own initiative. Trying to say who paid him the fifty dollars he had in his pocket is quite impossible. Clever of you, really, to put that dummy in the bed and change rooms." He paused. "Oh, I assume that you were the one who shot the bushwhacker."

"That's your privilege, Mr. Northcliff. I try not to question people about their assumptions. Shall we go inside and complete our transaction? I'm anxious now to get out to your spread and see just how big a job this is going to be."

Northcliff waved him ahead, and led the way into the Rawlins City Bank, the only one in South Junction, Montana Territory.

Ten minutes later, Spur took the five hundred dollars from Northcliff, all in U.S. federal greenbacks. There was no discounting problem with the paper money in Montana. He and Northcliff went to the livery, where Spur chose a good acting black gelding, purchased for $80 with the understanding he could sell the mount back to them later. The used California type saddle and tack was another $15, all in good condition.

The saddle was ten pounds lighter than the Denver cowboy-style leather. This one had fancy tooling on the sides.

Spur saddled the black and took him two turns around the back pasture. The gelding was deep, strong and sturdy; Spur figured it was even tempered. After a day or two to get acquainted, he would be a good mount.

They rode out the Pumpkin River road to the north, upstream along a small creek.

"My spread is six miles out," Northcliff said.

They moved at a gentle pace. The River road was a quarter of a mile from the wooded slopes of a low range of hills to the left. Once Spur thought he saw a sunflash over that way that could have come from a binocular lens. He looked around critically, and decided it could just as well have been a flash from a broken glass bottle.

They were in the open range now and saw many cattle. The Texas Longhorns originally brought to the area had been bred with the current favorite, white-faced red and white Herefords. The resulting crossbreeds were sturdy, wider, heavier and had much more meat on them. They also herded and drove more easily.

Spur had just turned to ask his employer what kind of cattle he had when he felt something strike his saddle horn and splinter it, and an object hit him hard in the belly. Only after he had jerked free and spun off the horse and dove behind a boulder on the ground did the report of a heavy rifle come.

"Hit the dirt, Northcliff! Somebody's shooting at us." Spur bellowed it and the tall Englishman dropped off his mount in a rush, tripped over the stirrup and fell flat in the road. A second later a rifle bullet tore through the side of his horse and it dropped into the dust, kicking and screaming in a furious death struggle.

Northcliff scampered behind some rocks before any more rounds came. Spur scanned the tree-covered hills, spotted a wisp of white smoke from the rifle round's black powder.

Wilderness Wanton

Trouble. Neither of them had a rifle. They were pinned down in the open. Whoever it was out there with a rifle was good with it. The big question was, who was trying to kill them this time?

Chapter Five

The village of Glenview, Montana Territory,
population 2014, 30 miles south and west of
South Junction, had two more residents this
Friday night in mid-summer. Folke Guthrie
and his wife Dianna were welcome guests in
some places, only tolerated in other parts of
town, and downright unwelcome with the more
gentile sector of the community.

   Tonight, their third full day in Glenview would
be their last if the game went according to plan.
Folke Guthrie wore the traditional loud, out-
landish, bright vest of the professional gambler.
His black suit was not new but carefully tended
and cleaned. He was a tall, slender man, wore
a white shirt and string tie, and his suit jacket
had sleeves that came conveniently close to his
palms.

Wilderness Wanton

Folke had a long, drawn face, but it was not the product of any sickness or dietary problem. He was born that way, as were his two brothers and one sister, who had since passed on to her reward. His gray and wary eyes were set deep in his skull, and he could pull his dark, heavy brows so low that he could barely see out. No one in a high-stakes poker game could look into those eyes to read his intentions. Long sideburns curved outward toward his chin, but he had no moustache or beard. He kept his full head of black hair neatly trimmed, but it was a little longer than that of most of the local businessmen. It was his trademark.

Folke glanced up from his five cards and stared at the dealer. He was a local merchant with a reputation as the top card player in town. In two nights of the friendly game, Folke had lost a little over $200 to the merchant. The man had arrived early at the game and fumbled with a deck of cards, waiting for the poker to begin. The merchant's name was Hans Tally, which was all Folke knew of him, all he wanted to know.

Tally was short and heavy, with folds of flesh under his chin and cheeks so fat they made his eyes all but vanish in their sockets. His hair was sparse blond wisps fighting for survival. He was clean-shaven and smelled of tonic water. Tally's hands were the most vigorous part of him, curiously lean and long fingered. They caressed the cards as if they were lovers.

Five players started the night's play. Now two of them had dropped out and it was down to

Folke, Tally, and another card player called Ike.

Tally had drawn two cards after carefully laying down his hand to deal. Ike took three. He had opened, and Folke figured him for no better than a pair of queens, and no possible luck on the draw. Tally had dealt himself only two cards, which meant he could have three of a kind. He wasn't the kind of player to keep an ace and a pair, nor would he gamble good money trying for two lucky cards to fill in a straight or a flush. He had three of a kind, not over an eight, Folke decided.

Folke looked at his own cards again, fanning them out for a quick peek one at a time from the closed stack of five. He had stayed in the hand and drawn two, which should have given Tally pause. He had held only a pair of jacks, kept a king, and doubled up on the king for two pair, but his fifth card was a seven of hearts. He had the lower hand, but he would win. It was bluff time.

Ike bet ten dollars and Folke tossed in a blue chip and then two more.

"See you and raise you twenty," he said, his voice as smooth, even and natural as ever.

Tally looked up quickly. Folke saw a small tick jerk at the merchant's left eye. He rubbed the eye with his right hand and it stopped. He nodded, then took out three ten-dollar chips and stacked five more beside them. Without a word he pushed the $80 worth of chips into the pot at the center of the table.

They were playing in the far corner of the

main room of the Draw Fast Saloon. It was a little after midnight, and ten drinkers scattered around the big room paid them no attention, lost in their own problems. Five watchers sat around the game, most on top of other poker tables, monitoring the play.

Dianna, wife to Folke Guthrie, relaxed at the table just behind Tally. She had been there since the game began and from all appearances was deeply absorbed in a book. From time to time she adjusted herself on the chair, moved her book on the table, and positioned the special kerosene lamp which the management had provided for her reading ease.

Dianna was in her mid-twenties, and long brown hair with tints of red in it swirled around her shoulders. Her face hinted at strong Irish-German stock, with wide-set, darting green eyes, a small upthrust at the end of her nose, and a mouth wide enough to be friendly and roar with laughter without looking untoward. The effect made her pretty rather than beautiful, but she far outshone any of the three fancy women who lounged about at a sofa at the rear of the saloon waiting for customers. She wore a dab of rouge at her cheeks and some color on her lips, but was far from being a painted woman.

Dianna stood barely five feet tall, still had her slender figure and large breasts for her compact size. She stirred, looked at the game, lifted her brows and went back to her book.

During the times she moved on her chair, it gave her a perfect view of one or two hands of

cards, those of Tally and one of the men who
had dropped out.

A simple set of signs, signals and body move-
ments communicated quickly the strength of the
hand or hands against her husband's play. Now
with only three players it was harder to get
the cards in sight, but she kept working at it.
Tally was not a close-to-the-chest player, and
that helped.

Folke Guthrie watched Ike. He shook his
head, folded his hand and lay it face down near
the edge of the stacks of chips in the center of
the table.

"So, Mr. Lincoln?" Tally asked. Lincoln was
the name Folke had chosen for his stay in
Glenview.

"Fifty to me," Folk said. He stared at Tally a
second, smiled and counted out five blue chips,
then ten more and pushed them into the pot.

"Damn me!" Tally said when he saw the size
of the raise.

"That's a hundred to you, Mr. Tally. How
say you?"

"What? Oh, yes, a hundred." He looked at his
stack of chips. He had more than a thousand
dollars worth of red, blue and white chips in
front of him. He counted out ten of them, then
another five and toyed with them, his fingers
clicking them up and down against the polished
oak table top. At last he pushed them all into
the pot.

"Your hundred, and fifty more to you, Mr.
Lincoln."

Folke didn't hesitate. He counted out the fifty,

then twenty more chips from his stack and pushed them forward. Tally watched him with surprise.

"That's two hundred to you, sir," Folke said.

Ike chuckled. "Glad I got out of this whirl-wind. It's too rich for me."

Tally shot Ike a dirty look, then stared back at his hand. He opened the cards slowly, showing just the barest edge of the value and suit before closing his hand. He sighed, counted out twenty blue chips, then pulled them back into his treasury.

Slowly he bunched his cards and pushed them into the pot.

"Fold," Tally said.

Folke's expression never changed. He simply reached out and pulled the pot into the area in front of him. The pot had about six hundred dollars in it, but he was getting impatient for a big score, one to wipe out the merchant's pile of chips. Ike was not a factor. He was playing conservatively. He started the game with fifty dollars, had over two hundred at one time, and was down now to about a hundred.

Ike dealt and Tally won the next pot, but Folke had dropped out after buying his three worthless cards. The pot had the $20 antes and ten dollar bets to get cards. Ike had folded when Tally backed his openers with a $30 bet.

Folke took his cards, glanced at Dianna and gently rubbed his left eye. This was the hand. She sat a bit straighter, adjusted her position, and waited.

The game was still five card draw, and Tally

couldn't suppress a small grin, which he quickly squelched. Folke was enough of a card mechanic to deal the merchant two queens. He had the other two himself, and an ace. He had dumped a worthless hand on Ike with only a pair of eights. Ike stayed in for the ante and the card-buying round, but still had only a pair of eights and dropped out.

Folke felt his senses sharpen. His eyes became more alert, he knew his heart beat faster, and his breathing tried to quicken, but he held it to a slow steady rate that he had developed over many years of practice in big games.

The draw cards had been exactly what he ordered. The markings on the back of the deck were subtle, but he knew them. He had substituted his marked deck three hands ago when he dealt before and no one had noticed the difference.

His own hand now was a full house, Aces over Queens. He watched Tally try to stifle his joy. Folke had blessed him with exactly what he wanted. Dianna had signalled that he had kept the three queens and the ten that he had been dealt originally. Folke hesitated as he read the cards but had a ten close by and dealt it off the bottom of the deck so swiftly and casually that neither player noticed. Then he dealt himself his two aces, and the betting began.

A short time later it had become interesting. Both players had closed their cards and placed them carefully on the table near their chips.

"Your two hundred," Tally said, and hesitated. " . . . And I'll raise you another four hundred.

Time to see who the real poker player is in this game."

Ike had dropped out after his first ten-dollar bet and now shook his head.

"Four hundred? Damn. That's more money than I make all year working at the hardware store."

Folke ignored him and stared at the chips, wiped what he hoped looked like a small band of sweat off his forehead, and coughed twice. Stall tactics he had learned years ago, but they still worked.

"You said . . . That was *four hundred?*"

Tally nodded, then grinned. "Yes sir. That's what I said. Four hundred United States dollars to you after I met your two hundred raise."

"Ike is right. Four hundred is a handsome sum." He checked his chips. He had more than fifteen hundred in front of him. Tally had about the same amount. "Damn," Folke said softly, and checked his hand. The full house was still there. He let a small smile slip onto his face, made sure that Tally saw it, and scrubbed it away at once. Slowly he counted out the chips, forty of the blue ones, then he counted out fifty more.

"Mr. Tally. I probably shouldn't, but I have faith in my five cards here. I'll see your four hundred and bump you five hundred more. It's five hundred to you, sir."

Tally's smile had begun to fade when Folke counted out the 40 blue chips. When Folke continued with another 50, he picked up his hand and checked it again. He put the cards down, then checked them yet again.

This time when he put the cards down a tight, grim line formed across his face as he counted out blue chips. He had just enough to make the $500. Then he added all of his red five-dollar chips until he had another $200.

"See it and raise you two hundred."

Folke didn't waste time now. He counted out his chips. He had the $200 left in blues, added another hundred dollars and pushed that into the stack. It would nearly wipe out the merchant if he met the bet and lost.

Tally pulled his tie loose and unbuttoned his top button. He shook his head twice, then counted his chips. He had $213 dollars worth.

He pushed every chip he had into the pot, then spoke in little more than a whisper.

"See your two hundred and raise you thirteen dollars." He put his cards face down in front of him and folded his arms. Then he shifted on his chair and rubbed his face. He folded his arms again and closed his eyes.

Folke pushed $13 into the pot.

"Call," he said. "What do you have you'll bet every cent on?"

Tally worked up a small smile and turned his cards over one by one. It was as it was supposed to be.

"Full damn house with three queens over tens," Tally said. "Been waiting my time for a goddamned good hand. This was it." Tally beamed and reached for the pot.

"Mr. Tally. Don't you want to see what my hand is? I would think it's customary, even if I have lost, that I can show my hand if I want to."

"What?" he asked, and his hands came away from the pot. "Yeah, sure, what got you so high money minded, a flush?"

Folke placed his cards face up one at a time, showing the two queens, then two aces. Tally frowned and stared at him a moment before Folke turned over the other ace.

Tally bolted upright, his hand darting for a hideout. The instant he had the weapon in his hand, Folke lifted a five-shot .32 caliber revolver from his lap and shot the merchant twice in the chest before he could bring the deadly little derringer around to fire.

Tally took the two slugs and crumpled, hitting his chair and sprawling face up on the floor. He took two long breaths, then stared at the two men before his head rolled lifelessly to one side. His bowel's emptied, fouling the air.

"Hated to do that," Folke said. He turned to Ike. "You better go bring the Sheriff. You were a witness. He pulled his hideout and was ready to kill me when I had to shoot him to stay alive. Self-defense, pure and simple."

Ike had pushed back in his chair when the weapons appeared. Some of the other men around the table came up and stared at the body. One of them ran for the sheriff.

Folke calmly remained seated, drew the cards together and shuffled them twice, then quickly substituted the house deck they had played with first when Ike looked away. The marked deck went deep in his pants pocket, and he laid out a hand of solitaire with the house cards as they waited for the sheriff.

Before the lawman came, Folke cashed in his chips. The watchers agreed that he had won the pot and there was no sense letting all those chips sit around without being counted. Mr. "Lincoln" owned them sure and proper.

The second barman counted them, stacking them in hundreds. The pot contained $2,483. Folke cashed in the rest of his chips as well and pushed the roll of bills into his pocket. He had almost $4,000 in cash.

A deputy sheriff came, took statements all around, and asked Folke to come into the sheriff's office the next morning to write out a statement. Ike would do the same thing, along with two of the witnesses who had been watching the game.

After he took the statements, the deputy had two men carry the dead man down the street to the undertakers. Then he looked at the cards. He examined the backs of them critically. He called over the barkeep, who also owned the establishment. The man looked at the deck and shook his head.

"Not a damn mark on them. One of my decks, I can tell by the pattern on the back. It's not a marked deck."

The deputy took the deck with him, reminded Mr. "Lincoln" to come to the sheriff's office the next day, and left. A few minutes later Dianna and Folke left as well. The woman had walked away from the table where she was reading as soon as she had signalled that Tally had kept the ten and thrown the other card away.

On the way to the hotel, Dianna grinned. "I

didn't think Tally would be a shooter."

Folke chuckled. "Same with me. I'm going to switch handguns. I'm going for a .45 with a lot more stopping power. I had to use two rounds to put Tally down."

"He wasn't even that big," Dianna said.

"Fat and gullible and now almost thirty-five-hundred dollars poorer as well as being dead."

"You going to see the sheriff tomorrow?"

Folke Guthrie smiled. "Of course. As a law-abiding citizen, I'm honor bound to do everything I can to keep this a crime free community."

Dianna giggled. "Like shit you will."

Folke caught her arm and nudged his hand against the softness of her warm breast.

"Yeah, you're right. I'd rather get to the hotel, lock the door and celebrate with my very own little whore. You never do talk much about those days. What was it like taking on one prick after another six nights a week?"

"You're right. I don't talk about that. Now, do you want to celebrate or don't you?"

Folke grinned as his hand closed around her big breast, and he laughed softly. "Oh, yes, my own little fucker. I want to celebrate with you five or six times, or until I can't stay awake any more or can't get it hard. Let's hurry."

Two hours later, they both lay naked on top of the white sheets in the hotel room. She took another pull from a bottle of whiskey, then returned it to an upright position between her legs so it wouldn't tip over and spill out.

"That's how you got through those long nights

in the whorehouse," Folke said. "Figures."

She nodded. "Get drunk enough you don't have to think about it, remember any of it, even feel what's happening. You're just there and they use you for a half hour and they're gone. Just be sure you never get too drunk to collect the cash before they get their pants down."

"That's why you married me?" Folke asked.

"You didn't know what I was back then. Damn, it's been three years. Not so much different, really. There I fucked for money, cash on the dresser before the pants came off. Now I fuck to please you because you keep me and take care of me and you even by goddamn married me. What the hell is the difference between me and them 'nice' ladies uptown?"

Folke sat up and traced a finger around her flattened breasts. "Difference. Not one fucking hell of a lot of difference. So what you're saying is that all women are whores, one kind or another. Some work for cash, some fuck to get married and have security and love and honor and all that shit, and some just fuck around and have fun until they get pregnant, *then they latch on to one of their bedmates* and make him marry her. Same fucking thing."

"So why do the 'nice' ladies in a town look down on the whores so much?" she asked.

"Why? Maybe they're jealous, maybe they're afraid the whores will get their man and leave them alone and unprotected and unsupported. Mostly I'd think they're just jealous. The whores get all those pricks all the time and don't even have to wash underwear and bear kids and work their youth off in a dozen years or fight with some bastard of a husband."

Dianna nodded. "So why did you marry me?" She frowned. "No, forget that. Would you have married me if you knew I'd been whoring for six months in that saloon?"

"Only six months? I didn't know that before. Would I have married you? Hell, I didn't think you were no angel. Remember the first night I met you at that street dance? We danced and every time I touched you I got a hard-on and pretty soon I talked you into the back of the barn and the haymow and we got it going right there in the damned hay."

"You thought you were seducing me and I squealed and protested and fought you just a little so you'd think I was a good girl."

"I didn't figure you was no virgin, but I guessed that you hadn't been around the back of the barn too damn many times. Yeah, after that first night I was hooked like an overbid bluffer. I'd have hitched you even if I'd known you'd been a working girl for a time."

"Good, now where is my five hundred dollars?"

He pulled her up so she sat beside him. "I keep telling you, you don't need to worry about that. It's our money, not mine. I'll take care of you."

"Nope, agreed, you did. Every time I help and you go over a thousand, I get a hundred."

Folke lifted his brows, bent and sucked on her breasts, came back up and kissed her cheek. "You still squirreling it away? You still have that bank account in Denver?"

"Yes. That's what I rely on to take care of me in my old age. That's just in case you kick my ass out of your bed sometime, or you don't get your six-gun up fast enough some night and some cowboy gets lucky and blows your brains out. This way I'll have some cash to get started again."

"You can always go back to getting poked a dozen times a night."

Dianna's face flashed anger so quickly he pushed away from her. "No, ain't never going back to whoring. I'll find me a little business or maybe open a room and boardinghouse. Now, give me the money."

He found his long, thick wallet and counted out some bills. She took them gently, stared at them for several seconds, smiled and tucked the bills in her reticule on the dresser.

"Now, I feel better. What are we going to do after you alibi your way out of that killing tomorrow with the sheriff? Will we stay here a while?"

"Dianna, we're on our way to a family reunion. You remember, we're heading for South Junction, about thirty miles up the road. There you'll meet my old Ma, and my two brothers, E.B. and Jefferson. I know they'll like you."

"So, we heading out tomorrow?"

"More than likely the sheriff will insist that we move out of his town. Gambling isn't a highly prized profession here in Glenview. I'd say by tomorrow sometime, we'll be in South Junction and having a reunion with my family."

Chapter Six

Spur pressed lower behind the rock as a rifle round whined off the top of it. He took stock of his position. He was on the flat ground in the edge of a modest valley. The trail was about 400 yards from a fringe of trees in the first upslope from the area to the left. His employer, Penley Northcliff, lay behind some rocks to his right.

Another shot came from the high ground and Spur ducked automatically. To his right was a small stream they had been following. It had a fringe of trees and brush and meandered to the north. He looked again. Less than 200 yards upstream a feeder creek came in from the left. He stared at the course of the stream. It branched sharply to the left and angled toward the low ridge of foothills, arriving a quarter of a mile north of the puffs of white smoke that betrayed the bushwhacker's position. He knew what he had to do at once.

"Northcliff, you stay put. No sense in both of us getting hit. I'm going to scramble for that brush behind us about thirty yards. I should be able to make it. You fire a couple of shots from your six-gun to attract their attention."

"The creek?"

"Yes. I can get behind the brush and work upstream, then along that creek that comes in from the left. I should be able to get into cover up there and work in behind the shooters."

"You sure it'll work?"

"Hell no, but at least I have a shot at it. We stay here long enough they'll get an angle on us and shoot us full of lead."

"Oh, well, old boy, in that case, *bon voyage*."

"Yeah, thanks." Spur pulled his feet under him, crouched low and called to Northcliff. "Okay, fire a couple of shots. As soon as you do, I'm up and running."

Spur drew his weapon to make it easier running. One shot jolted into the air from the Englishman. Spur sprinted away from his lifesaving rock and darted ten feet, then zig-zagged in quick spurts the rest of the way to the brush. Two rounds missed him, one kicking up dirt in front of him, the other sailing over his head.

He smashed through some brush and dove behind a foot-thick Douglas fir just as he heard two more rounds slice into the brush over his head.

Now he checked the growth more carefully. It

88

was no more than ten feet wide before it hit the
ribbon of water. The stream itself narrowed to
ten feet across here and he could see the rocky
bottom all the way.

Two more rifle shots zapped through the
brush over his head but 30 feet off target. He
waded into the stream, paused to bend and take
a long drink, then hurried on across to the bank
and turned north along the far edge of the trees
and brush.

He used the Indian trot he had learned years
ago. It was not walking, not running, a kind of
gentle jog that he used to cover long distances
quickly. In open country like this, he could do
a mile in seven minutes and maintain that pace
for two hours without stopping. He could do
fifteen miles in two hours and be ready to fight
when he arrived.

Once he had to duck low as the cover along
the creek thinned, but he made it past and soon
came to the branch creek. He waded across
the water again, staying on the far side of the
tributary, and now jogged to the left, which he
thought should put him close to the shooters
and behind them.

A few firs and pine had seeded down on the
slopes of the foothills, coming within 200 yards
of the valley floor. In that fringe somewhere the
bushwhackers worked. Spur heard a shot now
and then, so at least one man was still there
keeping Northcliff behind his rock.

The creek entered the brush of the foothills,
and Spur took a cautious look at his general
target area. Another shot sounded, and he saw

the puff of white smoke drift up from some brush. The shooter was 250 yards south of him and slightly uphill. Spur ran through the trees and light brush up the slope for 50 yards, then stopped and turned at a right angle and moved cautiously forward.

Now he became a Chiricahua Apache, moving silently, never putting his foot down firmly until he was sure there wasn't something underneath that would make a sound. He drifted from one fir tree to the next, pausing often to look ahead and listen. He came to a bare area 20 yards across. It took him ten minutes to turn uphill again and go around the opening, then back to his line of travel again.

A little over a half an hour after he turned south along the foothills, he stopped again to listen. This time he heard a voice not too far ahead. Spur doubled his efforts at silence and cut in half his forward speed. This was what he had spent all that effort to achieve, and he couldn't spoil it now.

Spur edged around a two-foot thick fir for a look ahead. Through light brush he saw two men lying on a slight lip of ground with an open field of fire in front of them. They shot just under a screen of small brush and were invisible from the valley below.

He worked forward again, silently, not fluttering a branch, not displacing a stick or a leaf. His six-gun in his hand was cocked and ready as he moved in a low crouch. Ten yards later his leg muscles threatened to cramp. He willed them to relax and knew he was in range. When he was

30 feet behind and slightly higher than the pair he aimed at the closer one, holding the Colt with both hands where he lay in the forest mulch.

"Freeze, you're covered, don't even look around." His voice came like a surprise thunderclap on a spring day. One man jolted to the side, turning with the rifle to find a target. Spur changed his target and pumped two rounds into the man's chest before he could get the rifle up.

The second bushwhacker turned and brought up his rifle. It fired a round that slammed through the air an inch from Spur's head. His third round thundered through the shooter's right shoulder, jolting the long gun from his hands, slamming him back to the ground where he screamed in pain and grabbed his wounded shoulder.

"Lay right there quietly and you'll live," Spur brayed. "Move just one hand and I'll kill you the way I did your buddy there. Who the hell hired you to bushwhack me?"

"Go to hell."

Spur fired again, and the precisely aimed round sliced through the flap of pants leg that showed next to the gunman's boot. He sucked in air and scowled at Spur.

"You wouldn't just gun me down in cold blood."

"Why not? You tried to shoot me out of my saddle."

"Different."

"Sure, you got paid to do it. Easy like, take a look at your friend there and tell me if he's dead."

The wounded man nodded, moved slowly to a sitting position, then crawled three feet to where the second gunman lay on his back.

"Yep, he's a goner. You ruined his whole day."

"You're next. Who hired you?"

"Nobody. Figured you were a guard for the boss man's payroll. It's due today."

Spur moved up on the man, checked him and found a hideout in his shirt and a knife in his right boot. He tied the man's hands and found out where the pair's horses were.

Twenty minutes later he rode into the valley on one horse and trailed the other one on a lead line. The second horse carried the dead shooter face down over his saddle. The other bushwhacker walked beside Spur's mount with a lariat around his neck.

Northcliff saw them coming and rose from his place behind the rock, dusted himself off, walked over and caught Spur's mount, which had grazed down the trail aways. When they met, Spur had a question.

"On payday, you bring money out to the ranch to pay your hands?"

Northcliff chuckled. "I don't have that many hands, not that big a payroll. I never carry large amounts of money to the ranch. They say they were after a payroll?"

Spur nodded, and they talked about what to do with the pair. They were two miles from the ranch, so they continued there. The dead bushwhacker over the horse created a stir when they rode into the Bar-B ranch yard.

Spur dismounted and pulled the bushwhacker along with him as he found some shade beside the ranch house. He pushed the man to the ground and tied the rope to a small tree. Then he stared at the outlaw.

"Easy or hard?" Spur asked.

"Huh? What the hell you mean?"

"You want to simply tell us who hired you to kill us, or do you want to make us force the words out of you the hard way, one during which you'll experience all sorts of excruciating pain?"

The bushwhacker snorted and stared at him. "You really don't expect me to rat on my boss, do you? You can't be that stupid. I do that, I never get another job."

"You dead, you'll never get another job either." Spur looked at him. "You'll hang for what you did, you should know that. A man died in your felony crime of attempted murder. That means you can be tried and easily convicted for his death. You're a dead man anyway you look at it. Now, are you ready to tell me who hired you to kill me?"

"Not a chance."

Northcliff had come out of the ranch house a few moments before and listened to the last of the questioning. He nodded and stepped forward.

"I say, I have an idea. An ingenious method was created some years ago, centuries ago perhaps, to help intransigent prisoners to tell the authorities what they knew. Would you mind if I tried it on this chap?"

Spur shrugged. "By all means."

Northcliff called two of his men over and talked with them a moment, then he motioned and Spur untied the rope from the tree and led the prisoner behind Northcliff.

A few minutes later they arrived at the stream behind the ranch house. The ranch hands had brought two doors from the barn. They lay one on the solid ground and then waited. Northcliff had the men position the wounded bushwhacker on his back on the door and then lay the second door on top of him.

The top of the second door came up to the man's chin and he stared at Northcliff with disdain.

"I'm really hurting so far, what the hell are you doing?"

"Patience, wayward one. Justice takes time."

Northcliff nodded at his men, who came to the door carrying 20- to 50-pound rocks and boulders from the stream. They put the big rocks gently on the door, making sure they wouldn't roll off.

Within a few minutes there were over 200 pounds of stones on top of the door. Northcliff called to the bushwhacker, who was staring with wide eyes at him.

"What the hell you doing?"

Northcliff smiled down at him. "An experiment, old chap. Won't take much more, I'd say. Any time you want to tell us exactly who hired you, we stop putting stones on top of you. It's called pressing, and I'm not sure who started it. Some say it was a form of persuasion used by the Spanish Inquisition back in 1483. Tomas de Torquemada may have used it to wring confessions out of the heretics and witches and Jews and Muslims.

"I understand you Yanks used the same device in Salem, Massachusetts, to get confessions from the witches before they were burned at the stake."

Northcliff motioned to his men, who put three more large rocks on the stack on the door. The bushwacker groaned when the last one settled down on him.

"Eventually, of course, the weight will crush your rib cage," Northcliff explained. "Then it's just a matter of a few hours before your crushed lungs stop working and you'll be dead. The pain, I'm told, is horrendous."

Spur McCoy watched the torture and knew that he should step in and stop it. He was an officer of the federal court, an agent of the United States Government. He had to stop it.

"Enough! Stop it," the bushwhacker screamed. "I'll tell you everything you want to know."

Northcliff motioned and the men began taking the stones off the man one at a time. When the top door came away, the bushwhacker told them in detail how Rawlins had contacted them, paid them $100 a man and set them to tracking the pair, but said it had to be done out of town. By the time the confession was finished, the outlaw was too weak to stand. He slumped against Spur as they led him back to the ranch house.

"We both knew it had to be Rawlins," Northcliff said. "That was interesting. No blood, yet effective." He turned to Spur. "What's your suggestion for the next step?"

Spur told him and the Englishman laughed.

An hour later, Spur rode hard for town with the dead bushwhacker still tied over his saddle. On the back of the dead man was a notice spelled out in bold block letters. It said:

"I tried to kill a man. That man killed me instead. I was hired to do murder by Stewart Rawlins. Rawlins is my killer. He paid me $100 to kill a man. I would testify against Rawlins if I could."

Spur pulled up in front of the sheriff's office and hurried inside to bring the lawman. When they returned, 20 people stood around the dead man reading the sign.

"Don't like this, McCoy, you bringing in another dead body." The sheriff read the notice and grinned. "Damned if you ain't got a pile of savvy about you, McCoy. You still aim to lead him down there?"

"Damn right, Sheriff. I want to see his face."

They led the laden horse down to the bank, and Spur walked it up to the front door. He tied the reins to the door handle, and by then someone had told Rawlins, who came out with a shotgun in his hands.

Spur stood beside the door and grabbed the shotgun and aimed it at the sky, then mashed the banker's finger down on the trigger. The exploding shotgun brought half the town running.

"Your employee came home to roost, Rawlins. I'd predict that any more episodes like this one would be extremely dangerous to your health and well-being."

Rawlins let go of the weapon and Spur tossed it to the sheriff. The banker stared at the message a moment, shook his head and waved both arms.

"Sheriff Halverson, I want you to arrest this man for murder. There is the victim. I want him jailed at once and no bail allowed. I want. . . ."

Spur caught the small banker by the shirt-front and backed him up against the door. He twisted the shirt tighter until Rawlins looked at him in anger and panic.

"Not a good idea, Rawlins. Not a good idea at all. You better take care of the funeral arrangements for your good friend there. The money you paid him is still in his pocket. That should pay for a funeral. Two if you want to join him. Now stop bothering me. I have important business to attend to."

Spur let go of the man's shirt, smoothed it out, patted him on the head as he would a puppy, turned his back and walked down the boardwalk to where his own horse waited.

Without looking back, Spur mounted and rode down the street to the north and the Bar-B ranch.

Back at the Northcliff spread, he and the rancher talked about the rustling situation. Spur had brought the maps and notes that the rancher had sent him. They spread everything out on a big table and colored the various spreads in different shades with crayons.

"Now, you've put the brands on each of the

spreads. Looks like seven different ones, including the Bar-B. Which ones have been hit by these rustlers?"

Northcliff folded his arms and scowled. "That, old boy, is the big problem. All seven of us have been hit by the rustlers. Most of us at least twice, some three or four times."

"Is there any pattern?"

"Not that anybody has been able to figure out. If we could find a pattern, then we'd go after them at the next ranch they might hit."

"The sheriff gave me a list of the reported rustling and the dates. I'll put a black date on each of the spreads that reported the rustlings."

"Good idea." Northcliff watched as Spur put down the dates in black crayon over the ranch affected. "I've been thinking about something else. This bushwhacker you caught. The slug went right on through his arm, so there's no problem there. But what are we going to do with him? I can't keep him here for long."

"How about for three days? That will make Stewart Rawlins sweat, wondering what's happened to him and if he's going to talk from a witness stand."

"Yes, I can keep him for three days."

Spur stepped back from the sheets on the table and studied them. "You're right, there doesn't seem to be any date pattern. Sometimes twice a week a raid is made. Last one was almost a week ago."

He studied the layout again. "Look at this, the Bar L spread has been hit only twice. All the rest show at least three attacks and some, four. I'd say the next hit could come at the Bar-L."

"That's the smallest of the ranches. It has the fewest cattle. Maybe the rustlers have given up on them."

"Possible, entirely possible, but I'm keeping it as the ranch they might rustle next."

Spur sat down and looked at the spread-out papers again. "Did you tell me that there hadn't been any extra cattle drives showing up down at the railroad cattle pens south of here?"

"Far as we can tell there have been only the regular ranchers from this area with their registered brands selling steers. I would say there's a chance the rustlers could drive the cattle another fifty miles along the tracks to the next town, but it doesn't seem like an option. Why would they do that?"

"That brings up another problem," Spur said. "Have the rustled steers actually been sold yet? Is someone simply keeping them in some out-of-the-way valley hidden away until the next roundup in the spring?"

"Hold them a year when they are ready for market now?" Northcliff asked. "What benefit would that bring?"

"It would be a cold trail, for one thing. Any rebranding would be harder to spot. It could mean a lot of money for every critter that came through the winter."

"Possible."

"So that's my next job, to check on the outback and see what I can find in the way of hidden valleys and places where those cattle could be hidden. About how many animals are we talking about?"

"From what I hear there are about three-thousand head involved," Northcliff said.

"So it would take a good-sized area to hold that many cattle and keep them fed and watered."

"Water is usually no problem in this country."

"Granted. Who is the man in your crew who's been with the Bar-B the longest? The man who knows every inch of this country up here on your spread and some of the others?"

"Easy, that would be Rusty Kahill. He's the oldest man in my bunkhouse, but he damn well knows the area. Wanted him to be my foreman, but he said he wasn't up to it. Needed a younger man. He was my trail-drive boss this year."

"I'd like to talk to him."

"I'll bring him right up."

Ten minutes and a cup of coffee later, Spur shook hands with Rusty Kahill. He looked about forty, but Spur figured he was closer to fifty. He moved with a labored grace that probably covered up some arthritis or possibly a slight limp. Rusty had graying red hair that had turned into a dull rusty color. It fit. His receding hairline left a patch of pure white scalp and forehead, and a sharp line across both cheeks and downward just below his nose was burned a rich golden brown from the sun. It was his "cowboy" tan produced by the wide-brimmed Stetson.

Rusty was a short, compact man without any spare fat; he looked tough and lean despite his age. His soft brown eyes sized up Spur, and he grinned. His teeth were white, with only two missing.

"Rusty, this is the gentleman I've been telling you about, Spur McCoy, a range detective out of Denver. Spur, meet Rusty."

They shook hands, and Spur liked the shorter man at once.

"I hear you know the back country, up to and beyond the line-shack area on some of the spreads hereabouts."

"Aye, that I do. Been in the valley for twenty years. Good country."

"How long would it take for us to ride over the area I just described?"

"On all the spreads that reach the mountains?"

Spur nodded.

"Four of them, the biggest four. I'd say we could do it in two days."

"We'll leave tomorrow at daylight." Spur looked at Northcliff. "Can your cook put together some no-fire food for us to last two days?"

"No trouble."

Spur nodded. "Oh, and if you have a pint of brandy, we'll take that along for snakebite. Never can tell in this Montana country."

Rusty grinned. "Aye, Mr. McCoy, you damn well never can tell."

"Keep it to Spur, and I'll be more comfortable. Oh, we'll need two rifles, repeaters if you have them, and a pocket full of rounds. No sense going out there without some protection against snakes, crawling kind and riding kind."

"Pleasure after what happened today," North-cliff said.

Rusty nodded. "I hear you kind of saved the ranch out there near Pigeon Creek."

"Just part of my job," Spur said. "I'm ready to get to bed if there's a spare mattress down in the bunkhouse."

"Find you one, no problem," Rusty said. "I'm about ready myself. Dawn, you said."

Spur nodded. He was going to like this sharp old cowhand.

Chapter Seven

Jefferson Ritter Guthrie stepped down from the stage, collected his bag and looked over the town of Forest Grove, Montana Territory. They were getting smaller and smaller, maybe 1500 people. At least there was no telegraph here. Those confounded wires would be the death of him yet. He liked a town of about ten thousand without a telegraph, but they were becoming harder and harder to find.

He didn't figure there would be a lot of business for him in this town, but he was on his way to the family reunion so he had to work the field as it came. He wondered if E.B. and Folke were in South Junction yet, and Ma of course. South Junction was less than 50 miles on down the stage line. Ma enjoyed going with E.B. and their Medicine Wagon show. He knew his Ma loved the play acting when they became rawhiders between towns. Ma was a corker.

Jefferson Guthrie, 36, was the oldest of the trio of brothers and looked somewhat like his siblings with his long, drawn face. He was tall and thin and was the best dresser of the three. Today he wore a new dark blue suit with a small stripe through the fabric. He had a white shirt, four-in-hand tie, and a matching vest. His work demanded that he dress well.

He had dark hair like his brothers, the same gray and wary eyes, and he was clean-shaven except for a moustache. His hair had been cut and trimmed the day before. He had a trim every week, so he always looked sparkling clean.

He picked up the sleek leather traveling bag and made his way down the boardwalk to the hotel. There appeared to be only one in town so he would be forced to stay there. He registered as Jefferson Ritter. It was not prudent to use his real name any more. Too many sheriffs and small-time marshals had his name and photograph, although that picture showed him with a beard and glasses.

He stayed in his room only long enough to deposit his travel bag and take from it a handsome leather letter case and a small flask of whiskey, which vanished into his inside suitcoat pocket. He added a .22 caliber, two-shot hideout in the other pocket and walked back downstairs.

The desk clerk told him he hadn't seen a medicine wagon in town, so E.B. and Ma must not have come this way. He toured the business district. He had been right, not much action here for him. Maybe a lonesome widow who needed some attention and some advice about her investments.

He checked the last six months of the newspaper, scanning the front pages of each weekly and a few inside pages. In one issue four months ago he found an interesting item.

H.B. Jordan, the owner of the Forest Grove General Store, had been taken in death before his time by the ravages of disease. His widow, Katherine, had sold the store but would remain in town to continue her community service work. Ideal.

He noted the name and address of the good lady in the small leather-bound notepad he carried in another suit coat pocket, and left the newspaper office with a nod to the young editor.

Outside he checked the numbers and streets, and ten minutes later knocked on the door of the best house on the block, a three-story wood-frame structure that was newly painted and in good repair.

A maid answered the door and let him in when he said he had business with Mrs. Jordan. She left him in the entrance hall and a moment later showed him into the parlor. Mrs. Jordan was about 40, he figured, a medium-sized woman on the chunky side but not actually fat. She had bright red hair and a delicate complexion. She nodded as he entered, and her stern expression warned him in advance.

"You have business with me? What business, sir?"

He extended a card to her and she read it quickly.

"The Homer Jamison Financial and Securities Organization. I've never heard of you."

"You're quite right, Mrs. Jordan. I'm Jefferson Ritter and I came searching for your husband. He's the one we had worked with, and it is only after I arrived here that I learned of your loss. Let me communicate the company's and my own deep-felt sadness. I had no way of knowing. Perhaps it's best if I pay my respects and retire."

Her pinched face deepened into a frown. "Business you said. Did my husband have investments or securities with you?"

"Yes, ma'am, at least he did. He spoke of cashing in while he was making such a good profit. I can't say for sure if he did or not. I have been in Washington D.C. for the past six months working with the president on a commission. Only now have I been able again to service some of my better accounts."

"His lawyer and I went over all of his business papers and investments, and I must report that he had no stocks or bonds of any kind. He must have sold them."

"Well, I see that my business here is over. If at any time we can be of service to you. . . ."

Her sharp look stopped him. "Why don't you sit down. I was about to have some afternoon tea and cakes. Wanda, you may serve both of us now."

Wilderness Wanton

The girl brought tea in a sterling silver tray and teapot. Jefferson sipped the tea and smiled. "Delightful, it's a tea you've mixed yourself, I would guess. An unusual flavor. Is it scented with rose petals or are those orange peel shavings?"

Mrs. Jordan smiled. "Yes, orange peel slices and shavings I dry myself in the sun. Quite good, I think."

They sipped a little more tea, and then Mrs. Jordan glanced at him and the expensive leather letter case that sat at his feet.

"You say my husband invested through your group in . . ." She looked at the card. " . . . in Omaha. Just how much money did he have with you?"

"At one time or another, around ten thousand dollars. We put him into some stocks that doubled in price in six months and advised him to sell and take his profits. It's quite the normal way to invest these days. Of course there are risks, too. Mr. Jordan selected his stocks with enough insight that he never lost a dime on them, as I recall."

"There is a risk, I know," Mrs. Jordan said. "I remember his talking about stocks. At one time he wanted to become a corporation, and sell stock, but the local banker said he didn't have enough cash reserves. Whatever they are. More tea?"

He smiled and held out his cup. Jefferson hated tea, but he'd learned to drink almost anything the customer offered and do it smiling all the way.

"Do you remember any stocks my husband invested in?"

"As a matter of fact I looked up his account before I came. The stock he liked over the years was Wyoming Mining and Minerals. That was the one that almost doubled in price in two years, and your husband did extremely well with it. You must be benefiting today from his marketing skills."

"Well now, that is nice. He never talked much about money and finances. He didn't think I'd understand him, I'd guess."

They sipped tea again and Jefferson waited. He'd been down this route dozens of times before, and it always worked best to let the victim suggest a stock before he did.

"I wonder if you know how Wyoming Mining is doing these days?"

"Why yes. I put a man in Cheyenne into that stock not a week ago. He invested about twenty thousand and figured if it doubled in two years he could retire and live the life of a grand potentate for the rest of his days."

"How is it doing? The stock?"

"I haven't had a quotation since I left the rail line a week ago. The telegraph keeps me current when I'm near it. My last report was that it was up about ten percent in a month. That is an amazing increase and it won't keep going up at that rate, but the company did have another gold strike, and one of copper and coal as well, so they are solid."

"Oh my. I'm only getting five percent in the banks. Most of my money is in a Cheyenne and

Omaha bank. H.B. didn't trust the local banker, but I have some money there. The banks are paying only five percent these days."

"Bankers say times are hard, but somebody is always saying that. Times are going great at Wyoming Mining and Minerals."

Mrs. Jordan sipped at her tea and took a dainty bite from a cookie on her plate. "I've never seen a stock certificate. Would you have any with you?"

"Usually I can't carry them because some are negotiable, just like a ten dollar bill. However I'm taking some to the office because we can't always trust the mail. They happen to be some Wyoming Mining, which is why I thought of them first."

He opened the leather case and extracted a file folder, from which he took out a gilded stock certificate. It was about the size of a letter and printed on a parchment like paper. The printing was delicate, intricate and bold in places to help prevent counterfeiting. It had a picture of a mining cart and two men pushing it on one side, and a child riding an eagle on the other. "Wyoming Mining and Manufacturing" had been printed in bold Gothic lettering, and a blank was left to write in the number of shares. Near the bottom were lines where the secretary and the president of the corporation had signed the certificate. This one was good for 100 shares.

He handed the certificate to the woman and frowned.

"I do hope you won't tell anyone about my

showing you this certificate. It has the man's name on it, and all our transactions are required to be in confidence. I'd appreciate it if this could be our little secret."

Her eyes flashed as she looked up. "Yes, of course. You said this stock could double in two years?"

"Well, we can't guarantee anything. It has in the past, but past performance can't be relied on to predict future growth."

"No, of course not, I learned that much from my late husband." Mrs. Jordan stared at the stock certificate, then looked out the window, where she could see the ridge of hills on the horizon across the valley. When she looked back she nodded.

"Yes, Mr. Ritter. I think I'd like to buy some of this stock. I know, I know. You can't guarantee the safety of my money, or any increase in stock price or any dividends. I can afford to gamble some money, and the return sounds wonderful."

"You realize my company has a commission charge on the sale. This means we charge a percentage of the sale, as our payment for helping you find the right stock."

"Yes, yes, that's reasonable. What's the commission?"

"Usually five percent, but if you wanted to buy in increments of ten thousand dollars, we would reduce our fee to three percent, saving you two percent right up front."

"Ten thousand," she frowned. "I was thinking more like two thousand. Let me look at some financial statements I have."

"Of course. Or I could come back tomorrow."

"No, I have the records right here. Just take me a minute."

Jefferson Ritter Guthrie sat there as calm as if he had just talked about selling a fifty-cent jackknife. Inside he was churning like a raging river. He hadn't made a ten-thousand dollar sale in almost a year, not since that first one ever in Denver, and that one had put him on the run for six months before he shook off the detective who had dogged him. It had taken a pair of bullets from his hideout to close out the chase.

Now he looked out the window, his mind a maelstrom of possibilities. If this sale went through he might just pass up the family reunion and the traditional activity. He'd have enough money to live for five years if he was careful. Why jeopardize a windfall like this?

The widow Jordan looked up. "Mr. Ritter, I do want to talk to my financial adviser down at the bank. That will take me about an hour. Why don't I see you back here at three o'clock. Then I'll let you know how much of that stock I'll buy."

"Mrs. Jordan, I'd be glad to come back. I'm delighted that you want to check out this stock a little more. I realize that in the past there have been unprincipled men on the loose selling worthless gold mining stocks and such. I can assure you that Wyoming Mining and Minerals is a legitimate company, with stock on the public market. Do you have any other questions before I go?"

She creased her brow a moment, then shook her head. "No, I think you have taken care of my questions. I'll see you at three. Can you find your way out?"

"That I can, Mrs. Jordan. Until three o'clock."

He rose, bowed slightly and walked to the door. It was a sale, he knew. She would ask the banker if he'd ever heard of the stock. The banker would look it up in the stock listings in the Denver or Omaha papers, and he would quote the current price. He had checked it for a week ago. The price had been $22.50 asked and $21.50 bid. He'd go with the $21.50 figure unless she brought back a paper with a lower bid price. Yes, it was going to be a delicious day.

He thought of the woman's surging breasts. He always had been a "breast man." Those female glands fascinated him. Any size any shape were marvels to him, and if he could see them bare he was carried away. Yes, he figured if he completed the sale, he would also suggest ever so casually that Mrs. Jordan was an entrancing woman whom any man would be delighted to be with. One thing could lead to supper and then some candle light and perhaps a gentle seduction. Time would tell. Without the sale, any such try would be a waste of time.

He retreated to a small cafe on the main street and had a cup of coffee and cherry pie, then took off down the street on a vigorous walk for what he figured was a half mile out of town and along the river. He turned at that point and walked back. A check of his gold watch on a gold chain at his vest pocket showed that he would just

112

have time to walk back to the widow Jordan's house and be there at three o'clock.

He arrived on time and before he could ring the bell, the widow herself opened the door. By the smile that blossomed on her plain face, he knew that she was hooked.

"Mrs. Jordan, I hope I'm not late."

"No, dear man, not late at all. Do come in and let's talk."

They went to a different room this time, a den with a couch and desk and many books. She settled down on the couch and patted a place beside her. When they came in she had closed the door behind him.

Now she smiled and nodded. "Yes, I've decided to buy some of the Wyoming Mining stock. I checked the Denver paper and found that the stock has gone up in the past two days. It's now selling for twenty-two dollars. My banker suggested that would be a fair price, as we don't know what it's done in the week since the date of the Denver paper."

"Yes, it's been around twenty-two lately. It did go down to twenty-one-fifty, but twenty-two is a fair price. How many shares do you want?"

"We figured it out. I want four hundred and forty-one shares. That comes to nine-thousand, seven-hundred and two dollars. Which leaves you with almost all of your three hundred dollar commission."

"Yes, ma'am. Only the commission goes to the company I work for, it isn't all mine. I do get twenty percent of it, however."

"I'm glad. You've been such a revelation to me.

I don't know how to show my appreciation."

"I'm pleased, Mrs. Jordan. You're an extremely attractive woman. I'm sure you won't stay a widow for long. Once your mourning period is over, men will be swarming all over this house."

Katherine blushed prettily and lowered her head. When she looked up, she was beaming.

"So, I have arranged for you to get the cash, ten thousand dollars. I hope that was all right. My friend said to be sure to get the stock certificates signed and numbered and the correct number of shares written in. I'll have to have that in hand before I can take you back to the bank and get you the money. We'll have to do that tomorrow. I'm sorry for the inconvenience. But this is a lot of money."

He evaluated the plan in an instant. No problems. The banker would be impressed with the stock certificates. There was no way he could check the fake stock-dealer company he represented. Nothing to spoil the sale.

"Mrs. Jordan, that would be exactly the way I would do it. You can't be too cautious these days. Now, let's get the stocks all set up for you. There will be four certificates, since no one may be written for more than a hundred and fifty shares."

They moved to the desk and he wrote out the stock certificates, which had been presigned with a different pen and in a slightly different colored black ink. When they were fully filled out with her name as owner, she beamed and reached in and kissed his cheek.

"I'm so thrilled. H.B. always said I didn't have a head for figures. I guess I'm going to show him." She stayed close after the cheek kiss. He reached up and turned her face to his and kissed her lips ever so lightly. She closed her eyes at the touch and they opened slowly.

"Oh my!" she said, taking a quick breath. "Oh, my goodness."

"I hope I wasn't too forward," Jefferson said. He put his hands on her shoulders and drew her to him gently. She gave no resistance. He kissed her again, pulling her full breasts against his chest; the kiss was firm and strong. She reacted, and her arms crept around his shoulders. When the kiss ended he held her tightly.

"Mrs. Jordan, that was delightful."

"It was better than that, it was wonderful. Could you . . . would you try that again?"

He kissed her again, his tongue brushing her lips. They opened and he stabbed into her and her breasts pushed harder against him. The kiss lasted a long time and when it ended there were tears in her eyes, tears of pleasure. He softly kissed her nose and her eyes, then her ear as he whispered to her.

"Would you mind going over to the couch?"

She looked at him seriously for a moment, then she smiled and nodded. He took her hand and led her there, let her sit down, then knelt beside her and gently pushed her shoulders down on the long couch and bent and kissed her again.

One of his hands rested on her breasts, and he stroked them easily. She murmured her approval and he caressed them harder. Her hands came up and undid the buttons on the front of the dress, and his hand moved inside. It worked under the camisole, and he fondled her big bare breasts. Katherine sighed, nodded and kissed him again.

Her hand crept down to his crotch. He unbuttoned his fly for her, and her hand edged inside.

A few minutes later she sat up and quickly finished unbuttoning the front of the dress and pulled it off over her head. Then she removed the two petticoats she wore, and the chemise. She sat there with only her drawers on; they extended from her waist to mid-thigh. She grinned as she began undressing him.

"I love this part. I always made H.B. let me undress him. He was always so impatient."

She stopped the undressing and hurried to the door and threw a six-inch bolt soundlessly then went back to her duties.

Soon they lay naked on the carpet next to the couch. He nibbled at her lips, then kissed her as she stroked his erection. Softly, gently he finished the seduction, warming her up with his hands down to her belly, then to her crotch. She murmured as he touched her private glory.

"Yes, yes," she said, so softly he could barely hear. He went between her raised knees and entered her with easy thrusts. Katherine moaned and then squealed before her arms came around him. Her legs went straight in the air, and he settled into position.

"Glorious," she whispered.

He stroked slowly, then faster, and she exploded with a climax almost at once. Her whole body shook and trembled, and then in a few seconds it was over.

"Your turn," she said, and he drove into her with excitement. It was over too quickly for him, and he rolled away panting. She sat up, patted his shoulder, and padded barefooted to the door. She opened it and called to her maid.

"Wanda, we'll be having Mr. Ritter for supper. You may start preparing it now."

She closed the door and smiled. "I couldn't bear to have you leave so soon. We'll have supper, then one more lovemaking before you go."

"I could stay all night."

"Oh, my goodness no. My reputation. Even now, Wanda is wondering what's going on in here. I'll tell her about the stocks, but that won't explain away my glorious smile."

"I guess not. I'll be more than pleased to stay for supper, and afterwards. When does Wanda leave?"

"She lives in, that's the trouble." They both laughed and began to get back into their clothes.

Supper was a vegetable beef stew that had been cooking most of the day—chunks of beef, carrots, parsnips, onions, potatoes, broccoli and cabbage. It was delicious. Homemade bread, butter, apple butter and three cups of coffee complemented the meal.

After both had signed the stock certificates, he put them back in his case. She nodded.

"Good precaution. I might feed you poisoned

117

coffee and take the certificates and never pay you. Prudent move, Mr. Ritter."

They sat in the parlor after the supper. Wanda asked if there was anything else. Katherine had her fix iced tea for them since the evening was warm; then she went to her room on the third floor.

That evening the lovemaking was fast and furious. He wasn't sure that she ever climaxed, but she seemed in a rush to end it, so he did. After they had dressed she reminded him to be at the Forest Grove Bank the next day at ten. There they would transfer the certificates and the cash under the banker's eye.

"I'll be there," Jefferson said. He reached in to kiss her goodnight. She turned her cheek and said something he didn't quite catch, then she had the door open and he walked outside. He turned to look at her once more, but she had closed the door. Why the sudden cooling, he wondered. Did she know the stocks were fakes on a real company? Had she arranged to have him trapped the next morning? Possible.

That night in the hotel room, Jefferson cleaned and oiled the little hideout gun. It would kill a man if he hit him in the head or the heart. The widow-maker would be ready for tomorrow in case he needed it.

Chapter Eight

Spur and Rusty left the Bar-B ranch house just at dawn after a big breakfast of hot cakes, bacon, eggs and country-fried potatoes. The cook made sandwiches of dried beef and cheese for the second day, and roast beef slabs for the first.

The food sacks included fresh and dried fruit, and a dozen crusty apple turnover pies. They would keep well for the two days in the hot sun. At the last minute, Spur decided they could take along a coffee pot and some pre-ground coffee to finish off the meals.

They rode at dawn, Spur on his gelding and Rusty on a feisty little pinto mare. Rusty grinned when she tried to nip Spur's leg.

"Yeah, she's a corker, a lot like me. Likes to get her own way most of the time. We get along. She understands me when I'm around her. I don't take no shit from her, and she knows it. I give her a clout across the side of the head now and then."

They rode at a gentle lope to achieve a six mile per hour rate as they headed due north toward the mountains.

"Four of the big spreads reach up to the foothills," Rusty said. "We'll head near straight north and get to the ranch that's east of us a bit. The Bar L is over there, about half the size of the Bar-B. We've got more critters. Both outfits control big stretches of land we don't own up north into the edge of the mountains wherever there's graze.

"Up in there is where there could be some steers hid out. Course you know about half the stolen cattle have been brood cows. A rustler don't have no problem with brood stock. Just change the brand or blank it out. In a year or two the hair will grow long enough to cover up the old brand and you got yourself a $200 brood cow. That's if you're starting a new herd on your own. Ain't heard of no new outfits starting up around here.

"Don't always work, but usual. The steers got to be marketed sooner or later. Don't know what the hell these night riders are doing with them. I hear ain't been no more sales down at the railroad pens on steers lately. Got to be doing something with them."

They were on the fringes of the Bar-B range, and now and then they saw Bar-L stock.

"Overlap here on the ranges. That's why we usual have a round-up with each of our neighbors. Easier than a whole range-wide gather. That gets too complicated."

"I've got to admit, this is a new kind of a problem for me," Spur said. "Usually there's a bunch of marketable cattle stolen, driven to a spot and then on to a market somewhere. Doesn't seem to be the situation here."

"So where are the damned critters?" Rusty asked.

"That's what I hope we can find out. Some grazed-down valley that should be untouched. Maybe the remains of a branding fire or two. Even some concentrated horse droppings and trash from a cooking fire. There's got to be some evidence up in here somewhere."

"Yeah, got to be, but let's face it, if these rustlers are as smart as they seem to be, you think they'll leave any easy-to-read clues like you been talking about?"

Spur chuckled. "Probably not, but we've got to take a look and eliminate any possibility."

They rode harder then, shifted out of the Bar-B land and snaked up a long draw that emptied out into some breaks that made the country look like a patchwork quilt of ravines, draws, small valleys, cliffs, bluffs and a dozen other types of terrain.

"Welcome to the breaks," Rusty said. "This is all on the end of the land the Bar-L controls. Logan is the gent's name and he runs a right respectable outfit. I worked for him one year back when he was getting started."

Spur studied the breaks that spread out for at least ten miles ahead of them and more than a half mile wide before the land rose sharply into the foothills. Behind them they could see the Rocky Mountain range to the far north and west. The white-capped peaks spread across the horizon in what looked like an unending display of majesty.

"Rusty, you heard any bunkhouse figures of how many cattle have been rustled from the seven outfits?"

"Yep. Gibber and guess. Figures run from fifteen hundred to thirty-five hundred. Probably somewhere in between."

"Sheriff says it's near to three thousand. Now a herd that big can't be hidden in a gully half mile long. Up here they'll need an acre a critter to keep alive and a lot of water."

"Water ain't no problem."

"True, which leaves us with a hide-a-way at least two miles long, maybe a mile wide. That would keep three thousand head happy for maybe a week before they had to be moved to new grass."

"Why the hell somebody going to all this hanging trouble and not making any money out of it?" Rusty asked.

"It must be a long-range operation. They figure they'll do the work now, take the risk and by roundup time next spring, they'll get the critters to market with no problems."

"That's a damn long-range operation and a big gamble. Half of them could be wiped out in a blizzard this winter."

Spur nodded and checked the breaks in front of him stretching to the northwest. He saw only two areas that looked promising, and he pointed them out to Rusty.

"Yep, been in both of them a time or two. Big enough for a holding operation for a time. Not easy to get to."

They rode. It was three hours later, past noon before they came to the first of the suspect areas. The grass was lush and tall and hadn't been violated by a single cow all spring.

"Logan always likes to keep this one for further along in the summer when the grass dies lower down on the slopes. He'll drive a lot of his stock up here in another couple of weeks or so."

The second valley yielded nothing, and they retraced their ride to where they had entered the breaks. Now they looked to the west more. These were the breaks topping out of the Bar-B range. There weren't as many possibilities here and the country wasn't quite so rugged.

Rusty knew this area better. They made good time and checked two spots where he thought there might be chances for a hidden herd. A few of the far-ranging Bar-B cattle had wandered into one of the valleys, but there was no concentration, no fence across an opening to contain them.

By that time it was the middle of the afternoon. They hadn't stopped for coffee yet.

"Where to next?"

Rusty pointed further west. "The Box C, Cuthright's outfit. Don't know much about him or the country."

"Break time," Spur said. They had just come

to a small creek bouncing down from the
mountains above. A clutch of trees offered some
shade and they dismounted and dug out the food
sacks. Rusty worked up a small cooking fire and
soon had the coffee pot boiling.

They munched on the roast beef sandwiches,
ate some of the fresh apples and some raisins.
Then Spur remembered the apple pie turnovers.
They each had two of the triangular little pies
and a second cup of coffee.

Rusty looked up. "True what they saying
about you and our friendly local money-
grubbing banker?"

Spur grinned. "Depends on what they're
saying."

"They say that you rousted him when he lit
into Ben the stage driver. Nailed him to the
wall, drew on him, made him look chickenshit
foolish."

"Guess it's true."

"So he tried to kill you twice and you nailed
the hired hands?"

"About the size of it, but don't tell the
sheriff."

"No chance."

They rode again soon after that. It was
nearing dusk when they got to where Rusty
wanted to go. It was higher on the slopes
than they had been before, but Rusty said it
would give them a fine view of the breaks
topping out the high range of the Box C
spread.

They stared into the growing darkness, and
Spur shook his head. "Too late today. Let's

find a campsite and we'll hit it at dawn in the morning."

They found a grove of fir trees, and Rusty leveled off a spot with a small folding shovel he had brought along. Then he dug a six-inch trench two feet wide and six feet long. In it he cut fir boughs, stripping the finger-sized branches off larger limbs until he had a fluffy bed of pine needles half a foot thick.

He lay two blankets over the needles and tested the natural mattress. A smile broke out on Rusty's face.

"Oh, yes, nothing like a nice pine-needle bed, if'n you can't get a feather ticking. Ain't done this for six or eight months. Not bad, not bad at all."

They had a small fire, more coffee and sandwiches, then both crawled onto their blankets. Rusty went to sleep almost at once. Spur put his shoulders and head on his saddle and stretched out with his feet toward the warmth of the few coals left from their cooking fire. They were at more than four thousand feet here and the nights could get nippy even in summer. He spotted the big dipper and the north star, then he slept.

Rusty had a fire going when Spur woke up the next morning. The coffee was boiling but not quite done yet. He rubbed the sleep from his eyes and went to the lookout and studied the land in front. He saw at least four spots they needed to check out.

They ate quickly and got away from their camp a half hour after dawn.

For six hours they rode, tracking the elusive valleys in the confusing, often dead-end draws. Once they rode higher again to get their bearings. By noon they had checked out the last of the four suspect spots and found exactly nothing.

Spur looked at the notes he had brought along from the big layout of spreads on the dining room table back at the Bar-B.

"Next one is the Circle-L, that's the Lathrup spread. I got them confused back there somewhere. Lathrup is the farthest west and Logan farthest East. Will we find anything there?"

"Not much chance," Rusty said. "The breaks tend to smooth out just past the Box C. I doubt if there's even one spot that would hold three thousand head. I worked for Lathrup for five years. I'd say it would be a waste of time to ride over that area. There's nothing at all south or west that would fit what we're hunting for."

"If we head southeast will we come in close to town?"

"Yep. Closer to town than to the Bar-B. Been a while since I been in town. I'm not much for drinking any more and the girlies don't get my blood boiling so much. That the way we're heading?"

Spur nodded and they rode out at their cantering pace.

They came into South Junction a little after three o'clock. Spur treated Rusty to the biggest early supper he could manage at the Mountain Cafe, then sent him back to the Bar-B.

After the meal Spur talked to Sheriff Halverson. The man knew nothing more about the rustling situation than when Spur had talked the last time. He thought of showing Halverson his credentials as a Secret Service agent, but decided this wasn't the best time. He gave up on the lawman and went to the First Class Saloon. Abby saw him come in and soon stood next to him at the bar.

"Where have you been? Three days and not a peep."

"Two nights. I was out on the range doing my job."

"Find out anything?"

"Found where three thousand cattle are not being hidden."

"So, that's progress."

He stared at her, not understanding.

"If you find out something isn't true about a mystery, that's one element you know about and you don't have to cover that ground again, so it's progress."

"Yeah. Have you heard anything about the missing cattle?"

She shook her head.

"Listen to some of the cowboys. Somebody might let something slip when he's been drinking a bit."

"I'll try."

"What's Rawlins doing?"

"He's so furious he won't even come out of his office. He's afraid people are going to laugh at him. The man is paralyzed. I'm sure he'd try to kill you if he had the chance."

"Good, I'll give him a chance. I need to pay him a visit. Want to come along?"

Abby shook her head. "I don't like to get blood splattered all over my new white blouse."

"A nice blouse. I especially like the way it outlines. . . ."

She held up a hand. "Later. Tonight for sure? In my house. Stop by here and I'll let you walk me home after closing. No, a long time before closing. Harvey can close up as usual."

He finished the beer he had started, nodded at her and left the saloon. It was almost time for the bank to close at four o'clock. He walked quickly and slipped in the door just as one of the clerks was reaching for the lock.

Spur didn't announce himself. Rather he walked straight to the door marked "President," and kicked it open. It hit the wall with a bang, and the man at the desk looked up. Somehow Rawlins looked smaller than his five-feet five today, sitting behind the desk. He glared when he saw Spur and reached toward a drawer.

Spur's .45 was out and centered on the banker's chest with the ominous click of the hammer cocking before Rawlins had the drawer open.

"No, no, Rawlins. No guns. This is just a friendly visit. I want to impress on you the idea that I'm getting mad as a wet setting hen about the way you're trying to kill me. Warning time. If anyone in this town or country tries to gun me down or blow me up, I'm coming straight for you. I don't care if you're behind it or not. If I get attacked in any way, you're a hanged man, hanged by the neck until dead, dead, dead."

Rawlins sat there trembling. He looked at Spur, then at the clerk who had come in the door, then back at Spur. He started to say something, then waved the clerk away.

"The corpse of one of your hired guns, I hope you gave him a decent burial. The other one in the team is incarcerated in a jail of my own making. He's waiting to testify against you on an attempted murder charge. If we need him, we'll have him. Anything to say, Rawlins?"

The small man started to stand, then changed his mind and remained seated. He picked up a cigar and tried to light it, but didn't. He put it down. "I. . . . I don't know. . . ."

Spur cut him off curtly. "Don't deny it. I have a confession, a live one. If I have to use him, you're a dead man, hanged. Remember, all those hundreds of thousands of dollars you have and all the people you control won't do you one damn bit of good when you're measured for a pine box and dug into the graveyard!"

Spur stared hard at the man, turned and walked out of the room, through the bank and to the front door. He opened the twist lock and barged outside, angrier than he had been in some time. He took a deep breath and grinned. That had been fun; he enjoyed chawing on the little man's ego for a while.

At least now Spur didn't have anything pressing to do the rest of the afternoon and night. A long hot bath at the hotel, a

129

drink, then a guided tour of Abby's house. Maybe even a little bit of squeeze and tickle before the night was over. He lifted his brows and headed for the hotel and that first-floor bathtub.

Chapter Nine

Jefferson Guthrie whacked the reins down on the back of the fancy black mare and rolled the buggy away from the South Junction livery stable. As it turned out, he had no trouble whatsoever getting his $9,700 at the bank the morning after his sex games with the widow, Katherine Jordan, and he took the cash in $100 national bank notes.

Guthrie turned one of the bills over in his hands as he drove the carriage. He enjoyed looking at it. It was one of the prettiest sights he could remember. This one bill represented as much money as a working man could make in three months.

He drove the horse to the left, down a street that led out of town toward the creek. E.B. said he would meet his brothers on a creek a ways out of town where he would park his Medicine Wagon and get ready for his grand entrance into South Junction.

Jefferson wasn't about to walk to find the place; neither would he ride a horse. He considered riding a horse the lowest form of transportation. After all, he had to establish his position as a man with money in this small town, and one of the best ways to do it was to dress exceedingly well and drive a fancy buggy with an outstanding horse.

As his rig rounded the last house in the town, he could look out the River road. He detected a small plume of smoke rising from a group of trees about half a mile upstream, so he headed that way. That looked to be a likely place for E.B. to transform himself from a rawhider into a medicine man. Jefferson wondered what kind of women E.B. had picked up along the way this time. He never was without some female for long.

As he rolled up to the trees, Jefferson could see the wagon. Must be the place. He came to a stop next to the tattered wagon and E.B. rushed around the tongue and waved. A moment later Folke and his woman came around from the fire.

"Looks like I discovered the Guthrie clan," Jefferson said. He tied the reins of the black to hold her steady and stepped down.

He shook hands with E.B. and Folke. E.B. was still in his tattered overalls and long-handled underwear. His beard was scraggly, and he was a damn mess. Folke, on the other hand, was dressed in his gambler's outfit, with a red checkered vest to go with his black suit. Without the vest he could have been a preacher or an undertaker.

"Where's Ma?" Jefferson asked.

E.B. turned away. Folke shook his head and closed his eyes.

A young girl came around the wagon combing out her long blonde hair, which she had just washed. Her still-wet blouse clung provocatively to her good breasts.

"They can't talk about it," Melody said. "You must be Jefferson. They said you'd be coming. Your Ma got shot dead about a week ago a piece south of here. Young kid with a shotgun. He got away."

"Ma dead?" Jefferson sagged against the buggy. "Somehow I just never figured that Ma would ever die. She's always been around for as long as I can remember. She had to go on living forever." He pushed away from the buggy. "Is it too late to go after this kid? How long ago? Tell me about it, E.B."

E.B. Guthrie, youngest of the brothers, shook his head and looked at his oldest sibling.

"Ain't nothing to say. She's dead and gone. My fault, I should have taken care of the nub when I first saw him. Didn't, and Ma got shot and that's that."

Jefferson listened and nodded, then he whacked his hand into the padded seat of the buggy and swore. When he turned around again some of the anger had drained from his face.

"Ain't like us to let this happen. I mean we

always say an eye for an eye. We usually even up the score damn fast. Remember when Pa died?" They nodded.

Melody frowned. "I don't know about that. What happened?"

"Who are you?" Jefferson asked.

"Oh, I'm Melody. I'm with E.B. Cook and things for him. What happened to your Pa?"

"Simple little poker game. Two strangers. They dumped on Pa good, cheated him out of his poke and then tried to take his horse for a marker he gave them. They shot him four times and rode off."

Melody pulled the wet blouse free where it stuck to her breasts and released it. It peaked again, clinging to her wet skin and outlining her mounds perfectly. She watched Jefferson staring and grinned. "So, you go after them?"

"Did. E.B. and I rode them down, cut their balls off and made them eat them, then we tied a half-inch rope to each leg of one of them and snugged the lines down around our saddle horns and galloped away in opposite directions."

Melody put her hands over her face. "Oh, God!"

"Yep, we ripped them legs right off the rest of him. Then we did the second one and left them in a trash heap. Us Guthries don't take kindly when one of our own is murdered."

Melody's eyes were large and her breathing came fast. One hand rubbed a breast as she looked at Jefferson hungrily. "Oh, damn, but that makes me excited. You busy, Jefferson?"

"Right now?"

"Uh huh. E.B. won't mind, over there in the woods."

He grinned, eyed her up and down, then shook his head. "Not now. Family business. Maybe later."

E.B. had gone back around the wagon to the fire, where he was in the process of heating some water to shave and wash up. Two saddle horses were tied on that side of the small camp. Jefferson squatted near the fire and watched E.B.

"You all right, little brother?"

"Fine. Still mad as hell, but I'm alive. That damn kid got away and I figured he had another gun. Not a damn thing I could do about him. He warn't more than twelve years old."

"That's a bad one, E.B. Maybe we can make up for it here in town."

"Oh, I burned out some of my hate on the next ranch we found. But it's still not all gone. We still working on that big project of yours?"

"You bet. Soon as you get presentable and we can establish ourselves in town."

"Two days and I'll be ready to go. You won't know me."

"What about Melody?"

"Damn, help yourself. I can get another one. Right now I want to hear more about the project."

Jefferson watched his brother clipping more beard. "When you're ready to be fit company for the gentle people of South Junction, we'll talk about the project. I need some time to scout out the place and make some contacts. We're not going to do this one all by ourselves."

E.B. pointed the scissors at Jefferson. "Told you before, I don't like sharing with outsiders."

"This time we need them. This is going to be bigger than anything you ever thought possible. Now, get yourself cleaned up and then paint your wagon and get out your big signs for the sides. We need the medicine wagon as part of our smokescreen." Jefferson paused and watched his brother. "You have any trouble with that, E.B.?"

The tattered, dirty, bearded man glared at his brother for a moment, then looked away and shrugged. "Just so we get to hit something really big and make a lot of money. I'm about ready to find myself a young whore and settle down. Whores make the best wives, you know that? They ain't all that demanding, don't give you a lot of mouth and they know they just lucky as hell to be married and not wind up with one of them diseases and die before they thirty-five. Yes, sir, a nice clean young whore only been working a year or two. Them's the best wives ever."

"Whatever fits you, little brother. Now, I've got to get back into town, find a hotel and start establishing myself as a man of means. Oh, in case you have some expenses getting yourself turned back into a human being."

Jefferson extended a bill that had been folded lengthwise. E.B. took it out of his hand disdainfully, then looked at the face of it and saw the figures.

"Be damned! For me? Never seen me a

hundred before. Is it good? Not one of them counterfeit ones?"

"Good as five double eagle gold pieces. You stop by for me at the hotel when you're fit and proper. Make it some time tomorrow." Jefferson turned and saw the young girl step down from the wagon. Her hair, now dry, was hanging around her shoulders, half way to her waist. It curled on the ends. She wore a white blouse without a spot of dirt or grime and a full red skirt that swept the ground. She even had shoes on.

She looked up. "Oh, Folke and his wife had to get back to town. He's setting up a poker game for tonight in one of the saloons. He said he'd leave word for you at the one hotel in town which room they was in. Said maybe the three of you could have supper together tonight."

"Thank you. Melody, wasn't it? What a pretty name."

E.B. came around the end of the wagon, saw Melody and laughed.

"Damn, you the same female I had in my wagon? Look a hell of a lot better now. She's wanting to go into town, Jeff. Told her to wait until you came. You mind giving her a ride in? She needs to buy a new dress or two so she can look proper at my medicine shows."

Jefferson looked at Melody again and nodded. "Seems I have room to take her to town. You giving her some money to buy those clothes with?"

"Nope. Figured you could do that. Know damn well she wants to do you soon as you get out of sight. Hold her off and show her what fucking is like in a soft, clean hotel room. After that you can get her some clothes, if'n you want to. One more screw don't make me no never mind. Hell, can't hurt it any. Bring her back or keep her there a couple of days. Up to you."

Jefferson snorted. "You always did have a smart mouth, E.B. This time looks like you figured things out about right. She's hot to drop on her back and lift her legs, sure enough. I'll give her a try."

He walked to the buggy and helped Melody step into the clean padded seat, then looked back at E.B., who had part of his face scraped clean with a straight razor.

"Still hate it about Ma. You say there's nothing we can do about it. Damn it. So the kid was only twelve, a life for a life." Jefferson frowned. "Oh, did you do his family?"

"Yep, three of them. Then I cremated Ma in the log cabin they built out there."

"Cremated! Jesus, E.B." He stared a minute longer, then untied the reins and turned the rig around and drove the high-stepping black back to town. They made one trip the length of town so some of the folks could see them, then returned to the hotel.

They signed in at the hotel as Mr. Reginald J. Archibald and daughter Rachel. He made up the names on the spot and liked the sound of them. The clerk never looked twice at the obvious young age of Melody. He had learned long before to be discreet, especially when the man tipped him two fifty-cent pieces.

Wilderness Wanton

Upstairs in the room, Melody locked the door, then turned. She had already opened the buttons on the white blouse from top to bottom and brushed her hair back over her shoulders. The gap between the sides of the blouse showed a generous glimpse of her young breasts.

For the first time since he had met her, Melody seemed a little nervous, unsure of herself. She walked back and forth and hardly looked at him. He sat on the bed and waited. At last she stared directly at him.

"I hope to glory, Jeff, that you like a whole lot what you see. Most older men like younger girls. I promise that I know a lot about fucking and can show you a marvelous time." She pulled back the sides of the blouse to reveal her up tipped breasts, which were larger than he had hoped. Her nipples were starting to pulsate and grow. She rubbed them gently, then walked over to him.

She put his hands on her breasts and let him caress them a little, then she sank to her knees between his spread legs and worked at unbuttoning his fly.

"I know how to get you warmed up all right and proper, and leave a lot of slippery juice on you," Melody said with a sweet smile.

"Show me," Jefferson Guthrie said in a husky voice.

Melody did, three times. She dozed a little afterwards, then came wide awake. Jefferson slept beside her. She lifted his arm off her stomach and lay it gently on the bed. He didn't wake up. She eased off the bed and dressed quickly, then took the wallet from his pants pocket and looked inside. She'd never seen a hundred dollar bill before. There were eight or ten of them there. She slipped three out and pushed them into the small pocket sewn into her skirt.

She put the wallet back in his pants pocket, and with cautious, soft steps moved to the door. It squeaked as she unlocked it and pulled it open a foot. She squeezed through, closed the door without a sound, and hurried down the hallway.

Three hundred dollars!

That was as much as some grown men made working all year. She considered for a moment what to do, then she walked out of the hotel and asked someone where the sheriff's office was. She found the place, went in and stared boldly at the man behind the waist-high counter.

"I need to talk to the sheriff," she said.

The deputy smiled. "What might a pretty young girl like you want to talk to the sheriff about?"

"Murder, rape, arson, burglary, everything a rawhider does."

The deputy came to his feet and stared at her, then walked to a door and knocked. He went in and a moment later came out.

"Right this way, Miss. Sheriff Halverson would like to talk to you."

She walked in with her head up and stood watching the sheriff for a moment. Yes, he would believe her. She could trust him.

"Now, Miss, what was your name and where are you from?"

"My name is Melody Parker. I growed up over in Idaho a ways, on a farm outside a little town called Salmon."

"Yes, I hear you. You said something about murder to my deputy. Tell me about that."

She sat down in a chair across the desk and stared at the man. Yes, he would believe her. "Well, one day about six months ago, a covered wagon pulled up at the farm and a man and a sick woman was in it. My Ma helped the sick woman and then the man shot my Pa dead on the spot. Then he raped my Ma, and the old woman messed with my twelve-year-old brother. She warn't sick at all, just pretending.

"They tied me up and then when they was done with Ma and Willy, they killed them and stole everything any good inside the house, then burned it down.

"They took me with them and the man. . . . he had his way with me that first night, with me tied to the bunk inside the wagon. After that, he took me whenever he wanted to. He said he kept me for . . . for his pleasure. This is the first time I had a chance to get away. I slipped out of the wagon about twenty miles south of here and been walking and getting rides ever since."

Sheriff Halverson had been writing on a pad of paper. When she stopped talking he looked up.

"Melody, how old are you?"

"I'm eighteen last birthday in April."

"You look more like fifteen."

141

"That's what everyone says. I'm just over eighteen."

"Melody, can I believe all of this story that you're telling me?"

"You sure as hell can. If'n you don't think so, you write a letter to Salmon, Idaho Territory to the sheriff there and ask him about the Parker family. Or you can look at a little ranch about twenty miles south of here. Don't know their names. Little spread, man, woman and two kids twelve and thirteen, maybe, a boy and a girl. All killed, house and barn burned down."

The sheriff growled deep in his throat and put down his pencil. He got up and went to his window and looked out.

"I know about the Vuylstekes, three of them dead all right along with another body."

"That was an old woman. She was this rawhider's mother."

"Did the rawhider use a name?"

"Ben, only name I ever heard. Now you don't need to worry about me. I didn't hurt nobody. I was trying to get away. Old Ben got drunk and I stole a hundred-dollar bill from him and ran away as fast as I could. I got kin of some kind here in town. I know how to find them, a cousin I think."

"You have a hundred-dollar bill?"

"Yes sir. You turn around and I'll show you."

The sheriff grinned and turned his back to the girl. She slipped one of the $100 bills from her hidden pocket and held it up so the lawman could see it.

"Can I look at it? Might be counterfeit."

"No sir. Not a chance I'll give it up until I get some smaller bills for it, like at a bank."

The sheriff sat down in his chair. "Miss Melody Parker, I believe your story. Happens more than I'd like it to in this end of the country. I'll put out a wanted on this Ben. How old is he?"

"A little over thirty, so dirty you couldn't tell most of the time."

"Describe him for me, big, heavy, skinny, tall?"

"Tall and thin, longish face, dark hair. About all I remember."

"Describe the wagon."

"Usual kind, had hoops and a canvas over it, some in tatters. Pulled by two brown mules. Ornery critters."

"Good. Anything else?"

"Can't think. We was heading south after that last ranch he burned down. Said it would be safer that direction. That's why I hitched a ride up north, away from him."

"Fine. Now are you sure you can find your cousin?"

"Yes, I'm sure. I got away from Ben. I can do about any damn thing I want to now. Pardon my swearing but I picked it up from Ben. Had to be tough to live that way for six months."

Sheriff Halverson grinned. "I can see that. Tell you what. I'll send a deputy with you to the bank to vouch for you. Over there they'll break that hundred-dollar bill into smaller ones, so you can spend it if you need to. In case you don't find your cousin right off. That sound fair?"

Melody blinked, holding back tears. No one had been decent and nice to her in a long time. She nodded. "Yes, Sheriff Halverson, that's fair."

She stood, and the sheriff held the door for her.

Ten minutes later, Melody had a wad of bills in her hands as she came out of the bank. The deputy suggested that she buy a reticule to put the money in so nobody would rob her on the street. He took her into a store and they came out a few minutes later with a small brown reticule with strings on the top she could tie to her wrist.

She thanked the deputy, told her she would find her cousin right away, and walked down the street away from the sheriff's office. The sheriff waited a minute. When she looked back at him he waved and walked the other way. Melody reached the far end of the business buildings and didn't find what she was searching for. She crossed the street and went the other way and walked almost to the end of town before she spotted the structure she wanted.

It simply looked like a whorehouse. She had decided what she would do long before her first good chance to escape. E.B. had watched her like a guard dog, especially since his Ma died.

She hadn't sent the sheriff out to E.B.'s wagon. She had better plans for E.B. than to send the law on him. She wanted to kill that dirty old man for what he had done to her. He'd turned her into a whore and nothing could undo it. Damaged goods. She knew what the proper ladies of even this small town would say if they knew. If she testified against E.B., everyone in town would know he'd been poking her twice a day and sometimes more.

She checked up and down the street, went to the door and knocked. Then she saw the sign that said: "Welcome, please come right inside." Figured. She turned the knob and stepped into the entranceway. It was a hall eight feet long, with three doors opening off it. Two were closed. The one straight ahead led into a parlor with fancy furnishings and paintings on the wall of half-naked women. Melody grinned. She'd picked the right place.

A woman stared at her from the parlor for a minute and then motioned to the other door.

"Honey, if you're looking for work, we're short-titted around here. You best talk to Noona, that door on the right. She's the one to see."

Melody looked at the whore a minute. She was in her twenties, had small breasts peeking through a lacy robe. She was thin, with a heavily painted face, and she looked as if she had dyed her hair. Melody figured she was twice as pretty as the whore.

She nodded, turned back to the entranceway and knocked on the door on the right.

She heard a sound from inside and pushed open the door. The wallpapered room was stark and prim and looked smaller than its eight feet square. A desk sat near the far wall. The big woman who stood behind the desk must weigh 200 pounds, Melody figured. She stared at Melody a minute, then smiled.

"Well, honey, if you come looking for work, we can use another pussy around here. One of my girls is six months pregnant and another one run off with some no-good cowboy. You are looking for gainful employment by selling your ass, ain't you?"

Melody giggled. "Yes, ma'am."

"How old are you, Honey?"

"Eighteen."

"Fifteen more likely. Some fuckers like them young. You got more tits than most of my girls. They won't like that, but the men sure as hell will. Two dollars a poke, you get one, and I get one. I charge you $8 a week for room and board and you buy your own clothes. You got any?"

"Just this."

"Figures. You get any tips, you split them with me down the middle. No holding back or I can get unpleasant. I'm good to my girls. Ask them."

"How many?"

"We got six here now. Could use ten."

"No, how many times a night?"

"For you, ten or twelve. Make it a half hour by your alarm clock. Each girl gets one. Keep it wound up tight and set the alarm. Get paid first and don't let them do anything you don't want them to. No rough stuff. You understand?"

"When do I start?"

"Relax, not until six o'clock. Oh, we get a matinee clerk or cowboy once in a while. Marsha takes care of them. I'll show you where you'll do your gainful employment. It's your room, too, where you live and sleep after the clients taper

146

off. About two A.M. Down this way, then up the stairs. You'll be on the second floor front. Not big, but homey."

Back at the hotel, Jefferson Guthrie came awake the moment Melody moved his arm off her stomach. He kept his eyes closed until she left the bed, then slitted one eye and watched her. He saw her dress, then lift his wallet. He saw her stare into it, then take out three of the $100 bills.

He grinned. She was being careful, taking enough to make it worthwhile, but not all of it so he'd track her down or stop her right now. He waited until she left the room, then dressed quickly and watched her out the front window as she walked down the street.

He saw her again when he walked up behind her just before she turned into the sheriff's office. Jefferson had a cup of coffee and a piece of cherry pie in a cafe across the street, down three doors as he waited for her to come out.

Was she ratting on E.B.? She was too old to train to be a rawhider, too young to be free to testify against E.B. He wondered what to do. When Melody came out 20 minutes later, she was chaperoned by a deputy sheriff. Jefferson saw the shiny silver star.

He followed them to the bank, then waited again and saw her come out with a fistful of bills. Broke up the $100 bill so she could spend it easier. He was surprised when the deputy led her into a store, but nodded when she came out with a reticule. Then the deputy left her and she walked the other way.

He tracked her from the other side of the street. She seemed to be looking for something. When she went up the steps to the big house at the end of town, Jefferson grinned. He could tell in a second what the house was, a bordello, and evidently the only one in town. The girls there had it better than the lower class whores in the saloons.

Jefferson Guthrie watched the whorehouse and the sheriff's office from a vantage point between the two. Melody never came out of the pleasure palace, and there was no special activity around the law office. Maybe little Melody had a change of heart and wasn't going to sic the law on brother E.B. after all.

He couldn't take the chance.

Jefferson went back to where he had parked the carriage, boarded it and snapped the whip over the horse's back as he drove out to E.B.'s camp. He'd have his little brother move his place three or four miles down the road on the other side of town and conceal it well in some woods. No sense letting some angry little girl put a crimp in the clan's grand plans this early in the game.

E.B. was angry when Jefferson told him about Melody going into the sheriff's office. He soon calmed down. "Hell, I'll get me another girl at the next ranch I visit. No big loss."

To make E.B. feel better, Jefferson sketched in his plans for the village of South Junction, and together they roared and laughed just thinking about it.

It was dark before Jefferson Guthrie drove

back to town, turned in the buggy and found out which room brother Folke and wife were using. They were in. He told them what had happened with Melody.

"I don't think there's any problem. I'll check with the madam at that house tomorrow, just to make sure our little soiled dove is working there. If so, her testimony now wouldn't mean a thing in court. Whores don't have much credibility in this wild west country."

They talked far into the night. Jefferson told the pair what he had planned for the town, and Folke agreed with the plan. His wife Dianna nodded, and said there were a few details she could help them with over the next several days.

Chapter Ten

The next morning, Spur found a message for him at the front desk. Northcliff wanted to see him for breakfast or sooner. Abby had been with him last night, but she had left late for her place to take care of some business. Spur read the note again, remembered where the Silver Spoon Restaurant was and headed in that direction.

Northcliff was on his second cup of coffee when Spur sat down at his table.

"Good, you received my note. A few things we should go over. I heard about your talk with our banker. Bully for you. That was well done. But that doesn't find our rustlers. There hasn't been any activity by them for a week now. Maybe just the fact that I brought you into town to hunt them down has put a damper on their activity. I certainly hope so.

Wilderness Wanton

"How did your survey of the hiding spots go with Rusty? He said you'd give me a report."

Spur outlined what they hadn't found and the area they had covered. "Rusty said we hit every good spot in the territory to hide a big bunch of steers and brood cows. That part stumps me. What in hell are they doing with the animals they steal? They must have them somewhere because they haven't been driven to market or driven into another state or territory that I have heard about."

"That is a problem. Another small task I want you to take care of for me. The South Junction Cattleman's Association is holding a meeting this noon in the meeting room at the First Class Saloon. The back room. I want you to go to the session, tell them who you are and what you're doing and ask them if you can sit in on their meeting."

"Will they let me?"

"Most of them are reasonable men. They hate me, but they'll have nothing against you. You're trying to help them solve their problem. I think they'll let you stay."

"What have they done so far to try to catch the rustlers?"

"Talked, mostly. They haven't hired anyone to try and solve the problem. Maybe they're going to now. In any event, I want to know what they're planning, and this looks like the best open-handed way of finding out. Maybe you can help them as well."

"I'll be there."

"So, do you have anything else to report?"

151

"Not a lot. I've been spending too much time trying to stay alive. I guess that has to come first or I won't be much good to you. I'm getting a feel for the country. Sheriff Halverson isn't much help, he may never be on this rustler problem. My next move will be to try to figure out a pattern by the raiders and be ready for their next hit. It's a long shot, but it's the only other step that I can figure out right now. Do you have any suggestions?"

Northcliff frowned, rubbed his jaw and looked out the window at an attractive woman who walked by. "My best suggestion to you is to find the culprits doing the rustling and hang them on the spot. Let's have some wild west justice here and be done with it. My financial backers want to make some money, not be worried all the time about being rustled out of half our stock."

Northcliff stood. The interview was over. Spur nodded at the Englishman, stood slowly and faced his employer. Northcliff spoke.

"I'll be in the Old Wrangler Saloon playing some solitaire and waiting for a rundown on what happened at the cattleman's meeting. After that, I want a report every two days. If I don't contact you here, come out to the ranch in the evening. For the kind of money I'm paying you, I expect results."

Northcliff frowned, nodded to himself, turned and walked out of the eating place. Spur sat down, signalled for another cup of coffee, and thought over the meeting.

Northcliff didn't seem as friendly as he had before. He mentioned "his backers." That was the first time Spur had heard anything about Northcliff not owning the Bar-B all by himself. Who were Northcliff's backers, who were so anxious to be making money off the cattle spread? He'd ask around; somebody might know.

Abby might know. He'd ask her. He still had three hours before the meeting time. He walked up the street to the newspaper office and went inside. No one was in the front.

"Hello, anybody here?"

"Oh damn!" He heard the words faintly from the back room.

"Opal, are you all right?"

"Oh, damn." The words came louder this time. "No, I'm not all right. I'm angry." The words came first, and then Opal came through the curtain between the front and back shop. She had a smudge of grease on her cheek, one side of her blouse had come out of her brown skirt, and her hands were dark with oil and ink.

She held up both hands and shook her head. "I'm trying to get the press working. Leroy is home sick today and we wanted to get the press working for a trial run. I'm just not that mechanical. I thought I had it, but something slipped somewhere."

Spur nodded. "A flatbed press can be a monster. You want me to look at it? I've worked a press or two in my time."

She looked up with surprise and pleasure. "Really? Mr. McCoy, Spur, I'd be ever so grateful. Let me show you what I think the problem is."

She grinned and led the way to the back shop and the press. It was a kind he'd never seen before. He looked at the workings and turned it by hand until it ground to a stop. He backed it up, then moved it forward.

"Oh yes, I know the problem. See this socket? You need a rod to fit in there and be bolted on to the driving section of the press ram. Without that, there can't be any forward and backward motion."

"Mmm. Yes, I see. But where's that rod?"

They looked around the press for five minutes and didn't find it. She gave up.

"Leroy will know where it is. He's good with machines. Let me wash this grime off. I need to talk to you about the work you're doing for Mr. Northcliff. It'll make a good story when we get the press working."

She went to the side, where there was a metal washpan and some soap that looked darker than the grime on her hands and arms. It worked. She lathered it on and rinsed off twice, and her hands and forearms were clean. She looked in a small mirror, cleaned the grease off her cheek, and then wiped her hands dry.

"Now, there's something else I want to talk to you about. Back here. We made up living quarters so we can stay here if we have to work late some nights. We have lots of room in this big old building we rent."

She took him through a partition into the deepest section of the building. It had been fashioned into a small kitchen, living room, and to one side behind curtains, two bedrooms.

They sat on a couch and she held up one hand. "Now, I want you to let me have my say.

Wilderness Wanton

When I'm through you can talk. I am so deeply grateful for what you did for the three of us out there on the stagecoach. No, no, let me finish. I know they would have killed us. The other, what the big one was going to do to me, that I could have endured, but being killed. . . ." She took a deep breath. "I've tried to think what I have that I could give you or do for you to show you how strongly I feel about this. At last I decided. Just a moment." She turned away from him, and when she turned back her blouse was open. She held it open on each side to show her bare breasts.

"Opal, I told you. . . ."

"Hush. I get to finish my say. I decided the only thing I have I can give you is myself. You can have me any way you want, now and any time in the future. It's something I owe you that I can give you. I'll always owe you for as long as I live. Remember, any time, anywhere." She let the blouse slip off her shoulders and fall to the couch.

She wore no wrapper or chemise. Her breasts were much larger than he had thought. They had faint pink areolas but large nipples now turning pinker by the second.

"Please, Spur. Let me do this for you."

He smiled and looked at her breasts, then up to her eyes. "Opal, you are a beautiful woman, but this isn't something you need to do. What about your husband?"

She smiled, and it transformed her plain face into an amazingly appealing picture. "I thought you'd figured that out by now. Leroy is my brother. We thought we'd be safer that way if we said we were married. Leroy isn't aggressive, and I didn't want to rely on a brother to protect me. But a husband has a certain amount of built-in defenses." She paused, took a deep breath, then moved closer to him, caught his hands and put them on her breasts, then pushed in again and kissed his lips. She came away reluctantly, her eyes glowing.

"Spur, I don't know a lot about making love, but you go right ahead. You do want to, don't you?"

He bent and kissed her eyes and then her lips for just a second. Her eyes closed and her breathing rapidly increased.

"Opal, any man alive in my position right now would want you. But it isn't right for you." He kissed her again, then took her in his arms, crushing her breasts to his chest. He spoke to her with her head on his shoulder.

"Pretty, marvelous Opal. I understand how you feel. It's natural. I appreciate the offer and your debt, if there ever was one, is paid in full. You have no more obligation to me."

She pulled away and stared at him. "But . . . but we didn't do anything."

"You did a wonderful thing, Opal, *you offered yourself.* That is doubly wonderful because you'd be giving up something greatly prized and precious. You're a virgin, aren't you, Opal?"

Her eyes went wide and she hugged herself tightly to him again and kissed his neck, then she sighed. She spoke over his shoulder.

"Yes. How did you know?"

"Never mind, you'll find out soon enough."

He bent forward and kissed both her breasts, then lifted her blouse and helped her into it and buttoned the fasteners up to the top. He tipped her chin up and kissed her, hard and demanding. When he came away from her she sagged in surprise and wonder.

"Oh my goodness. Let's do that again."

Spur caught her shoulders and held her. "No. That was a goodbye kiss. I have a meeting to go to, and you have a newspaper to get ready to publish."

"But I thought. . . . I mean that last kiss." She reached toward his crotch but his hand caught hers. "You're ready and you want to, so why not?" She sighed and reached up and kissed his chin. "You're right. I have a lot to learn about men. Oh, I've seen that part of a man, his privates. This one was all hard and ready. A boy I knew wanted to do me but I wouldn't let him. I'm glad now I didn't. But this grown up . . . lovemaking. Wow, it's a lot more complicated."

"A lot more, young lady. The next time you whip off your blouse and offer yourself, you be sure it's not until you get that wedding ring on your finger."

He kissed her forehead and stood. "Now, back to work, all right?"

She sighed. He caught her hand and helped her stand. She was a bit unsteady for a minute and looked at him with a grin.

"Takes me a couple of minutes to come down off a highly emotional experience like that."

"Good," Spur said and led her out to the front

office. He went on the other side of the counter and nodded. "You're going to be fine, and do great. One of these days the right young man will come along. Save everything for him. Oh, about that interview. We never did get to it. We'll save that for next time."

"Yes, next time. You come back and see me. I want to write a story about your detective work here."

"Promise," he said, waved and walked out the door.

For a moment he had a pang of regret. She was luscious, with breasts like a man didn't see often. He admitted that he was a breast man. They were without question the most beautiful part of a woman. . . . He amended that, of a young woman, before they started to sag out of sight.

Stripping her clothes off and introducing her to the wonders of sexual intercourse would have been a delight to him, but he was not fourteen anymore. He could control his sexual drive a little better than that.

Spur grinned. Damn. Some of the things he did just to stay on the good side of his conscience. They were amazing. He'd think about this day some time down the road when he hadn't seen a bare breast in a month or two and had no opportunities, and he'd kick his own ass from one side of the road to the other.

In the meantime, he had a case to work. How in hell were they doing it and not getting caught? What worried him more, and had him totally at a loss, was where in hell were they holding the stolen cattle? It would take three or four men to

158

ride herd on a batch that big, and at least five or six square miles of graze to keep them going for more than a month or two.

The rustling here started over three months ago. Where in hell was that stolen beef?

He went down the street to the First Class Saloon and walked in. It was still not eleven o'clock and business was light. Two drinkers at the bar, half a dozen tables populated, and only one card game in progress.

He didn't see Abby. Montrose, the apron behind the bar, recognized Spur and waved him toward the door at the far side of the saloon marked "Private."

Spur headed that way, knocked and pushed the door open. Abigail looked up and smiled.

"Well, stranger, I haven't seen you with your clothes on lately." She smiled, remembering. "I like you this way, too. How goes the detective business?"

"Slow. It seems I'm fumbling around in my own pocket and can't find a way out."

"I thought I helped last night when I got you all relaxed and the tensions all out of you until you were sleeping like a newborn babe."

"You did. Got some new tensions this morning. What do you know about this cattleman's association that's having a meeting in your back room this noontime?"

"Not a lot. The Silver Spoon is bringing over dinner for the seven ranchers. None for Northcliff. I don't see many of them in here. Ingram now and then from the diamond spread, and Cuthright from the Box C. He likes to gamble. I don't know if he wins or loses but he's usually here on Saturday night and well into Sunday in a game. I've heard the stakes get kind of high. They use the back room for that game."

"I'm going to crash my way into the Cattleman's Association party today, right after they finish eating. So why don't you and I go out for an early dinner and then come back and wait my turn in the back room?"

They ate at the Silver Spoon, and Spur soon found that Abby had a lot of friends. Men said hello, waved and smiled at her. Some of the women stopped by and talked, a few women walked by with their collective noses in the air. Abby chuckled about that.

"You see, I'm not quite fully respectable. I'm not a whore and I don't run a whorehouse, no girls upstairs in the saloon. But I am a *saloon owner*, and for that some of the 'perfect ladies of the town' look down their noses at me. It doesn't bother me."

Abby stopped and blinked. He thought he saw some moisture in her eyes.

"Oh, hell no, it doesn't bother me at all. You probably have never cried yourself to sleep after getting snubbed at some social event." She wiped at her eyes with her hand and cleared her throat. "Didn't mean to get so personal. I'd like to scratch a few old biddies' eyes out around here. Like that one in the expensive blue dress. I'd battle hand-to-fingernails with her any day." She took a deep breath. "So, stranger, how's your love life?"

160

Spur laughed softly and grabbed her hand. "It couldn't be better. I even got propositioned today by a blushing virgin."

"Spur McCoy, you lie." She frowned. "A virgin? I didn't know there were any over twelve left in town. Damn men have been getting married to thirteen year olds so they can homestead twice as much land. A damn crying shame. Course most of them leave the girls with their mothers for a year or two. But some don't. Say they train the young things to do what they want them to do in bed and it works out fine. Damn, I'd like to go hand-to-fingernail with one or two of them baby-snatchers as well."

"Maybe I could be your manager and I could arrange a bare-knuckled fight for you."

Abby lost her pique and laughed. "Sure, I'd go topless, and while he was still looking at my titties, I'd scratch both his eyes out and win."

They grinned, let the waiter put down their dinner and dug into the food. For her size, Abby put away a lot of victuals. Just before dessert, she looked up.

"I've been trying to think what I've heard about the association and the rustling. About all is that Cuthright is the chairman of the group. About the only thing they do is set up rules for area roundups and now this rustling thing. He's the main push from what I hear."

"He also gambles in the big-stakes games."

"He's in the room and buys chips and cashes in. I'll ask Montrose if he wins or loses. Montrose has a memory like a printed book."

Back at the saloon, Montrose sipped a glass
of ice water and nodded.

"Oh, yes sir, Mr. Cuthright is a big player. I
usually don't tell anybody if a man wins or loses,
but it's well known that Cuthright's not a good
poker player, and usually loses what chips he
buys. Seldom does he ever come by the window
to cash in. Always waves and says he'll keep his
chips for next time. To me that's the same as
losing your whole stake."

"How many chips does he usually buy?" Spur
asked.

Montrose looked at his boss. She nodded.

"He almost always buys two hundred dollars
worth."

Spur whistled softly. "Two hundred. That's
eight months pay for a cowboy, runs to over
ten-thousand dollars a year. How long has he
been doing this?"

Montrose frowned a minute. "Cuthright. He
took over the Box C ranch three years ago.
Bought out Larry Box. Larry was getting old
and wanted to move to Helena where his kin
lived. Cuthright didn't start gambling until a
year later. Started slow, twenty a night, then
to fifty. When he hit a hundred he graduated
to the back room. You've got to buy a hundred
dollars worth to get a chair in the game for
eight."

"So he could be loser for over twenty-five
thousand dollars," Spur said. "Who are the big
winners at those games?"

Again Montrose looked at Abigail. "We're trying to help Mr. McCoy here, Montrose. Anything

162

you can tell him is appreciated."

"Jordan, the general store man, used to win a lot. He died six months ago. Now the saddlemaker takes his winnings, and so does Stewart Rawlins."

"The banker?"

"That one."

"Any others?"

"Now and then Sheriff Halverson wins a bit. But I'd say he breaks even week in and week out."

"Stewart Rawlins, that surprises me. Most bankers stay a mile away from any hint of gambling."

"Hell, Rawlins brags about it. What's he got to lose? He's the only bank in town."

"Maybe not for long."

Three men pushed through the swinging doors, nodded at Abigail, walked to the rear of the saloon where double doors stood open, and went inside.

"That your famous big-stakes back room?" Spur asked.

Abigail said it was. "Those three were Lathrup, Cuthright and Tabler. They don't stick together, must have just happened to come in at the same time."

"Four more to go," Montrose said.

A boy about fourteen came out of the back room and looked at Abby. She shook her head.

"Wait until all seven of them are there, Philip. Then you can bring over the dinners. That way they'll stay hot. Did you pour coffee for those three?"

The young waiter shook his head and rushed back into the room.

"He's from the Silver Spoon. Makes it nice this way. I don't have to worry about cooking and I still get to sell them the drinks."

A few minutes later the other four members had arrived and had their dinner served. An hour after that, they pushed back from the table as the two waiters cleared away the dishes.

Spur McCoy walked into the room and stood beside the eight-foot-long table until the men looked up. They did so one or two at a time, and as they did they stopped talking. Soon the room was quiet.

"Good afternoon, gentlemen. My name is Spur McCoy. I'm a range detective out of Denver. As you know, I'm here about the rustling problem that you gentlemen all seem to have. Yes, I'm working for the man who's not a member of your group, Mr. Northcliff. You see, what I'm doing here will benefit all of you. That's why I wanted to talk to you, and what better time than when you're gathered here?

"First a few questions. Do any of you here think that my investigation could hurt rather than help you?"

"Hell no," said the man Spur remembered as being Cuthright of the Box C. "You nail these rustlers to the wall and stop them, I'll give you a $500 reward from my outfit."

"Anyone disagree with my work here?" Spur asked again. A few heads shook. No one spoke.

"Now, to cases. Have each of you reported to the county sheriff each time cattle were stolen from you, giving the date and the number of lost animals?"

"Damn right, we all have," another man said. His range hat had a Triangle brand burned into the felt. He must be Quail. "Damned sheriff doesn't seem to do anything with the information."

"I'll do something with it. I'm working out the frequency, date and the time in days between the rustling. Perhaps that way I can predict when the next raid will be."

He watched them a minute.

"I understand most of the rustling has taken place at night and usually on the far end of your ranges between the main herd and your line shacks. Is that true?"

"Yeah, right, and the bastards split up a hundred head into groups of ten and drive them every which way until it would take a seeing-in-the-dark Apache Indian to track the critters, even come daylight." Spur had no idea who the man was who said it.

"But do the trails gradually work north?" Spur asked.

"Sometimes I've seen them go south, sometimes east. Hell, I have no idea where those stolen steers and brood cows are by now."

"Another interesting point. Do you all agree that no extra herds, beside your own and Northcliff's, have been driven south to the railhead and sold?"

"Know for damn sure," Cuthright said. "I talked to the cattle buyer down there warning him about what was happening up here. He's

165

watching for overbrands, and running iron work, even blankouts without ear-cuts."

"Good, that eliminates one possibility. Rusty Kahil and I rode over the northern sections of the four biggest outfits that butt up to the mountains. Up there in the breaks we did our damnedest and we never even found where a herd of twenty-five hundred to three thousand head had passed the time of day, let alone where they are now. Which makes me ask this question: If three-thousand head of your cattle have been rustled, where the hell are they?"

"Maybe they drove them to Idaho or Oregon, sell them there," a new voice said.

"Hell, they could drive them fifty miles down the tracks to the next town and cattle pens and sell them there."

"Have they? Mr. Cuthright, you must have checked that with the cattle buyer down at the railroad."

Cuthright nodded. "Yeah, I wired the buyers along the tracks a hundred miles each way. None of them had seen any of our brands, or brands that could be run from our brands."

"Which makes me believe those cattle are still in this general area," Spur said. "All we have to do is find them."

"Which is your job, Mr. McCoy. I'm Farley from the Double Bar, one of the smaller outfits. Losing a hundred head hits me like a sledge hammer into my skull."

"All right, I wanted to get the feeling of your group, see if I could pick up anything new, and let you know I might be showing up around your spreads one of these days, so don't shoot me as a rustler."

"We hang rustlers in Montana," another man said.

Spur thanked them and said he'd let them know if he solved the puzzle. He turned and left the room. Outside, Abby cut him off as he headed for the saloon's door.

"Not so fast, cowboy. What happened in there? I didn't hear any shots."

He told her. "So, I learned almost nothing new, I met the men directly involved, which could be helpful, and I have a better idea how they feel. Definitely not a waste of time."

"Okay, I'll keep my ears open." She paused. "Tonight?"

"Not sure. If I don't get tied up, I'll be at your place by nine, fair enough?"

"Can't wait, but I guess I better."

"Right here in the middle of your saloon would be bound to attract attention."

Abby giggled. "Maybe we could sell tickets."

"That's been done, too. It was a special peep show in Atlanta. You paid a dollar to watch. The billing was that this was a sweet young thing losing her virginity. The sweet young thing had to pretend to fight off the guy four times a night. They had this small bedroom built with peepholes bored in the walls all around. They wouldn't put on the show until they had sold all sixty peepholes."

"The same girl every night?"

"Oh, they rotated three of them when they found ones who could act well enough. The watchers didn't care who the girl was. Some of them watched two or three times in a row."

"I'm not applying for work there. See you later, and I'll give you a private audition to play the part of the seducer in Atlanta."

Spur went to the Old Wrangler saloon and found Northcliff. He gave him a quick report.

"They wouldn't let you sit through the meeting?"

"I figured I'd pushed them about as far as Cuthright would let me for one day. He wasn't friendly. Now I'm going to check the sheriff's reports again and see if I can figure out some kind of a sequence."

Northcliff played a red jack on a black queen and nodded. "Keep me informed of anything important. I've taken a hotel room for a few days. I'm in 301 in case you have something to tell me."

Spur nodded and headed for the door.

Chapter Eleven

Spur hadn't been out of the Old Wrangler Saloon more than two minutes when he saw a rider charging down the crowded street yelling at people to get out of his way. He pulled to a stop in front of the sheriff's office. Spur ran that way.

"Rustlers north and east on the Bar-L!" the rider shouted at the quickly growing crowd. He ran for the sheriff's office, and Spur jogged down to the livery and saddled his horse. He was a half hour ahead of the others. The members of the Cattleman's Association heard about it right after the cowboy told the sheriff. They all rode for the Logan ranch, just east of the Bar-B on the far eastern edge of the range.

The cowboy who had ridden into town changed horses at the livery and led the sheriff's deputy and the association leaders toward the site of the strike.

Spur heard something about the north pasture near the Bar-B line. He remembered the area he had ridden a couple of days before with Rusty and angled that way. He rode part way on the trail to the Bar-B, then cut across country to the stub fence that lasted only a half mile, dividing the two spreads. It was a bow to the idea that all the cattle ranches should have their land fenced in so everyone knew exactly where the boundary lines were.

Most cattlemen called the idea crazy, saying it was just a plan by the surveyors to get more work. Spur tended to agree with them. Where there were tens of thousands of acres involved, a few dozen or a few hundred feet one way or another made little difference—unless there was something vital like a spring or a water hole or a river involved.

Two cowboys waved as he came north along the border boundary that Rusty had shown him. He turned into the Bar-L land and rode another half mile to where the cowboys waited.

"Rustlers?" Spur asked as he rode in.

"Yep, not sure just when, probably last night. You can look at the tracks yourself."

The cowboy pointed to a swarm of cattle and horseshoe prints in the dust. Spur got down and checked them carefully, walked along the edge of the marks and nodded.

"Has to be from last night. Even the horseshoe tracks have little trails across them made by night crawling critters. They wouldn't come out

in the day if they were starving, cause then the
hawks and other birds would eat them like
candy."

"Last night then," the cowboy said. "They
drove about a hundred head due north, but
the main group don't get far before it breaks
up into six bunches. Go take a look."

Spur rode alongside the trail, and a half mile
north found where it divided. He picked the
largest branch and kept following it. For a while
it went due west, straight for the Bar-B range,
then turned north again and swung to the east.
Spur figured from the tracks that there were
about 20 head of cattle in the mix and three
riders pushing them along.

Another two miles of eastward tracks before
they angled north again and then due west,
reversing their direction. It was then that the
20 head split again into half that many, and
he found tracks of only two riders driving the
animals forward.

Twice he dismounted and studied the horseshoe tracks. He could find nothing unusual
about any of them. No broken shoes, none
missing, no special design or type of shoe. They
were like hundreds of thousands of shoes that
blacksmiths pounded out every year.

The tracks kept moving. Far behind him, Spur
saw the other riders arriving at the main point of
rustling. He pushed on. The tracks kept up their
western route, and soon they were across the line
and into what he figured must be Bar-B range.

Spur stopped and checked the range ahead. If
they continued on the same course, they would

have to angle more to the north to get into the edge of the breaks. There was no other way through except the long, narrow valley that led almost to the point where the breaks stopped and the upthrust of the range of foothills began that would eventually rise into the main ridges of the Rocky Mountains.

Making his decision, Spur kicked the gelding in the flanks and galloped a quarter mile due north for the mouth of the valley, then let the animal trot for a half mile and let him walk again. The opening of the valley looked to be only three miles away, but distances out here were still fooling people. It was more than six miles. He arrived at the start of the valley, got off and walked across the quarter mile stretch. In three places he saw where strings of animals had entered the neck of the valley, all moving up the stretch north and then west.

"Gotcha!" Spur bellowed into the sunlit afternoon. He galloped another quarter mile, then studied the thin vegetation. Now the three groups of steers and riders had come together, and he could see the signs of the larger herd from his saddle. He galloped, then let the animal canter for a while, then walked him.

The valley was another six miles long, and never more than a half mile wide. It acted as a funnel, and he remembered seeing it a few days ago, but it wasn't one they had concentrated on. He had no idea where it led or what the outlet might be.

If the rustlers used it, they must know they could get out on the other end. He rode hard now, pushing the big strong gelding as much as he could. He'd run out of light in another two hours.

Spur came to the end of the valley with an hour of sunlight left. He sniffed and then knew what he smelled. Charcoal. Not smoke, but the last lingering odor of the end of a campfire. He lifted in his saddle and stared around the end of the valley. He found what he wanted where the small stream came down a series of small hills into the low land.

A half dozen campfires had been used recently. He dismounted and touched the coals. Cold. He used his boot knife and dug into the ground an inch and then touched it. His hand came away quickly. The soil there was still hot. The fire had not been out for more than 12 hours.

Spur rolled back on his heels and squatted beside the fire. Grab the cattle, force-march them up here, have the fires going and the irons hot, rebrand or turn the Bar-L brand into something else. Finish the branding by daylight and drive the cattle through the end of the valley and back into the open range, where the cattle of two or more outfits were bound to commingle.

He now saw more evidence. Some trash from a meal, signs of many horse droppings in one place, and small logs near the fires where the hot handle-ends of the branding irons could have been placed for quicker use.

It wouldn't take long to brand a hundred head, even in the black night. The campfires would provide enough light. Now he had to ride the trail again, and see where the rustlers took their newly branded critters.

A fresh brand was easy to spot. It would scab over and the scab would fall off in three or more weeks, leaving the scar tissue and the hairless fresh brand. If he could find fresh brands out there somewhere, he might have a case.

He rode hard now, following the trail while he still had light. His close examination of the prints looked as if the critters were driven out at different times, in bunches perhaps, and probably to different areas of the range. But where were they now?

The valley turned west and opened into a low pass through some breaks, then down into another chute-type valley that would take them all the way to the main plateau of the beginnings of the great plains to the east.

Spur sat on his horse and stared at the darkening miles and miles of range in front of him. He was probably 15 miles from the Bar B ranch. The range through here was 60 miles wide. Say an area 20 miles by 60 miles for the workable range around South Junction.

That was 1,200 square *miles* of land. He could make a guess at how many acres, over 750,000. How would he find even ten newly branded cattle in a space that large? They could be anywhere, everywhere. Was he that good at picking out a new brand? Rusty could. He thought about it.

He rode back in the direction he thought the Bar-B spread was. Spur had come in north and east. If he headed south and west he should find habitation somewhere.

Now he knew one new fact. He wasn't going to find 3,000 head of the stolen cattle penned up anywhere. If they had been in the area, Rusty and he would have found them on their search. They were either out of this end of the territory, or they were still right there under their noses but with different branding.

That meant nobody would profit from the rustling until after the next spring roundup and a trail drive to the railroad a month or so later. Just didn't make sense. There had to be a better explanation. He had to find it.

After two more hours of riding, he saw lights ahead. By the time he rode into the ranch yard, he knew he wasn't at the Bar-B. Somebody hailed him and he called out who he was.

"Yeah, boss said you might be coming back. He and some of the others are inside. You find any of our critters?"

"Afraid not," Spur said. He left his horse tied to a rail and let the cowhand lead him up to the back door and into the kitchen.

Six men sat around smoking, drinking and swearing. They all quieted as he came in and took off his hat.

"Find them?" one man asked.

He had long before decided not to tell them everything he had learned, just as an ace in the hole. He shook his head.

"Found where they split up, then figured out where they had to be heading and rode up that

175

long finger valley that extends way up into the breaks."

"Yeah, know the spot," the same man said.

"Evidently they gathered there, then drove them through that low pass into another long valley and back into the open range. By that time it got dark. Your cattle could be almost anywhere this side of the railroad."

"Oh, damn," one of the men said. "I figured maybe we got here quick enough this time."

"From the tracks I saw earlier, I'm sure the rustling was done sometime last night," Spur went on. "Probably they began as soon as it got dark enough to cover them. Hard work driving cattle in the dark, but looks like they can do it."

"So we're right back where we were." The speaker was one Spur recognized, Cuthright of the Box C spread.

"Afraid so. Anybody going back to town? I'd just as soon not get lost. Too big a country up in here for me in the dark."

Five of the men finished their drinks. One brought Spur a cup filled with whiskey. He took a couple of pulls and said that was enough or he'd fall off his horse.

There was little talk on the way back to town. Most of the men still had eight or ten miles to ride after the seven from the Bar-L ranch house. They were sullen and angry. Spur didn't want to stir them up.

In town he waved farewell to them and put his gelding in the livery. He paid his bill up to date for grain and stable space, then walked back to the hotel. He had no messages in his box and went on up to his room.

When he came to his door, he saw that it was open an inch and there was a light on inside.

"Anybody home?" he asked, pushing the door in another inch.

"Just us chickens," a voice he recognized as Abby's said. He holstered his six-gun and slipped inside. Abby sat on the bed with a filmy nightgown on. It was so thin he could see right through it.

"Fetching," he said.

"I hoped you'd like it. You have any success on your wild ride?"

He told her.

"Maybe next time."

"This isn't a game of chance. I'm supposed to know how to catch these guys and put a stop to it. Uncle Sam says I should know how and General Halleck is going to be blowing his hairpiece off if I don't come up with some answers pretty soon."

"So what can you do tonight?"

"Have a bath, get dinner and get some sleep."

"Bad planning. The bathroom closed here at eight. It's near ten o'clock now and only one cafe is still open. You want me to go get you a steak dinner?"

He shook his head and grinned. "Hey, I really don't think that you'd make it past the first saloon dressed that way. I may be wrong, but you could meet with some notice once you got into the light down there."

Abby nodded, her grin larger now. "Maybe so.

Your alternative is to come over here and let me help you get to sleep."

Spur stared at her. Might be a good idea. He could dominate the hell out of her, have his way with her, and maybe take a little edge off his anger at himself for coming up empty again.

"Let me wash my hands and face first. You don't like to kiss dirty faces."

Abby slid off the bed and walked over to him. She reached up and kissed his lips and smiled.

"Big guy, I like kissing dirty any time. You just give me a call."

She poured water into the crockery bowl from the big pitcher and handed him a small washcloth. Ten minutes later he stretched out on his back on the clean sheets. Abby rolled over and lay on top of his naked body.

"Yes, now this is more like it. I heard what happened, saw the ranchers all steam out of the saloon and grab their horses. You must have been a bit ahead of them."

She reached down and kissed him. He didn't have much of a reaction, so she felt his forehead for a fever.

"You sick or are you just too tired?"

Spur gave her a weary grin. "I have a rule. When a naked, beautiful girl with big tits is lying on top of me, I'm never too sick or too tired."

"Hot fuck, I'm gonna get poked tonight."

"Twice if you're lucky, then I really do need to get some sleep."

She pushed up on his body until she could lower one breast into his mouth. "You can have a few bites of these instead of that supper I talked you out of. Chocolate on the right and vanilla on the left."

"Oh, yes," Spur said around her breast. He chewed on her nipple until she yelped.

"Speaking of chocolate, you ever done it with a black girl?"

Spur pushed her up a little to change breasts. "You ever fucked a black man?"

"Asked you first, whitey."

"Yes. She wasn't black though, kind of light chocolate brown, with little tits that had almost black nipples and a round ass that could do things I had never heard or even thought about before."

"I'm jealous," Abby said.

"Hell, girl, you asked. Now what about you?"

"A black man? You think I'm crazy? I could get knocked up with a black kid and then where would I be? I couldn't get somebody into my bed and say he was the daddy and force him to marry me. No thank you. Is it true, though?"

"Is what true?"

"That black men have huge, long, thick whangers?"

Spur laughed in spite of himself. "Truthful. I never asked any black men I've talked to that question. Just a rumor. Black women aren't that different from white women. Why would black men be different from white men?"

"Just wondered."

"There's one way you can find out next time you take the train into Chicago. There's a whole lot of black men there you can experiment with."

She punched him in the shoulder, then rolled off him and lay on her back. She spread her legs and held out her arms.

"Spur McCoy, don't want no black stuff, I want you to stuff me full right now. Do me quick and hard and then we can pretend that we're old married folks and go to sleep the rest of the night. I don't want your shooting hand slow if'n you have any gun work to do tomorrow."

Spur lay there a minute, then came over her and kissed her nose, and then her mouth. He kissed her hard, and then she guided him into the perfect spot.

"Oh, yes!" Abby said, sliding off his mouth. "Why is it always so damn fucking wonderful?"

"You know why? It's called the preservation and continuation of the species."

"Right now I don't feel like a species."

"That's the big trick that mother nature plays on all of us."

"Not on me. I have ways. Now shut up and let me enjoy this."

She pumped upward at him, then ground her hips around in a circle underneath. Her inner muscles clutched at him, grabbing him on every thrust, milking him and then letting him go. Spur knew he couldn't stand much of this kind of expert treatment.

Abby climaxed. She wailed softly, then humped at him a dozen times. Her whole body spasmed and jolted, then did so a second time before she gave a long sigh and closed her eyes, breathing deeply.

A minute later she snapped her eyes open and

her hip motion continued. It took longer this time, but Spur knew he was in the game, and then the floodgates exploded off their hinges and the surging, roiling mass of fluid jetted downstream and swept away everything in its way. He gave six more mighty thrusts and then came down gently on top of her with all of his weight, pressing her deeply into the mattress.

"Feels wonderful," she said, "being buried like this with you on top of me. I might put that in my will."

"Shut up," Spur said. She did. Five minutes later they came apart and she snuggled next to him.

"What are you going to do tomorrow?" Abby asked.

"I don't have the slightest idea. Get back to trying to predict where the next rustling will be. So far it hasn't done me much good."

"You wouldn't have picked the Bar-L for tonight?"

"Actually it was last night. I hadn't really had time to do any kind of projecting. My only thought was that they would probably hit the bigger ranchers more often simply because it would be easier to get their one hundred animals. Now I'm not sure."

"You still planning on taking me back to Denver with you when this is all over?"

He rose up and stared at her light blue eyes and her wide grin and that glorious dark hair tumbling around her face and down over one breast.

"Will you always dress like this?"

"Whenever I get the chance. Say twice a day?"

"You trying to kill me off early?"

"Then once a day, just to keep you in practice." She watched him closely and her grin faded. Her serious expression surprised him.

"Hey, big guy. Would it be too forward of me to ask you to marry me? You know, I could propose and you could say yes, and we'd get it done here by the judge when he comes to town."

Spur stared at the ceiling. "Last year three Secret Service Agents were killed in the line of duty. Two of them were married. The agency doesn't disapprove of marriage, and doesn't prohibit it, but for active field agents, they suggest that it's not the best idea."

"That's the longest damn 'no' I've ever had to a proposal."

"You do this often?"

"Just once so far. Could I kiss you anyway?"

She rolled over and their lips met. A tear squeezed out of her eye and rolled down her cheek and dripped on the sheet.

"Damn you, McCoy. You fuck me and make me the happiest female in the world, and now you won't marry me."

"True. We could live together . . . whenever I'm here in South Junction."

"If you were serious I'd pay to put in a telegraph just so I could hold you to that. I hear it's on the way, but not going to make it here for two or three more years. With a telegraph here you could get all your orders from your damn general."

"You can wait two years. You're young."

"Damn you, Spur McCoy. One more time? I'll be on top and do all the work."

"One more, then we'll play married and go to sleep."

"Deal. Now be gentle. I'm a virgin."

"Again?"

"For as many times as I want to be before I wear my white dress and white wedding veil. Now be nice."

He was. They were. They got to sleep just before midnight.

Chapter Twelve

J.R. Guthrie put on his best suit that morning and took special care with his shaving. He combed his dark hair precisely and inspected his appearance in the hazy hotel mirror over the dresser. He picked three spots of lint off the deep blue fabric and smiled.

It was his best suit, the one he took out especially for impressing the local citizens. It had cost him $45 in St. Louis, ten times what the average man's suit sold for. Time and again it had produced results, and by now it had paid for itself a hundred times over.

He was not really looking for a "client" this morning, but if one should step into his path, he couldn't very well pass the opportunity by. The timing would be important. He'd have to

be able to coordinate any "client" with the final
phase of the program he had been working out
for the village of South Junction. Oh, what a day
that would be.

J.R. had a late breakfast in the hotel dining
room. By then the working people were gone,
and those with more time at their disposal were
up and around. He had made some interesting
contacts this way over the years.

He had an omelet with cheese, bacon and
sunflower seeds. They made it to order for him
and even put in a touch of basil and tarragon.
He enjoyed the contrast.

Breakfast came and he luxuriated in it, but
it produced no interesting contacts. A half
hour later outside the hotel, he moved his
gold-headed walking stick forward as he strolled
sedately down the boardwalk. He had thought of
stopping in and having a chat with the banker
about the stock market, but that would be a bit
too ironic, so he moved on.

The careening buggy came out of nowhere,
it seemed to J.R. He had moved close to the
street to avoid three men talking just ahead,
when a buggy slanted directly at the edge of
the boardwalk. The big black horse foamed at
the mouth, eyes wild, a runaway!

Not six feet from the flashing hooves of the
big black horse, just off the boardwalk in the
dirt street, stood a small girl, looking back at
a woman ten feet behind her. The child was
not more than three or four. A woman on the
boardwalk screamed. J.R. didn't think about
what he should do, he simply darted forward

half a dozen feet, lunged into the street and grabbed the little girl.

He could smell the sweat and fear on the horse that loomed over him, its deadly hooves pawing the air as it smashed forward.

J.R. held the girl tightly and dove to the side, utilizing his momentum from the surge into the street to help carry him out of the path of the horse and buggy. J.R. cradled the girl in his arms, held her tightly against his chest. He sailed six feet through the air and came down on his shoulder on the hard-packed street.

The horse screamed in fear and anger as it flashed by. It missed J.R.'s trailing legs by inches but caught one boot, slamming his foot forward in an arc but not damaging it. Then the hurtling buggy bore down on him and the girl. The black rig was three feet wider than the horse. J.R. swung his feet upward as he hit the ground and tried to roll.

The steel-rimmed wheel of the buggy hit him just below the knee on his left leg and spun him another two feet out of the way of the trailing wheels as the buggy flashed past and careened down the street. A small woman inside the rig screeched for help and tried vainly to pull the reins hard enough to stop the crazed animal.

J.R. Guthrie lay there in the dirt and offal trying to get his wits about him. He'd nearly been trampled by that big black, but he'd escaped. The buggy had almost cut him in half but one last twist of his long body had saved him. He had little more damage than a bruised leg.

He tried to sit up. A dozen people crowded

around him. The voices came but he couldn't say for sure who said what.

"You all right, Mister? Bravest damn thing I ever seen."

"You see that? He saved that little girl's life, no two ways about it."

"Julie! Julie!"

He was aware of the woman kneeling in the dirt beside him, her gentle hands reaching in and loosening his fingers where they still held the small child.

"It's all right, I'm Julie's mother. How can I ever thank you for saving my little girl's life?"

He blinked, rubbed his eyes to get some of the grime out of them, but only made it worse. The woman's hands came up with a white handkerchief and gently wiped the dirt from his eyes and mouth. He could see her clearly now.

He groaned and let go of the small child. Her white dress was powdered black on one side where they had rolled to escape. His clothing was filthy, grime-smeared, and smelled of horse dung from the street. He had probably ruined his best suit. The woman watched him closely.

"The wheel. I thought it hit you. Did the horse kick you or Julie as it swept by you?" He shook his head. "Thank God. Can you stand? Are you hurt seriously?" The woman said it all with a soft, concerned voice.

"Let me through here," a voice loaded with authority called. "Let me see the injured man."

"He don't need nothing but a medal and a bath, Doc," another voice called. "He saved that sprout there sure as there's a heaven. Saved her life, you can bet on that."

The man knelt beside J.R. and looked in his eyes, then asked him questions about moving his arms and legs. A moment later he stood and helped J.R. up. Guthrie winced when he put weight on his right leg.

"Leg. Could be some problem. Let's have a look. Don't think it's broken or you'd be screaming by now." He lifted the fine cloth of the dirt-smeared pants leg and looked at the bony front section just below J.R.'s knee.

"Yeah, you're lucky. Nothing there but a few inches of skinned bone. You'll be right as a Texas thunderstorm in two or three days. Come over to my office and I'll clean that up and put some bandages on it. Nothing to worry about."

The doctor turned and led the little girl and her mother back to the boardwalk.

"I'd say she had a soft pillow to land on, Ma'am. No harm done. She might be a bit skittish around horses for a time. Just treat her natural. Oh, a dish of that newfangled ice cream might help her forget all about this." He brushed the soil off her dress and she looked up at her mother, who smiled. The little girl smiled back.

The woman turned to J.R. She was in her thirties and tallish, with eyes that had seen too much and a trim body that wore better than the average clothes. She touched his shoulder.

"Sir, I wish to thank you again for what you did for my daughter. You did save her life. Her father will want to know who you are."

"J.R. Archibald, ma'am. I'm new in town. I'm an investment counselor on my way to Omaha."

"J.R. Archibald. I'll remember that. Oh, pardon me. I'm still a little bit shaken. My name is Victoria Openlander. My husband is a lawyer here in town."

"Pleased to meet you. I really should get back to my hotel room and change my clothes. I must look a mess."

"You look like a hero to me. I turned around to talk to a friend and Julie scampered ahead of me. We were going to cross the street but I didn't think that she would. . . ." She sighed. "I'm sorry. I don't need to trouble you with my explanations. Excuses, really. You're staying at the hotel?"

"Yes, ma'am. I'm glad your small one is safe. Now I better be going."

"First, let me shake your hand. I'm sure my husband will want to do something for you."

"No, nothing. I'm glad I was there at the right place. Goodbye." As he said it he studied her face critically. Pretty, high cheek bones, olive eyes, long lashes, a softly curved mouth that had a touch of color added, a few smile lines around her mouth, and soft, unblemished cheeks that he suddenly wanted to touch. She smiled and her eyes brightened.

"I'm sure we'll be contacting you again, Mr. Archibald. You saved our only child's life. We owe you a great deal."

She nodded. All this time she had been holding the little girl to her bosom, not letting her move.

Julie wasn't crying, but all this serious talk must have bored her. She wiggled in her mother's arms, at last won the right to walk. She held her mother's hand tightly. Mrs. Victoria Openlander led Julie down the boardwalk, but they stayed as close to the store fronts as they could get.

J.R. Guthrie nodded as he watched them. It could be a contact worth saving. A lawyer. Sometimes they had lots of power and lots of money. This one would be on the young side, about Victoria's age, thirties. He pondered it a moment.

He glanced down at his trousers. When he saw bits of horse manure on them he almost gagged. He turned around and walked quickly back to his hotel and ordered a hot tub in the first bathroom available. Upstairs in his room, he shrugged out of the suit, put on a robe, then stuffed the fouled suit in a pillowcase off his bed. He selected clean clothes and took them with him down to the bathroom.

The bath water was hot and he soaked for as long as it stayed warm, then washed vigorously. When he came out he was pink and clean. J.R. dressed and returned to his room. An envelope had been pushed under his door. He saw it at once when he entered.

It was a long business envelope. Inside was a note on printed stationery. The printing said: "Alonzo Openlander, Attorney at Law, 114 Broadway, South Junction, Montana Terr." The note was short.

"Dear Mr. Archibald. My wife tells me you saved the life of our daughter this afternoon.

Please let us show you our appreciation. We invite you to our home tonight for dinner, cigars and a good brandy. We will expect you at 6:30. Our home is on Second Street, two blocks over from Broadway. The number is 237. We hope to see you." It was signed by the lawyer.

He turned the note over and nodded. His ploy with the stock certificates might work with the wife, but the lawyer would want to check and double check. Of course without a telegraph, it would take him several days by mail. Might work.

He went to the bed and lifted a locked leather case out of his traveling bag. He unlocked it with a key from a chain around his neck and opened it on the bed.

J.R. examined the prepared stocks and bonds he had left since his last trip to the printer in Philadelphia. He used only the best: Top flight stocks and bonds "borrowed" from the printer who had one assistant pressman who could work wonders with the count on stock certificates printed before they were hand-numbered.

His were absolutely authentic; the only slight discrepancies were the numbers written in by hand and the signatures. J.R. had no way of knowing what numbers had been used. He had the right names on an up-to-date basis on the more popular stocks, but the correct penmanship was a guess. Still, they fooled 95 percent of the legitimate stock salesmen even in Philadelphia itself.

Out here in the wilds of Montana, he would have no trouble even with a sassy lawyer.

He selected carefully. He would go with the conservative Central Pacific stock. It was still a good buy on the open market and one that was easy to check on for price. He looked over the last Denver quotation he had and saw it was bid for at 34 ¾ and sold at 33 even. That would be the stock to be sold to the lawyer's wife, but not tonight at supper.

Tonight he would be humble and gentlemanly. He would barely mention his profession and let matters take their course. If he was right, he had seen a deep desire and wanting in those olive eyes that had locked with his for only a few seconds today. There was gratitude and excitement, and a rush of emotion at the danger he had been in. Given the chance, the lady might show her appreciation in a slightly more intimate and physical way. It would be up to him to give her that chance.

Satisfied with his decision, he took his pillowcase filled with the suit and asked the desk clerk if there was a Chinese laundry in town. The clerk said yes, but few people used it. It was a block off Broadway and down three blocks.

J.R. found it easily and stepped into the establishment. Incense wafted through the outer room. He could also smell the sweet smoke of an opium pipe somewhere, and he smiled. These Chinese probably didn't care how much business they did as long as they could keep their water pipe going.

A small bell had tinkled when he came in the door, and a moment later a young Chinese

dressed in western clothes but with the traditional long black pigtail came through a curtain
from the rear.

"Ah, yes?" the young man asked. It might be
all the English he knew, J.R. thought.

J.R. showed him the suit. The young man's
eyes went wide when he saw the quality of the
cloth and the needle work. He spoke quickly in
Chinese to the rear and another man came out.
This one was older. He glanced at J.R. and then
at the soiled suit.

"Ah, hero. Small girl. I see."

"Yes, thank you. Can you clean the suit? It
can't be washed. Could it be brushed and cleaned
with spirits of some kind?"

"Yes, yes, kerosene."

"Kerosene? That'll melt the fabric."

"No, kerosene. Guarantee."

"That's a fifty-dollar suit," J.R. said. "Boston.
If you ruin it, you'll give me fifty dollars?"

The older man stared at him a minute. He
exploded with a rattling shower of Chinese and
the younger man winced and moved away.
The older man looked at J.R. again after the
outburst.

"No fifty dollar. Thirty-five. Used now. Thirty-
five for you if we ruin. Guarantee. Make like
new. You see."

He pinned a number on the pillowcase, pushed
the suit back inside, and gave J.R. a matching
number.

"Tomorrow morning, same time," the Chinese
man said, and carried the suit into the back
room through the curtain.

The young Chinese bowed low. J.R. snorted and walked out of the small store. Then he began establishing himself as a well-to-do stranger in town. He bought the most expensive white shirt that the Johnson Apparel store had. He had them add a fifty-cent black string tie, then a pair of stockings for a dollar. The price was outrageous, which made it all the sweeter.

He spent more of the $9,000 he had cleared in the stock deal in Forest Grove. He found a home-made candy store and bought six kinds of hand-dipped chocolates and a dozen pralines guaranteed to be from an old New Orleans recipe. By the time he left the candy store he had spent more than five dollars. It was more business than the lady had probably done all day. Her mainstay was horehounds, which he avoided. They were a nickel a dozen.

J.R. had lunch, as he studiously called it, in the best eatery in town, which he determined was the Silver Spoon. There he had roast pheasant on a special order. He asked them to bring him the whole bird and he demolished it before the delighted eyes of the cook. It cost him $3.25, an outrageous amount for a dinner, let alone a lunch. A small bottle of a fair wine went with the complete luncheon, and he was satisfied. He left the waiter a fifty-cent tip. He knew most tips at good restaurants in that area were a nickel or a dime.

Outside again he checked another clothier, but they had no gentleman's trousers he would be caught wearing to a cock fight, so he passed, bought only a three-inch-wide black silk tie that would make a loosely tied muffler-type knot at his throat. The store owner apologized, saying it was the finest he had. The price was a dollar and fifty cents.

J.R. paid the bill with a smile and left another surprised and impressed store owner.

Word of mouth travels fast in a small town, and before he had finished his shopping tour, he was sure every merchant in town was waiting and hoping that he would stop in his store.

J.R. went back to the hotel and took a nap. He wanted to be sharp and ready for any opportunity that came that night.

About four o'clock, a knock on his door awoke him and he let in Folke and Dianna. Both were dressed well. Folke had been scouting the chances at a few games of poker and found the biggest game at the First Class Saloon. It would start about ten that night.

"You going to play?" J.R. asked.

Folke shrugged. "Might, if the mood strikes me. I wondered when we're going to make our plans for our big hit here in town?"

"How about tonight?" J.R. asked. "I have a dinner engagement, but any time after, say, ten."

"Where? Out at the medicine wagon?"

"Sounds good to me. I still have the buggy. We can all ride out in style. Be here at ten and we roll out there. If E.B. is drunk or sleeping, we'll wake him up and sober him."

They agreed. Dianna nodded and grinned at J.R., and when Folke turned to leave, she stared at his crotch. She made the stare obvious. When J.R. looked at her she lifted her brows and tilted her head. Then she grinned. J.R. laughed softly and walked them to the door. As they went out the door, he patted Dianna's round bottom. She looked back over her shoulder at him, then hurried to catch up with her husband.

"See you later tonight," J.R. said and closed the door.

He was right on time at the Openlander house for dinner. Victoria wore a sleek blue party dress that clung to her body, flared at the hips and came tight around her waist before it stopped short of her shoulders, leaving her arms and shoulders bare and showing a thin slice of cleavage.

"What a beautiful dress, Mrs. Openlander. That blue is your color."

"Thank you," she said. "I'm so sorry about that fine suit you must have ruined today in the street. I'd noticed it as you walked toward us. It looked expensive. Is it ruined?"

"Your Chinese laundry and kerosene cleaners are going to tell me in the morning," J.R. said.

A tall man with a full beard hurried in from another room and held out his hand. "Evening. I'm Alonzo Openlander. I thank you a million times for rescuing our little girl from that runaway horse this morning. You tell them and tell them. . . ." He stopped and grinned. "Thanks again, Mr. Archibald." ·

"Dinner is ready," Victoria said. "Why don't we go in and sit down. Julie is already there, I'm afraid. She doesn't have much patience at this stage."

J.R. smiled and watched her. She was beautiful, with the kind of sleek, athletic body that a person didn't see often. Good strong shoulders, fine breasts, a flat belly, and hips that weren't too wide, but just wide enough for the rest of her. He suddenly wanted to paint her in the nude.

They went in and sat down at the four place settings. J.R. was across from the little girl, who was scrubbed to a sparkle, her soft brown hair combed and held in place with barrettes.

"Hello, young lady," J.R. said as he sat down. She smiled and waved.

"We're in our not-talking stage right now," Victoria said. "In ten minutes it will be can't-stop-her-from-talking time."

Dinner was a roast, with all the vegetables and side dishes that went with it and a particularly strong horseradish sauce that left J.R. gasping after the first bite.

"Oh dear. I forgot to tell you that we like our horseradish almost straight, we cut it only a little with some fresh potato."

She smiled at him as he had a drink of coffee, then of water. He used a white linen handkerchief to dab at the tears in the corners of his eyes.

"I'll know where to get the recipe for horseradish now," he said.

Halfway through the meal, Alonzo caught J.R.'s attention. "I understand you're on your way to Omaha. You have an office there?"

"Yes, of sorts. In my line of work I do a lot of traveling. Have to go where the business is."

Alonzo nodded, had a bite of the roast and

then continued. "Victoria said you were an investment counselor. Are there that many folks here in South Junction who need help in making their investments?"

"That's what I'll be finding out, Mr. Openlander. Sometimes you just can't tell how a town is set up."

A few minutes later, just before the dessert of cherry pie with whipped cream on top, J.R. tried a question.

"From your letterhead I see you're a lawyer, Mr. Openlander."

"That's right. A small town practice."

"He's also the district attorney, but it's only a part-time position here in this county, so Alonzo can have a private practice on the side."

"Not only can, I have to in order to make a living."

J. R. took the news that he was sitting down to dinner with the district attorney of the county without an outward sign. Inside he was chuckling at the irony of it. If this man only knew what he had planned for their small town.

A knock sounded on the door, then came again more insistently.

Alonzo excused himself and went to the door. He came back a minute later with his hat.

"Business down at the jail. Some fool shot up a saloon and killed a man at the bar. Sheriff wants to get the paperwork done tonight because the circuit court judge will be in town tomorrow. Sorry, Mr. Archibald, but I'm going to have to leave. You finish your dinner. We owe it to you." He bent and kissed his wife on the cheek.

"I'll be back just as soon as I can."

They finished dinner and cleared the table. He helped over Victoria's protests.

"This is woman's work," she said, smiling at the same time. A few minutes later it was time to put Julie to bed. Victoria insisted that he stay.

"I need to talk to you for a few minutes. I won't be but a second or two. Julie is a big girl about going to bed. Thank goodness for small favors."

While she was gone, J.R. looked around the parlor where she had left him. It was well furnished, not richly done, but with one breakfront of a much earlier vintage, perhaps an antique of some sort. A middle-income family. Not rich, but not on the verge of starvation either. Victoria came back as he looked at some photographs on the spinet harpsichord.

"My mother and father just before he died last year. They thought sitting for a photograph was a waste of time and foolishness. Now I'm so grateful that I talked them into it. Mr. Archibald, please sit down." She motioned to a small couch and they sat a few inches apart.

"I . . . I want to talk to you. That little girl in there is the joy of my life. My whole existence centers around her. I haven't told anyone else, but I'm not right inside, female wise. I can never have another child. So you see what that small little human being in there means to me and why she is as important to me as life itself."

She moved toward him until her upper leg brushed against his. "Mr. Archibald, I'm not usually a forward person. I sometimes find it hard to voice my feelings. However, today there in town when my heart stopped and you charged into the street to grab Julie and rush her away from danger, I knew I would do something for you I've only done for one other man." Her hand fell to his thigh. "Do I have to say the words, to spell it out for you?"

"Mrs. Openlander. . . ."

"Victoria. Please call me Victoria."

"Victoria, this isn't something you have to do."

"Oh, but I do, and I'm sure if my husband ever found out about it, he would understand the deepseated, impossible-to-repress need for me to do this."

She leaned toward him, her lips brushing his cheek. "What I do is a true gift of love." Her lips brushed across his mouth, then she kissed him hard, her lips parting. His hands remained at his sides.

She ended the kiss and leaned back. "Do you find me so repulsive?"

"Oh, no! You're one of the most beautiful women I've ever seen. What a perfect face, a marvelous body. . . ."

"Then?"

"Your husband could come through that door at any second, and I'm sure he would shoot me dead before you could even start to explain. He would be right."

"Then tomorrow. He'll be in court all day." She caught his hands and put one over each of her breasts. Her hand moved to his crotch and up to his fly, where she found a long hardness.

"Oh, yes! I hoped that you would want me. Tomorrow. You come at ten o'clock to the back door. No one is about then. Come in as if you belong here. The door is never locked."

She moved his hand and pushed it under the soft blue fabric of the dress, directly on her bare bosom. For just a moment, Victoria trembled, then smiled. "Oh, yes, I must repay you in the only way I can. You saved not only Julie's life today. I know that I would have killed myself if I had to bury my baby daughter."

His hand caressed her breast gently, and he felt its stiffening nipple.

"One more kiss," she said. This time their lips parted and their tongues twined, then fought and battled. Her breathing surged, and she broke off the kiss and stood. She held his hand on her breast as they walked to the front door. Victoria Openlander rubbed the erection under his pants and smiled.

"I think he likes me." She hugged him, removed his hand and arranged her dress. "Tomorrow, at ten. I want to see you here. Don't fail me. It's one of the most important things I'll ever do in my life."

Chapter Thirteen

The three Guthrie brothers met later that night
on schedule. J.R., Folke and his wife Dianna rode
into the camp where E.B. had set up a mile north
of town on the creek and found him halfway
through a bottle of whiskey. They sobered him
up, and an hour later got down to business with
steaming cups of coffee and cookies Dianna had
brought from the bakery in town.

J.R. was pleased to see that E.B. had
transformed his rawhider's rig into a brightly
painted and sign-covered Medicine Wagon.
"Dr. Snodgrass and his magic elixir," one
sign boasted. "Dr. Snodgrass's elixir will cure
anything!" another said. The wagon tongue,
wheels, spokes, even the canvas in back had
been decorated with fresh paint. It looked ready
to go on display.

"So what the hell we going to do to this little bitty, rundown, goddamned town?" E.B. asked. He was on the verge of sobering up and hating it.

"Gonna surprise the hell out of them," J.R. said. "The bank is ripe for picking. That will be our primary target. But we do it smart. We set up the bank the way we always do. We all carry two sawed-off shotguns on straps around our necks. All loaded with double aught buck."

"Blast hell out of anybody who crosses us," Folke said grinning. "Lordy but I like the sound of that." He scowled. "But what's going to keep the lawmen they got in this town from moving in and blasting at us with their own shotguns?" Folke asked.

E. B. belched, had a drink of his coffee and stared at his older brother with delight. "Yeah, J.R., you old sod. What's gonna keep the law busy in this little town while we do the fucking bank?"

J.R. grinned and sipped the coffee. "Figured you were going to bring that up. You probably remember the bank at Centerville two years ago. We learned a lot there. This is what's going to happen. I'm going to hire us some helpers."

"Don't like helpers," E.B. said, reaching for the whiskey. Dianna lifted it out of his reach and patted his hand.

"These helpers will be working on their own," J.R. said. "They get no cut of our loot. I'm paying eight of them fifty dollars each to do the work."

Folke sat up straighter in amazement. He

snorted and looked at his brother. "You spending four hundred dollars for some help and let them work on their own?"

J.R. laughed. "Right as rhubarb. We want to keep the law off our backs, right? So we arrange some work for the lawmen to take care of. I'll hire these eight men, and up and down Main street on a given day, and at precisely three o'clock, all eight will hold up a big store or saloon."

Folke chuckled, then laughed. "Damn, J.R., might work. We have the holdups set for three, and at five minutes after three, when the sheriff and his two deputies are busy chasing robbers, we hit the bank and take off the other direction out of town."

J.R. had more coffee, tried one of the cookies and grinned. "That's about it. Not sure just how long after the robberies that we go for the bank. Want the people on the street yelling for the sheriff. We'll have the robbers all leave town going south. That will make the north route open for us."

"How long after three should we hit the bank?" Folke asked.

Dianna spoke up and they all looked surprised. "Why not just wait outside until you hear the sheriff called for, and when he gets into action, then you go into the bank."

J.R. nodded. "Sounds like a good plan. We get him busy, then launch our own attack on that strongbox. We want to get inside before the bank people hear the word and wonder if they will be next."

Wilderness Wanton

"When we gonna do it?" E.B. asked.

"This is Tuesday. Say we set the program for Saturday about three. Gives me time to round up my eight robbers. Fifty dollars each should be plenty. Don't bother trying to share the expenses, brothers. I'll stand the four hundred. I made a big haul down the road a ways."

E.B. grabbed his bottle. "How 'bout a drink to celebrate?"

Folke nodded. "Sure as hell, why not? What do you think this bank will have in it, cash money?"

J.R. pushed some small branches into the campfire and watched them blaze up. Amazing what fire could do.

"How much? I've been considering that. Town this size, and just one bank. I'd say he should keep about five thousand dollars in cash on hand for emergencies."

"We gonna give him one damn big emergency," E.B. said. He pulled on the whiskey bottle.

Folke grabbed it away from him and matched him drink for drink. Dianna sat near the fire across from her husband. J.R. sat down nearby and she watched him.

"Shouldn't take long," she said, loudly enough for him to hear but too softly to carry across the crackling fire.

J.R. smiled and agreed. "Not much time at all." He stared at the woman. "It's been a hell of a long time, Dianna."

"Since Ohio, I think it was. That was so good." She smiled at him, and her hand stretched out and touched his thigh. He pushed closer to her. On the other side of the fire the drinking brothers were still at it.

Ten minutes later, E.B. sighed, handed the bottle to Folke and slid sideways, passed out.

Folke sang a little song chiding his brother, then tipped the bottle on his own. His eyes went wide, he blinked, then he took the bottle down and tried to sit it up. It fell over with some of the whiskey dribbling out the narrow neck.

Folke watched it, tried to stand the bottle on the bottom. He reached for it, misjudged the distance, and lost what little balance he had left. He sprawled forward on his stomach, his head two feet from the fire.

Dianna hurried around the fire and pulled Folke back out of any danger. Then she went back and sat down beside J.R.

"Now, I'd say it's our turn to celebrate, wouldn't you, J.R.?"

"Just what kind of a celebration did you have in mind?"

"Something under the stars. Something on a blanket. Something with both you and me just as buck naked as we can get. Something a hundred yards upstream where our squeals and sounds of rapture won't wake up our two sleeping friends over there."

She moved over and kissed J.R. on the mouth. Then she moved down and kissed the bulge just behind his fly.

"Oh," J.R. said. "That kind of something. I think you're right. I'll get a blanket from inside the wagon, then we'll find a fine little nest under some trees and below a lot of stars. I've been waiting for this for two years."

"I'm not waiting any more," Dianna said. "You hurry up or I'm going to start without you."

When Spur McCoy awoke the next morning, Abby was still in bed beside him. He kissed her eyes and she came awake slowly.

"Morning already or do you have the lamps lit?"

"Morning."

"Short night," Abby said and sat up. She was still nude, and Spur smiled at the way her fine breasts bounced and swung with her motion.

Abby grinned. "You like that?"

"Any time, all the time."

"You wouldn't get much work done during the day."

"All night."

"Then we wouldn't get much sleep."

"Compromise. You cover both of them up and the rest of your lovely little body, and I'll take you to breakfast right here in the hotel."

"Won't people talk?"

"Not if they know what's good for them."

After breakfast, Abby went to her saloon and Spur checked his maps again in his room, trying to make some sense out of the dates of the various raids on the individual ranches. There was no pattern.

Then he cut out the smaller three ranches and concentrated on the largest ones. They had the most raids. Four each, and each raid a week apart, rotating from one of the larger ranches to another. Rustling on the smaller ranches had been sporadic, and usually after the large ranch sequence had finished.

He grinned and checked the four previous weeks. They went from the Circle L to the S-T, then to the Box C and on to the Bar-B outfits. The last one of the four hit was the Circle L, which meant if they kept on schedule the S-T Tabler ranch should be the next one to be rustled.

Spur felt he had a good shot at figuring this mess out. But what if he was wrong? He'd be wrong and sit outside all night or for two or three nights for nothing. No big loss. He put on his hat and gun belt and headed for the sheriff's office. He needed someone else to take a good look at his data just to be sure he hadn't messed up somewhere.

Spur was halfway to the lawman's office when he saw a commotion down the street. No gunfire, just some firecrackers going off. They had a lower popping sound than a heavier .45 or a rifle. He went to the edge of the boardwalk and looked to the north.

A colorful covered wagon came down the street, and he knew by the size and the big signs on it exactly what it was: A medicine man and his wagon had come to town.

Spur watched as the wagon rolled down the street. When it reached him, it was halfway through the three-block-long business section, and already there were 30 children screaming and yelling and following the wagon. The driver reached down and passed out suckers on sticks covered with bright paper.

Spur knew the wagon would go to the far end of town, then turn and come back for one more display before the good "doctor" set up for business in a vacant lot as close to the center of town as he could.

Spur watched him for half a block, then crossed the street and headed for the sheriff's office.

E.B. Guthrie, now known as Dr. Snodgrass, waved and called to the children, tipped his tall black hat to the ladies on the boardwalk, handed out his suckers to the children flocking around his wagon, and genuinely enjoyed being the center of attention.

He had shaved closely again this morning, his hair was slicked back, and he'd given himself a haircut. He had on a presentable suit he had stolen two months ago. He even wore a pair of half spectacles. The lenses in them had no correction of any kind since they were stage glasses he had picked up in St. Louis.

He made a turn at the end of the street and came back close to the other side, stopping along the boardwalk where there were no other rigs to pass out the candy.

He found the spot he wanted halfway down the street. It was a vacant lot between a millinery store and the big general store. There would be a lot of activity around these places and foot traffic past his display.

He drove the wagon in so it sat sideways to the street, then unhitched his two mules and tied them to a stake driven into the ground near the back end of the lot on the alley. Back at the medicine wagon, he let down a platform from the side of the wagon. It rested on stilts and perched four feet in the air. It was his sales platform. He brought out a table loaded with his wares, including his Magic Elixir. It was set up on the street side, where he could stand and make his pitch to those who passed by.

His main product was his elixir, made from sugar water, food coloring, and one ounce of cheap bourbon whiskey to seven ounces of water and a sprinkling of herbs. It came out a healthy red color. It sold well.

He sat up and began hawking his elixir. In five minutes he had 20 people crowded around his wagon. He gave candy to all the children, and most of them scurried away. Then he spotted a man in the small crowd.

"You there, sir. I'd like to shake your hand. The last time I was through town here you appeared to be on your last legs. You took a dozen bottles of my Dr. Snodgrass's Magic Elixir, and I see today you're hale and hearty. I want to give you—yes, ladies and gentlemen I said GIVE, this amazing man a free bottle of Dr. Snograss's Magic Elixir as a gift, so he can try it and see if it's the same and then tell you how good it's made him feel.

"No charge, not fifty cents, not two dollars and fifty cents, which is my usual price for this Magic Elixir. Today, and today only, I offer it to you, my good friends, for only a dollar a bottle. Yes, all of this Magic Elixir power in one small bottle. It will cure dozens of diseases including lumbago, back pains, gout, rheumatism, the palsy, the common cold and hundreds of other dastardly ailments.

"Here, sir, come right up and let me give you this free, no strings attached bottle of Dr. Snodgrass's Magic Elixir."

The man came to the front, reached out his hand. He was about 30, alert and dressed the way the others were. He stared at the bottle.

"You say it's free?"

"Absolutely free. I just ask you to have a swallow or two of this Magic Elixir and see how it tastes and how it feels in your belly. Can you do that, kind sir?"

The man nodded, took the bottle and un-screwed the cap. The elixir he sampled was not the same as the other bottles. This one had been juiced up with three ounces of bourbon whiskey and was almost surely to be greatly appreciated by the drinker.

The man tipped the bottle and had a sip. His eyes lit up and he grinned. He took another shot at it, and this time he came away with a huge smile. Dr. Snodgrass held his hand as he started to drink again.

"Tell these people, young man. Tell them what you think of Dr. Snodgrass's Magic Elixir. How do you feel?"

"Terrific elixir. I'm gonna buy a bottle myself, right now. Makes me feel good right off. Can't tell you the jolt of energy it gave me. I want one—no, make it two bottles of that wonderful elixir."

He gave E.B. Guthrie two dollar bills, accepted his two bottles of the Magic Elixir off the supply, and slipped away through the crowd.

The man had not been a shill. Guthrie had never seen him before, but from long experience he could spot a man who needed a drink. The whiskey in the Elixir almost always did the trick.

He sold 20 bottles of the elixir and then closed up for a moment to come down to the boardwalk and pass out his candy. He'd bought the suckers in Columbus six for a penny, and always made good use of them.

One small girl, about ten, hesitated, then took the sucker from him. She opened it and put it in her mouth, then came back and asked if she could have another one.

"For my sister," the girl said. She was so young she had no breasts at all, but E.B. wasn't choosy right then.

"What's your name?" he asked her. The others around the wagon had wandered off, and he hadn't worked up a second crowd.

"I'm Phyllis."

"Well, Phyllis, I have some more suckers, but they're in the back of my wagon. Come back there and I'll find two for you." The girl smiled and looked up the boardwalk.

"Is your mother here somewhere?" he asked.

"She's shopping in the store. I told her I'd be right here."

E.B. walked to the back of the wagon and stepped in close so he was out of sight of the boardwalk. Phyllis stepped in beside him and waited.

"Can you give me a hug for two suckers?" he asked.

She shrugged, then nodded and stepped forward and hugged him. His hand slid between her legs and rubbed her inner thighs. She stepped back without complaining.

"One more hug for another sucker," he said as he held it out. She laughed and moved toward him again. His hand flashed upward under her skirt to her crotch and rubbed.

"You shouldn't do that," she said, not moving.

"I know. Does it bother you?"

"No, but if my mother knew. . . ."

"Phyllis!" The word came like a marauding clap of thunder. The girl jumped away from E.B., who turned and took out three candies from the wagon.

"Just getting this nice little girl some candies," E.B. said.

"Phyllis, come here at once," the mother brayed. She was a large woman, with heavy arms and ponderous breasts hidden by a print dress.

"I told you about men like him. Never, never take candy from a foul old man like that."

A man came into the scene. "What's the trouble here?" he asked. The woman spoke to him softly and his eyes flared. He advanced on E.B. and swung before he was within range. E.B. pulled his boot knife, a six-inch blade he used for skinning, and faced the angry father. The man made one more charge and took a wild swing.

E.B. waited, dodged the fist, and cut the father's wrist to the bone with one slice. The father screeched in pain, held his wrist with his hand and glared at E.B.

"Old man, I'll be back. I'll be back with my gun. You better watch every step you take."

"Get out of here. All I did was give her some candy. You can't prove I did anything else. Get out of here or I'll get the sheriff and charge you with assault and battery. Then you'd be in big trouble."

E.B. watched the furious father walk away. The mother held the little girl tightly as they went up the street. Phyllis turned at the last minute and grinned at him. He waved at her and smiled. It might have been. He'd never tried one that young before, but it might have been.

Spur McCoy walked into the sheriff's office with his sheaf of paper and his projections and laid them out on the desk. Sheriff Halverson looked at them. He saw the lists and the progression.

"So, you're saying if it all goes according to some strange, wild plan, that the Tabler spread will be the one that gets hit by the rustlers next?"

"What it looks like to me, Sheriff."

The sheriff shook his head and shuffled some papers on his desk. He stood and walked to the window and looked out, then came back.

"Even if we knew for sure that's the ranch they would hit, we don't know where. That ranch has borders of what, twenty-five miles or so. Not a chance everyone in the county could patrol all that distance to catch them."

"Same thing I decided, Sheriff Halverson. At

least we have some kind of a theory. Oh, let's not say a word of this to anyone else. You agree?"

"Right. At least we can see if your idea is right."

Spur left the office and walked down the street past the bank and on toward the hotel. Spur wondered what devilment the banker, Stewart Rawlins, was up to. He must be working on some dastardly plan. A man as self-centered as he was wouldn't give up this easily.

Inside the bank, Rawlins looked out as Spur McCoy walked by. The banker opened a desk drawer and took out a .38 French revolver, then slowly put it back.

There had to be something he could do to get back at that damn range detective. How dare him, coming right into the bank and threatening him. Just who the hell did he think he was, God himself?

There had to be a way. Had to be, and a method that couldn't be traced back to him. No hired guns this time. He had to do the job himself, which meant a lot of planning, stealth, late at night when he had an alibi.

It had to be a plan that couldn't fail, that was safe, that was deadly and created no suspicion about him. Rawlins walked around his office trying to think. At night, that was for sure. A gun? An accident? Drowning in the creek? Shot while cleaning his revolver?

Rawlins snorted. Nobody would believe that even if he could make it happen. A woman. Yes, maybe one of the whores down at Noona's place. Only she said McCoy hadn't been in. She could invite him, give him an all nighter on the house. Why? No, he'd be suspicious.

An unsigned note about knowing who was doing the rustling, and asking him to meet at the edge of town or well outside of town. Pin it on the rustlers that way. He frowned at that. The idea was the best he'd had so far. But would it work? Would a smart guy like McCoy fall for the old set-up? He might have seen it a dozen times already. Still, it was better than nothing. He'd ponder it.

Rawlins went to the window and saw McCoy cross the street and go into the hotel. No more tries in the hotel itself. Could give the place a bad name. He'd ruled out the Silver Spoon as well. Business was business. He'd think on it some more.

Spur McCoy walked through the hotel door, checked his box and found a note. "Spur. See you upstairs soon as you get in. Just had a brilliant idea." It was in a sealed envelope and the only signature was a big A.

Upstairs he tried the door. It was unlocked. He knocked. Abby opened it, smiled at him and held the door open. She closed and locked it.

"Hardly recognized you with all those clothes on," Spur said.

She grinned, gave him a hard, hot kiss, then whirled away and sat on the bed.

"I've been thinking," she said.

"Damn, we're all in big trouble."

She stuck her tongue out at him. "Really. Thinking about the rustling problem. You said all of the seven ranches are losing cattle to the rustlers. One of the problems is you haven't seen anyone who knows anything about any steers being driven out of this range and heading for market."

"So the cattle must all be here, hidden away," Spur said. "I simply can't figure out where they are."

"What I think is that nobody is rustling any cows. I think those good old cattle ranchers are making the whole thing up. I don't know why."

"What about those cattle tracks I followed yesterday, or was it the day before? Somebody drove that stock off the Bar-L Spread. I was there. I saw it. I saw the rebranding fires."

"But did you find any fresh brands?"

"No. That's probably what I should do, go back up there and ride the range until I find some. Maybe I'll get Rusty to help me. Now, you interested in having some lunch? I'm getting hungry again."

Chapter Fourteen

On Wednesday afternoon, Abby watched the poker game in her First Class Saloon with a touch of awe, surprise and honest fear. She hadn't seen so much money on a poker table out front in her establishment since she took it over three years ago. The last pot went to more than a hundred and fifty dollars.

That was half a year's pay for a working man. When the next pot was won, she stepped up to the table.

"Gentlemen, I can't guarantee your safety out here in the open saloon with so much money on the table. I suggest you move to the back room. You'll have some privacy and not twenty gawkers, and you can concentrate on the game."

"Damn good idea, Miss," Folke Guthrie said.

He'd come out of his drunk early this morning, ridden into town on the buggy, had a hot bath and clean clothes, and gone looking for some gambling action. He lucked out at a big game in the afternoon here in this saloon.

"Fine with me to move on back," another of the players said. The two others in the game nodded. Everyone gathered up his chips, and Abby grabbed the deck of cards. She glanced at the backs of them, but couldn't see any obvious marks. Even so she substituted a fresh deck with the seal unbroken from the small apron she wore.

The four men and a woman who had been hovering about the game went into the back room.

Abby frowned at the woman who followed the group. "Miss, are you playing?" Abby asked. Dianna Guthrie showed her wedding ring and shook her head.

"I'm with Mr. Guthrie, there."

Abby looked at the other men. "Do you mind if she's in the room?" None of the men responded. They sat down at the green felt-covered poker table under the twin kerosene lamps hung from the ceiling and arranged their chips.

"All right, Mrs. Guthrie. You can stay. Usually house rules don't allow anyone in here but players. As long as the others don't object, you can stay. However, you'll have to sit directly beside or behind your husband and make no comments and not move around during a hand. We don't want to risk any chance that someone might think you were spotting for your husband."

"Well, of all of the . . ." Dianna began. A quick look from Folke stopped her.

"Mrs. Guthrie, I've been around poker players half my life. I understand them. I can tell you fifty ways to cheat at this game, and I watch players back here for every one of them." She tossed the cards on the table.

"New game, new deck, seal unbroken. Enjoy yourselves, gentlemen. As I said, I'll be watching."

"You've no right . . ." one of the men began.

"I own the joint. I have every right. If you don't agree, cash in your chips and get out of my saloon."

The player lifted his brows, shook his head and settled into his chair. The game continued.

Folke had been using Dianna now and then in the saloon to signal what cards the other players had. Now he had lost that advantage. The deck of cards he had put some thumbnail marks on were gone, and he didn't have a marked deck in his pocket that matched the color or pattern on the back of the cards they now used. It all meant he had to play honest poker, and good poker at least for a while.

He played smart for three hands, won two of them, both on bluffs, and was well ahead. He wanted a big score. Each hand that he played he watched for big cards, and as he worked his hand in his lap he would spike out an ace or king and let it fall, then slip it up his sleeve. This worked only on losing hands, when he didn't have to show all five of his cards.

Several hands later, when he had two aces

hidden away, he made his move. The pot went up dramatically. He had been dealt one ace and a pair of eights. With the two aces he had up his sleeve, he would have an Aces over Eights full house, good enough to win most hands of five card draw.

He raised the bet $200, and the big man with the smashed nose sitting across from him growled and put his cards on the table face down.

"Got to go take a piss," he said, with no hint of apology to the two women. He stood and went around the table. When he came behind Folke he grabbed the gambler's left arm and pulled back his suit-jacket sleeve. The two hidden aces fell out of the sleeve and onto the green felt table.

"By damn! No wonder you been winning so much," the big man roared. He fumbled in his vest and pulled a hideout derringer. He had backed up from Folke, and just as he brought up the small gun, Folke shot him twice in the chest with his own .22 derringer. He had readied it the minute his cheating was unmasked.

One of the rounds jolted through the big man's lung. He dropped his weapon, clutched his chest, and sat down heavily on the floor. He began to wheeze and cough. His eyes went glassy and he coughed up blood, then slowly he fell to one side. The second round from the derringer had sliced through just below the heart, tearing apart one of the large arteries leading away from the blood pump.

The big man lifted one hand toward Abby, then dropped it. His head rolled to one side, and a last breath whoosed out of his lungs as he died.

The door opened and the barkeep charged in with a sawed-off shotgun in hand, ready to fire.

"Go get the sheriff," Abby said. She stepped over to Folke, who hadn't even stood. "I'll take that weapon. You've done enough damage with it already."

"It was self-defense," Folke said, his words calm and precise. "You saw him draw down on me. He was ready to blast me right into hell."

Abby shook her head. "Not necessarily. He might only have been going to keep you covered until the sheriff arrived. You didn't give him a chance to explain himself."

"If I'd given him that chance, then it would have been me, not him getting ready to change his address to the boneyard. I don't take that kind of chance."

"You take that kind every day when you cheat. I saw you using your wife as a spotter in the other room. That's mostly why I moved you in here. I don't care who you are, I don't want you in my saloon any more. You come in here again, I'll have you thrown out and arrested. Is that entirely clear, Mr. Guthrie?"

"Entirely."

Sheriff Halverson arrived a few minutes later with a deputy. The deputy took statements from the other players and from Abby. He stood over the chair where Folke sat playing a game of solitaire.

"Guthrie, I've heard from the witnesses. Turns

out you were cheating in a high-stakes game. Turns out you got your shots off a little bit before anyone was sure that the man intended to shoot you. Technically it was self-defense, but between you and me, Guthrie, it was one hell of a lot closer to murder.

"We don't like card cheats in this town. There's a four o'clock stage south. You be on it or you be out of town on your own by four-thirty. If I find you still in town, I'll jail you for murder. Our circuit judge is in court here today, and he might just hear your case and have you hung by tomorrow. I hope we understand each other."

"Oh, understood. People in this town are easy to understand. I'll cash in. . . ."

"You'll cash in only those chips you bought, Mr. Guthrie. Not a cent more. The rest of what you have and the pot on the table goes to the man's widow. I know her and she can use the cash. You have any objections to that?"

"Seems quite fair under the circumstances."

Spur came in after it was over. He saw the sheriff having one last talk with Guthrie, then they went outside.

Abby had pointed out the killer. "You ever seen him before? Is he on some wanted poster somewhere? He was so cool, so matter-of-fact. It was like, ho-hum, I just killed another man who caught me cheating."

Spur raked over the stacks of wanted men he kept catalogued in his mind. He had a good eye for faces. He couldn't place him.

"The name does sound familiar, but he's not on any poster that I remember."

"Too bad. I could use a couple of thousand dollars reward money. You're sure?"

"Near as I can tell. Wanted to tell you that I'm going to ride out to the Bar-B and see if I can borrow Rusty for a few days to help me check out some things. Should be back before dark."

"Don't step in any gopher holes," Abby said. She watched him a moment and wished she could tell him exactly how she felt. But this wasn't the right time.

"Be back soon," he said and hurried out the door.

At the livery, he saddled his gelding and was ready to leave when a prancing black stepped up towing a fancy black buggy. The driver was overdressed for the town, a dandy. The suit cost three times what most men could pay. He wore a fancy town hat and sported a walking stick with a gold head.

Spur paused a moment. Something about the face. The man turned, saw Spur and nodded, then stepped back so he could ride past. That was when the face registered. He couldn't remember the name, probably not the one the man used now. Something like Gentleman Dan or Fancy Dan, something like that. He was wanted in at least three states and territories for bank robbery. Often worked with a pair of brothers.

The man in Abby's saloon. He had the same kind of long, drawn face, same glint in his eyes. They had to be brothers if they weren't twins. Yes, brothers. Well, Fancy Dan was in town, and the only bank was surely the target. Unless Fancy

Dan had turned over a new page in his life, which Spur doubted.

He rode past the man without looking back. Well, well, well. More business than he had figured. Now he was sure that he wanted Rusty to help him, back him if needed.

Spur grinned now as he rode. He felt more relaxed than he had since he arrived. A bank to protect against robbery was a concrete job, a practical under-control kind of a situation. This rustling was as nebulous and unspecific as punching holes in a fog bank. He didn't seem to get anywhere on it.

At the Bar-B ranch, Spur talked with Northcliff. He said he hadn't made much progress, and asked to borrow Rusty to help him get around the local geography.

"Calling in a second man, eh? Well, old boy, I can't blame you. But since I'm already paying Rusty wages, I don't see how I can lose. If he wants to go, he's yours for as long as you need him."

Rusty couldn't get his gear together fast enough. "I been wondering how you're doing. Heard you went on a long ride the other day up Five Mile ravine. That's what I call that long, thin valley you tracked the cattle up. I can't figure out why they went up there and then down that other slot over the low pass. Must have had some plan."

"That's what we need, a plan."

On the ride back to town, Spur told Rusty what he had figured out about the regular way the ranches had been rustled.

"You say it looks like the Tabler spread for the next heist?"

" 'Peers as how."

"We going to sit on guard out there?"

"What do you think? Where along a twenty-mile stretch do we wait for them?"

"Easy, wait where the most cattle are. Where the rustlers can grab their hundred head the easiest."

"Makes sense."

They got into town just after dark and headed for a cafe Rusty liked that had Greek food. They were riding down Main Street when they heard shouting ahead. Spur saw the glow of flames, then smoke and a crackling fire.

They rode up fast and saw the medicine wagon totally shot through with flames. It burned as if it had been soaked with gallons of kerosene. The mules were well away from the flames, and no one seemed to be on board.

Nothing could be done to put out the fire. It was well away from the stores on each side, and most of the people simply stood around and watched.

Soon a man ran up and Spur recognized Dr. Snodgrass, the so-called medicine man. He screamed and wailed and yelled and charged some of the people, asking who had set his wagon on fire. Once he tried to rush in to save some items, but the blaze was too hot and drove him back.

Spur and Rusty rode on to the livery and put their horses away, then had their supper. After the meal they sat in the chairs tipped up against the front of the cafe and watched the small town slow down to a few hardy souls venturing out in the darkness.

Spur heard the hoofbeats before he saw the horse. He came to his feet and looked to the north. Soon a rider materialized out of the dim light and came to a stop near the sheriff's office.

"Rustling!" the man bellowed. His lathered horse stood there blowing hard. "Rustlers! I just saw six of them out on our spread, the S-T, the Tabler ranch."

It took the sheriff ten minutes to gather a six-man posse. By that time Spur and Rusty had saddled their mounts in the livery. They weren't tired, just warmed up from their evening walk. The two joined the posse.

They took the road north and then west at a walk, and soon they were on the wagon trail that led to the Tabler ranch. It was seven miles almost due west of town. The rustling took place three miles west of the ranch buildings.

Jeremiah Tabler and three men from the S-T joined the group when they passed the ranch buildings. They all carried rifles and six-guns, an unusual package for most cowboys in the Montana ranges.

Jeremiah and the sheriff talked as they rode. Spur and Rusty talked to the cowboy who had ridden for town with the alarm.

"I seed them with me own eyes," the cowboy said. "They was six of them damned owlhoots. They hurrahed about a hundred head together and took off with them, walking them due north.

227

They go much over five or six miles and they out of our spread into the Circle L land. I don't know what the hell they doing."

"All steers?" Spur asked.

The cowboy shook his head. "Not a chance. They swung a fast loop around them critters fast, sweeping up steers, brood cows, even some heifers. I saw them cut out one range bull and send him running."

"Same kind of operation. They were heading north?"

"Was when I seed them. They could change directions minute I was out of sight."

After the three miles west, they turned and rode north. The sheriff had brought five coal-oil lanterns along, and they stopped when they got to the spot near where the cowboy said he saw the rustlers. Three men used the lanterns, walking slowly, watching for any sign of tracks.

It took them two hours to find the tracks. The whole herd had been driven north. Tracking was slow, and by foot. Then Spur suggested that they follow the general direction and send two riders out a quarter of a mile and try to cut the trail with the lanterns. If they found the trail again, it would speed up the night-tracking process.

It worked eight times, then they couldn't find the tracks. It seemed as if the entire herd had been split up into units of two or three and scattered in the range.

Twice they came onto clumps of cattle, but the lanterns showed that they all had the Circle L brand on them. None of the S-T cattle were seen.

By two A.M. the sheriff called off the search. "We ain't doing nobody any good out here at all," Sheriff Halverson said. "Time we head back for town."

"What about my cattle?" Jeremiah Tabler asked.

The sheriff took a long breath. "Tell you what, Jeremiah. You can stay out here all night if'n you want and track every trail you can find. Me and my posse are going back to town and try to get a little sleep before we have to get to work tomorrow."

Jeremiah took off his high-crowned cowboy hat and wiped the sweat away from his forehead. He was about 50, had been a cattle man all his life.

"Guess, you're right, Sheriff. We'll come back this way tomorrow in the daylight and see what we can find. We must have scared them some, since we didn't find anywhere that they stopped and did any running iron work."

The group broke up back at the Tabler ranch, and the town folks kept moving toward the distant shimmer of lights. They were another hour and a half from home.

It was nearly five A.M. when Spur checked his horse in at the livery and then rented a room for Rusty at the hotel.

They both slept until noon, then met in the hotel dining room for stacks of flapjacks, bacon, eggs over easy, jam, syrup, and coffee.

"Your theory about the next strike held up," Rusty said between bites.

"Held, but we didn't have time to get there."

Spur pulled out the paper with his summaries on it and read the dates. "They struck a day earlier than usual. So let's say their next hit will be in five days instead of six. That puts them at the Box C ranch next."

"Wasn't that where we ended up last night, over on the Box C spread range?"

"No, we were on the Circle L. They could have been out there at dawn rounding up those S-T cattle and driving them somewhere else. Just where is what we don't know."

"Damned strange," Rusty said. "Something damned peculiar about this whole damn rustling situation. In thirty years of pushing cattle, I've never seen anything like it. Usually there's a clean-cut raid, cattle stolen, driven off and sold. That last part is what bothers me considerable."

"Part of the reason I wanted you with me. I have another adviser who says there isn't any actual rustling going on at all. It's all just a show staged for somebody's benefit."

"Could be," Rusty said. He finished the stack of food and eased back from the table. "Don't eat quite that good out at the Bar-B."

"Why stage a rustling show?" Spur asked. "Could be to convince partners that there wouldn't be any profit this year. Or to show the bank that the note that was due couldn't be paid because of the losses to the rustlers."

"But then why involve all seven of the outfits in the whole damn area?" Rusty asked.

"You're right. Damn, we're right back where we started. With one exception. I did spot a notorious bank robber in town."

Rusty grinned. "Don't suppose he's planning on wiping out old bastard Rawlins, do you? Wouldn't hurt my mind at all."

"Yeah, I know what you mean. But it would bankrupt half the town, and kill off half the ranchers. I can't let anything like that happen."

Rusty looked up quickly. "Can't let it happen? That sounds like lawman talk. You some kind of a marshal or something?"

Spur showed him his identification and explained the whole reason he was in town.

"Damn. Thought you had to be more than just a range detective. He said he'd pay you *how much?*"

Spur told him and Rusty laughed. "Don't spend the money before you get it. Know for a fact that our Englishman brother is short on the English pound sterling."

"Maybe he's the one trying to show the bankers he can't meet his loan payments?"

"Doubt it. Something else, somewhere."

Spur moved back from the table. "I better go talk to Sheriff Halverson about our bank specialist. I know that he'll be thrilled right down to his underwear."

"What do you want me to do? I don't cotton to just hanging on to your shirt tails."

"Good point. Box C. Closer to town at least. Slip out there so no one sees you and check out the range. Figure where you would do some rustling. One thought. From what I've seen, the tracks of the cattle rustled seem to be turning toward the center of the range, rather than to the outside.

231

"The Bar-L cattle from the ranch on the far right side of the range were lost from sight and tracking somewhere in the upper Bar-B spread in the middle of the range. Last night the far left ranch, the Tabler outfit, had its stolen cattle moved north and then toward the middle of the grass again toward the Box C range, where we lost them. My guess would be that the next rustling will be on the Box C and along the part of the range that meets with the Bar-B borders. Just a hunch."

Rusty stood as well, finished the coffee and went outside with Spur. "I'll take a ride. I better rent a fresh horse. You have a bill there I can put it on?" Spur said he did and they went their separate ways.

Twenty minutes later, Sheriff Halverson sat back in his chair. "I'm not much good on three hours of sleep any more. When I was younger I'd snap back fast." He handed back to Spur his identification and nodded. "Seemed to me you was more than just a range detective when we talked. Now I understand. So that's why you know about this Fancy Dan, fine-dressing bank robber. You say he's in town?"

"He sure is. Must be staying at the hotel, but I don't know what name he's using. So what we have to do, or you better do it, is to warn Rawlins so half the town doesn't go broke. Have him keep just enough money to do business, and put all the rest of his cash hidden away somewhere outside the bank. Tell him you saw the robber's face on a wanted poster."

"I'd like to take a look at the gent, so I'll know

him and can try to keep tabs on him."

"Eat supper downtown tonight. He eats at the best place in town, I'm sure, which has to be the Silver Spoon. I'll be there to point him out."

"Some fancy-dressed man saved a little girl from a runaway yesterday. I'll find out who he was. People said he had a fifty-dollar suit on, extremely well dressed."

"Could be our man. But you said he saved a little girl from a runaway horse? That doesn't sound in character for our bank robber friend. He's killed six people in his shootouts."

"Sudden impulse maybe. Little girl was the district attorney's. I'll ask him about the gent."

"Now, about the rustling. That's still my main job here. From my guesswork, I'd say they will hit the Box-C next, strike somewhere along the Box-C and the Bar-B common boundary." He told the sheriff his theory about driving the stolen cattle toward the center of the group of ranches.

"Five days from now, you say?"

"Yes. It charts out that way. This is Thursday, the eleventh. Let's plan on doing some field work the night of the sixteenth, which is Tuesday, five nights from last night."

The sheriff nodded, made a note on his pad of paper, and Spur left for the street. He forgot to tell the sheriff about the man in the rented buggy. He headed for the livery. They must have the name of a man who rented a horse and buggy. At least he hoped that they did.

Chapter Fifteen

Spur went directly to the livery stable and rousted out Old Harry, the owner, who really didn't care if he did much business or not. His wife had inherited $50,000 two years ago and they had all the cash they wanted. Old Harry wasn't old, not more than 35, Spur figured, but he had a son called Young Harry, so he had to be the other extreme. He wore only the top of his long handled underwear and a pair of dirty old pants. He spit tobacco juice at a coffee can, missed and swore.

"I'm gonna practice until I get as good as those gents who use a spittoon on their fancy carpet. Never miss in a month they tell me. Dang me but they is good."

"Harry, I have a small problem," Spur said.

Old Harry grinned. "Not the way I heard it,

friend. Hear tell you got no problem at all with that sweet little gal who owns the saloon, Abigail. Hear you bouncing her regular like."

Spur grinned. "Caught me. I figured nobody knew."

"Everybody who ever wanted to hump her himself knows by now, I'd say. She looks like one sweet di-de-do. But you said that ain't your problem."

"True. You rented out a black carriage and a prancing black horse couple of days ago. Almost ran me down when I left yesterday on my gelding. I need to know who the gent was who got that fancified rig."

"On that one I can help you. Signed his name and put down a deposit and all. Don't want some yahoo running off to Clinton or Amarillo or even Butte with my horse and rig. Nosireee. In the office."

They went into the office, which had been closed off on one side with bales of hay. Old Harry looked in a ledger and then in a smaller notebook.

"Yep, here it is. He wrote it, then I had him print it so I could read it. Look for yourself." He pushed the smaller notebook across a grimy desk at Spur.

The name printed was Reginald J. Archibald. It wasn't a name Spur recognized, but he wasn't surprised. Confidence men and bank robbers were usually smart enough to change their names between jobs. Archibald, no, nothing came to mind. At least he had a name to go with the face. He went back and told the sheriff so he'd have a name to watch for.

"What about the bank?" Spur asked.

Sheriff Halverson squirmed. "Damn, I hate doing that little shithead any favors, but I guess I got to. Can't let the town go bust just because I hate that little bastard. We ain't got along for years. He even ran against me for Sheriff last election, three years ago, but I whupped his ass good."

"Leave me out of it, remember."

"I remember."

It wasn't time for even an early supper. Spur spent an hour at the sheriff's office writing out a report to General Halleck in Washington, mentioning the bank robber and saying he was working on both problems at the same time. He sealed the letter in an envelope, enclosed a five dollar bill and sent it by mail to the nearest telegraph office down on the railroad line.

At five-thirty, he and the sheriff went for supper to the Silver Spoon. They went early so they could get the table they wanted. It faced the door about fifteen feet away, and they had a perfect look at everyone who entered.

Their backs were against a wall, and no tables were set in front of them. They started with a beer and made it last. By six o'clock the place was half full but the robber had not come in for supper.

They ordered, and when the food came they took their time eating. By six-thirty the man had not arrived. Spur told the sheriff about the episode with the black buggy and the name the

Fancy Dan had put down on the record.

They had dessert and then coffee. Spur was getting fidgety by seven o'clock, when he looked at the doorway and saw the man come in. He touched the sheriff's arm.

"That him?"

"Yep."

"Same dude who saved that little girl. Fancy dresser, ain't he? You say he's got several notches in his gunstock?"

"Last I heard of. He's a shooter. Loves to blow people through windows, down stairways, that sort of thing. Uses a sawed-off shotgun. The last word I heard on him was that he was trying to branch out into selling fake stocks and bonds, but I've never seen any follow-up wanted on him that mentions it."

"The ritzy clothes would set him up to sell stocks for sure," Sheriff Halverson said. "I'll talk to some folks in town who maybe could afford to buy some such items."

They watched the man walk through the restaurant, turn down the table first offered, and sit with his back to the wall, well to the far side of the eatery. He was alone.

"A cautious man," Spur said.

"Must have a lot to be cautious about. Well, I guess I have his face in my memory now. It won't go away for some time."

Outside they left each other and Spur went down the street two doors to the newspaper office. The bell tinkled as he entered, and Opal's face came up from behind the counter.

"Oh, Mr. McCoy. Your cards aren't ready yet.

237

We haven't got the small press going. Leroy is working on it."

"You're here late."

"Not much else to do in this town but eat and work." She looked up and blushed. "I mean, you know, not much theater, or musicals, or even a good library."

"Why don't you help start a library?"

She nodded. A wisp of long blonde hair strayed over her left eye and she blew at it, then moved it back with her hand. Smudges of ink showed on her fingers.

"How's the first edition coming along?"

"Fine, but no press. We got that push bar put in you showed me, but now something else is wrong. I don't think that press has been used for at least a year. That salesman who sold us the paper lied to us."

"Been known to happen."

Opal motioned him around the counter, and when he came back she moved up close to him. She caught his shirt and reached up and kissed him. He had no reaction.

"I still owe you, Spur McCoy. At least twice to make up for . . . for what you saved me from on the stage."

He kissed her cheek and stepped back. "Forget about owing anyone anything."

"But am I so ugly you don't want to make love to me?"

"No, we covered that before. You're delicious, remarkable. You have an appealingly sexy body. But. . . ." He held up his hands as she reached for him. "There's more to making love than just the

physical part. Two people have to be involved
with each other, know and respect one another
emotionally and intellectually, and then want to
make love. Without that kind of understanding,
sex is like two dogs mating on the lawn outside
your window."

Opal nodded. "Yes, you're probably right. But
the other day you did get . . . excited, hard,
didn't you?"

"Yes, an automatic physical response in men.
There's a lot more to it than that."

"Do you like my breasts?"

"A woman's breasts are one of her most beautiful features."

She caught one of his hands and lifted it and
put it under her soft white blouse and closed it
around one of her bare breasts.

"Does that feel good, Spur?"

"For me, yes. How does it feel for you? Does
it make any difference to you? Does your heart
beat faster or your breathing speed up? I don't
see any reaction. Not even a physical one."

She put her hand on his crotch and found
the hard lump that grew by the second behind
his fly.

"But you're reacting."

"Easier for a man. He usually has to be
the aggressor, as in the animal kingdom, to
perpetuate the species."

She smiled. "Spur McCoy, I want you to be
aggressive with me." She caught his hand and
pushed it down and lifted her skirts and slid his
hand up to her crotch.

He bent and kissed her cheek. "Sweet Opal.

You're not ready to make love. None of this has moved you. None of it has excited you. I've known some young girls who would be stripped and have climaxed three times already doing what you've done." Gently he pulled his hands away from her.

"It's nothing about your physical appearance or your wanting to. It's just some emotional corner that you need to turn yet. You have plenty of time. A complete sexual experience right now probably would do you much more harm than good. Believe me."

He went to the other side of the counter and held her hand.

"Believe me, Opal, there'll come a time. It just isn't here for you yet. For some it comes early, for some about now, and for others, both men and women, much later. Be patient. Your time will come."

She tried to smile, but it didn't work. He leaned in and kissed her cheek. "Now, you do your job here and enjoy life and be ready for the emotional aspects of love whenever the chance comes."

She lifted her brows, took a deep breath. "Spur, do you remember back at the stagecoach robbery when I told that awful man that I wasn't afraid of him and that I wasn't a quaking virgin?"

"Yes, I remember, and I thought it remarkably brave of you. Now, I have to be moving. I'll check back later in the week and see about the cards. No, on the other hand, you have enough other problems, let's just forget about the cards. That will be one less thing you'll have to worry about. Now, I need to go. Great talking to you again. I'll be back, don't worry. Maybe next time I can work a while and help you get things moving. Oh, I can case type if you still have some pied."

"You can?"

"Learned the type case when I was a kid. Kind of thing you never forget." He turned and waved, then walked out the front door.

Spur checked his pocket watch. Slightly after seven-forty-five. Rusty said he would contact him in his room or at the First Class Saloon when he got back. It might not be for several hours.

A short time later, Spur stood at the end of the bar and ordered a draft beer. It was cold and good.

Somebody bumped him on the side and he looked around cautiously, not in the mood for a barroom brawl. Abby chuckled at his slow response.

"No, I'm not a saloon bully with an axe about ready to chop you into small particles of human flesh and feed it to the fish down in the creek."

"It is an idea, though," Spur said. He took his beer and they went back to the "owner's" table, where no one but Abby ever sat unless she was there.

He told her about finding the name of the bank robber and pointing him out to the sheriff. "He's using the name of Reginald J. Archibald. At least some of the time. He probably has half a dozen names he uses."

"At least we got rid of one troublemaker, that Guthrie guy who killed a poker player in here. I told you about it. I haven't seen him around."

"That the same one you showed me the other day? Don't get your hopes up. If I'm right, he's a brother to the bank robber. They used to work as a team, three of them. They'd sweep into a town, rob the bank and be away before anyone knew what happened. What I can't figure out is why they seem to be settled in for a longer stay here. Are the two of them going to take down Rawlins' bank? Are they taking their time to get it set up properly?"

"You said three brothers. Where's the third one?"

Spur shook his head. "He might be dead by now. Or he might be here in town waiting. My bet is that this card-playing Guthrie and his wife didn't go far and that we'll see them again here in town on the business end of a twin-barreled shotgun spewing out double-aught buck."

"McCoy, you're a bundle of laughs today." She lowered her voice. "Are you going to be this much fun in bed tonight?"

Spur grinned. "Hell, a lot more fun than it's been today, I hope. Just have to wait and see. I might even have a bad headache, and my sore back will just render me helpless and unable."

Abby laughed. "That will be the day. I'm waiting to see that one."

"Why don't we wander over to that little house of yours and lock the doors and pull down the blinds and see what develops?"

"Fine idea, cowboy. Would you mind if we ran

instead of wandered? I've got a sudden need that just won't be put off."

Outside the saloon and in the darkness of the streets, they ran. Both were out of breath when they came up to the front door of Abby's house.

"You own this?" Spur asked.

"Yep, and three other houses that I rent out. That little saloon is making me a bundle of money. I'd have enough to keep you in style if you ever want to quit playing lawman and settle down to be an honest saloon man."

They went inside and she locked the door. Spur went through the dark house pulling down blinds as he went and met Abby in the bedroom, where he'd been before. She lit two lamps so they could see exactly what they were doing.

She had already unbuttoned the front of her dress and now tugged at it.

"Whoa there, woman. A man likes to have a little to do with all of this unwrapping of a precious present."

Abby grinned. "Precious present. Damn, but I bet you've used that one a thousand times." She smiled. "It still works. Yes, a precious present and I'm giving it away. What's that old one about the cow? Why should your neighbor buy your cow if you're giving away the milk to him."

Spur snorted. "I never have liked that. Too much of a play on words. Anyway, you haven't come fresh yet."

Abby pouted. "If you do me right, I could come fresh in about eight months, then you could have some breast milk, if you would share."

He caught her around the waist and pulled her to him. She clung to him, her hungry lips found his and then she tipped them over so they fell on the bed. One bed-board bounced out of place and hit the floor, but the other three held the mattress and springs in place. They both laughed.

The first time was fast and furious. They ripped clothes off each other and threw them around the room. They came together, panting and scratching, and they both climaxed almost at the same time, crashing the springs against the bed-boards and making a terrible racket.

A half hour later they slowed down the lovemaking. They experimented a little and listened to the needs and wants of the other person.

Abby broke off a long passionate kiss and pushed away from him and got on her hands and knees. "This way, Spur. Do me this way. We haven't tried it yet." Spur went behind her, knelt between her legs and adjusted himself lower, then found the slot and eased into her. He reached around her back, caught one breast in each hand and balanced himself.

"Oh, lordy, but that feels fine," Abby said, looking over her shoulder at him. "It's so different that way, the angle, the depth, something. Just marvelous."

Spur fondled her breasts and felt her motor get going again. He stroked gently until the angle affected him, then he drove in hard and rocked back and forth, almost knocking her flat on the bed. She went down on her forearms and lay her head on the pillow as he stroked faster and faster.

She keened high and long and loud as the movement touched her off, then she spasmed and shook as he came to his own climax. Together they rocked the bed again until the spasms all passed. Then she slid down to the bed with him still in place. It was five minutes later before either one moved.

"What was that?" Spur asked.

"I didn't hear anything."

Spur listened again. "Somebody kicked something at the back door." He jumped from the bed, pulled on his pants and his boots and a shirt, and strapped on his six-gun.

"Get dressed, fast. Somebody is out there and I don't like it." He sniffed. "Smoke! your house is on fire. Front door. Now somebody is at the back door."

She dressed quickly and they ran toward the back through the kitchen. Before they got there, smoke poured in under the kitchen door from the porch. They turned and ran through the parlor to the front door but the glass in the window had broken out and flames licked the inside of the door all the way to the ceiling.

Spur could smell the kerosene. "Which bedroom is farthest from both doors?" he asked.

"The one across from mine. This way." She led him through the smoke that now blew into all of the rooms. Spur lifted the bedroom window and looked out. He saw no one. He vaulted through the window, drew his gun and looked around. Then he helped Abby through.

They both crept around the burning house, staying back in the shadows away from the firelight. On the far side, Spur spotted a man near a tree in the yard. He held a six-gun. Spur threw a rock at the nearest window. It broke, and the man by the tree fired five rounds through the broken window.

Spur pulled the trigger on his .45 once. The man near the tree screamed and went down, slammed backwards by the force of the heavy slug. Spur surged up to him and kicked the gun out of the arsonist's hand, then dragged the man forward so he could tell for sure who he was.

"Rawlins, you slimy bastard." Spur punched him in the jaw. Abby ran up and kicked him twice in the stomach. "You burned down my house. Nothing can save it now. I'm filing charges against you, you maniac."

"I'm shot," Rawlins howled. "You've got to stop the bleeding. You shot me."

"Lucky I didn't aim for your heart," Spur said. "You got a slug through your shoulder. It won't kill you. But I might before I get you to the jail."

By that time two dozen people had gathered around the street side of the house. It was too late to save anything. It was all gone, clothes, furniture, everything.

Abby dropped to her knees and cried. One of the town women came up and comforted her.

Spur grabbed Rawlins and twisted his good arm behind his back and marched him toward the sheriff's office.

"Hey, I'm shot, I'm still bleeding," Rawlins wailed.

"Good, maybe you'll bleed to death before we find the sheriff and save the county the cost of a trial and a hanging."

"Trial, what for?" Rawlins bleated.

"What for? Arson for one, attempted murder of two persons, shooting into a residence with intent to do murder. Rawlins, you better have a good lawyer, you're going to need one."

They met one of the deputies on the way down Main Street. He led the way, sent for the doctor to wrap up the arm, then put the town's richest man in the first jail cell.

Sheriff Halverson came out of his office and stared at the bleeding banker. He looked at Spur.

"Charges?"

"Arson. He burned down Abigail's house with her in it. Kerosene at the front and back doors, then he fired a six-gun through a window. I'd say arson, attempted murder, shooting into a residence with intent to do murder. That should hold him for a while."

"Any witnesses?"

"Half the town must still be up there. Sure, we can find half a dozen witnesses. Somebody must have seen him torch the front and back doors."

"He'll want bail. Judge is in town through tomorrow. He'll be on the street by ten o'clock."

Spur snorted. "Maybe a slug in the shoulder and a night in jail will beat some sense into his skull."

The sheriff shook his head. "Don't count on it.

I haven't told him about the threat to his bank yet. Now might be a good time, while he's feeling bad already."

Spur hurried back to the fire. It was burning itself out. Half of the walls had fallen into the flames. A few blackened timbers stabbed into the dark sky. He could see the mattress on the bed they had used so short a time before. It was still burning brightly.

He found Abby and put his arms around her.

"I had a lot of keepsakes in that house. Things I'll never be able to replace. Gone, all gone."

"You can stay in my room tonight," Spur said. "Then tomorrow we'll go house hunting. Must be something for sale in town. All three of your other houses rented?"

"At least I have a little luck. The first house I bought here in town is empty. It's furnished. I can move in there tomorrow."

"Then you get to start buying a whole new wardrobe. Now that will be fun."

She nodded. "He's in jail?"

"Yes. Lots of charges."

"I want to sue him for my house. Ten thousand for the house and furnishings and family heirlooms and irreplaceable treasures. Then I want punitive damages of another thirty thousand. I want that old bastard to pay for what he did to me."

"He will. Believe me, he'll pay. I'll see to that. It was me he was after. I'm sorry to cause you this trouble."

"Trouble is what I'm going to cause Rawlins from now on. He'll never hear the last of this,

not for two or three years. He's going to pay and
pay and pay."

She looked at the smoldering, flaring up ruin
of her house.

"Let's go, I can't stand watching it any more.
I want to be inside somewhere and feel safe and
know that nothing else is going to threaten me
tonight."

"My job," Spur said. He put his arm around
her and led her down the dark streets toward
the hotel and his room on the second floor.

Chapter Sixteen

Friday morning, the 12th of June, Jefferson R. Guthrie, going by the name of Reginald Archibald, slipped into the rear door of the Openlander's house. It was just after nine o'clock. He had seen the District Attorney leave for work a half hour before, and by now the lady of the house must be impatient.

Two mornings in a row he had entertained the neglected wife. Today she met him in the small woodshed and had her blouse open. His hands found her breasts and she moaned.

"The little princess, Julie, is safely tucked away?" he asked.

She nodded. "I gave her a sleeping powder. She won't be awake for three hours." Victoria threw her head back and moaned. "That just sets me on fire, your glorious hands on my . . .

tits." She looked at him quickly. "Alonzo doesn't like me to say dirty words. Sometimes I love to." She trembled. "He never lets me do anything unusual. He won't even let me take him in my mouth." She let go of him and slid down his frame, kissed the bulge at his crotch and opened his fly. She worked until she got his underwear pulled down and let his erection swing out.

"Oh . . . oh, my, so glorious. So hot and throbbing, so . . . so marvelous." She kissed the purple head, then looked up. He nodded. She licked the head, then down the shaft. She kissed the very tip, then let her lips part slowly. He thrust forward gently, and his erection slipped easily into her waiting mouth.

She made a small cry of joy and gulped more of him into her mouth. Then she turned and looked up. He nodded again.

"You can do anything you want to, pretty fucking lady," he said, his voice soft, gentle.

She began to bob up and down, and he thrust with short, cautious strokes into her wet, warm chamber.

He humped faster and she moaned. He cried out and his hips hit so hard she had to hold him with her hand so he wouldn't choke her. J.R. felt the whole world explode. He cried out and then knew he was melting into the furnace of the sun. His hips pounded again and again and she swallowed quickly until he quieted.

She came away from him, stood and leaned hard against him. His arms went around and held her as if she were a just-picked flower.

"I'll give you ten minutes, Reginald Archibald, then it'll be my turn."

They sat on the woodshed floor talking quietly. Twice before they had discussed the railroad stocks. Good as gold, he had told her, and ones that would be easy to sell when she wanted to. Their price was going up in value on the stock exchange every week. The stock issue was to open a new feeder line the railroad Central Pacific owned, which would stretch their monopoly over another three states.

"It's called the Central Pacific Railroad stock issue. My customers have been pleased with the semi-annual dividends. I brought some of the certificates with me."

She looked at them, nodded. "I have some stock in an electric company in Chicago. They say it will be worth a fortune some day. We'll have these newfangled electric lights in every town and village and house even."

He kissed her and stroked her breasts through the soft blouse.

"Yes, Reginald. I know the railroad is a good investment. We won't tell Alonzo about this. I'll take a thousand dollars worth. I have the money in my bedroom. Could you risk going in there with me? I'll get the money for you and you sign over the stock, then we'll take another turn on the bed. As I remember, it's going to be my turn this time."

Two hours later, J.R. Guthrie left the Openlander house through the rear door and alley and hurried back to the hotel. His sale to the unfulfilled housewife had netted him a thousand dollars in good greenbacks. He wouldn't see her again. That part of the work here was done.

Now he had to do some thinking about the raid on the bank. First he needed his eight men. He would find all eight today. The saloons were the best place to look. He changed clothes in the hotel, putting on the most common, everyday pants and shirt that he had.

He checked his best suit where it hung in the closet. It had come from the Chinese laundry looking as good as new. They tried to charge him fifty cents for the job, but he surprised them and gave them a dollar. They bowed him out of the store.

He knew there would be a need for the suit later. He'd made his score today, a thousand dollars. The stock certificates had cost him five dollars each in Philadelphia. Not a bad profit. He had written in a total of 14 shares on the stock certificate, and then signed where it showed a name for the treasurer.

In the first saloon he came to, he found an unusually rough crowd. Just the kind of men he wanted. There were only two poker tables, and eight whores standing and sitting in the back of the room looking for some afternoon work.

A half drunk man at the bar moved backward suddenly and crashed into a smaller man. The bumped one's beer sloshed over his hand and he snarled at the other man.

"What the hell you doing?" he bellowed.

The larger man turned around, and his fist smashed into the small man. He didn't say a word, just attacked, knocked the man down, and when he hit the floor, he kicked the downed man.

"Keep your damn nose out of my sight!" the attacker said. He glared at the smaller man on the floor, drew back his foot, but the downed man rolled away, scrambled to his feet, and scampered out the door, forgetting his town hat, which lay on the bar. The larger man snorted and returned to his beer.

J.R. Guthrie grinned, went to the bar and spoke to the barkeep a moment, then returned to his table. The barkeep took a fresh mug of draft beer to the big man and talked a minute. In answer to a question, the barkeep pointed to Guthrie's table.

The man was over six feet tall and broad. He was clean-shaven and dressed reasonably well. He looked at Guthrie a moment, then picked up the fresh beer and walked over and sat down at the table.

"Names aren't important right now," Guthrie said, watching the man's reactions. "What I want to know is if you want to earn fifty dollars for a ten-minute job."

"Hell yes," the big man said. He hoisted the beer and drained half the mug before he put it down. "Just so I don't have to kill nobody. Not that I mind, but them damn lawmen won't give up sometimes. I'm not happy about being on the run all the damn time."

"Nobody gets killed. All you have to do is rob a store. The deal is that you rob it exactly to the minute on the day I want you to. Understood?"

"Hell yes, I'm no dummy. When?"

"Tomorrow, Saturday. This is Friday. We do it tomorrow. Yes, this little bank stays open on Saturday. I checked. Now, are you going to be in town tomorrow?"

"To make fifty dollars, I'll plan on staying."

"You get to keep the fifty, and whatever you get out of the cash box and off the store owner. Oh, when you leave the store, I want you to put at least two shots into the ceiling. Have your horse right outside so you can ride like hell to the south and out of town. Go south."

The big man grinned. "Sounds like my kind of job."

Two hours later, J.R. Guthrie found a second robber to add to his list. He wrote down their descriptions and first names. Told each one that he'd meet him in the pasture behind the livery the next day at two o'clock, pay them and give them final instructions. They should come with their horses, packed up and ready to travel, and a working six-gun. If they took his money and didn't rob the store on schedule, he'd track them down and shoot them dead.

He found six more before the night was over. All were violent types who would fight at the hint of an insult. Just the men he needed for the job.

In his hotel room, he checked the bulk of the nine thousand dollars worth of one-hundred dollar bills he had slipped into the lining of his traveling case. All was in order. He put in $600 of the $1,000 he'd taken from Victoria. He grinned, thinking about her reaction when she found out the Central Pacific Stock certificates were forgeries and of absolutely no value whatsoever. Then she'd know she'd been swindled. She might not even tell her husband. She'd paid $1,000 for some wild lovemaking. She just might decide it was worth it.

J.R. Guthrie felt fine. He had worked another confidence game successfully. There was a thrill in fooling people the way he did. It was for more than the money. That's why he was switching from banks to bonds. Safer in the long run. This would be his last family affair bank robbery. He wasn't sure how he would tell his brothers. He'd contact them both that night in the hotel and set up the time of the bank robbery. Each would buy his own shotgun and get them sawed off the next morning.

With the medicine wagon it had been easy. Now they'd have to buy their own hacksaw. He caught Folke and Dianna in their room about midnight. They were in bed, and Dianna wore nothing under the sheet, he was sure.

"Yeah, E.B. slept here last night on the floor. He didn't have no place to stay after his wagon burned. He's down at a saloon getting drunk."

"We do the bank tomorrow at three o'clock. We each need to buy at least one shotgun. I'll get a hacksaw at the hardware and we'll saw the barrels off here in your room. No big story, you just need a shotgun and a box of double aught buck rounds. Got it straight?"

"Easy as filling in a straight flush," Folke said. "Now let me go find E.B. before he gets soused."

"Keep him here tonight, and keep him sober."

Wilderness Wanton

That same Friday morning, Circuit Court Judge Quinlin J. Sturdivent listened to the presentation of evidence in the case of the attempted murder and arson against Stewart Rawlins, bound him over to trial, and set his bail at $5,000 cash.

Rawlins posted the bail with the court and was released. His trial was set in two months, when the judge would return on his rounds.

Just before noon, Penley Northcliff hailed Spur as he came into the hotel.

"We need to talk, old boy. Some things have come up and we need to discuss them. Are you free?"

Spur allowed he was and they went to the Silver Spoon for lunch and conversation. After they ordered, Northcliff got right to it.

"I've been waiting for the results of your investigation, Mr. McCoy, and so far I've found little, if any, progress. I'm thinking of discharging you, paying your expenses and writing off the whole idea of a special detective as a bad business arrangement."

"I'm making progress. I've determined that the rustlers strike at five-day intervals. The next rustling should come on Saturday night. Now all I have to do is figure out where it will be."

"You're sure of this?"

"Right. I've charted the attacks by the rustlers in the past, and they work out dramatically evenly spaced, every five days. That much I'm certain. You should be especially alert on Saturday night, in case they hit your ranch."

"Yes, yes, I'll take note of that. But I'm

afraid that isn't quite enough to justify your expenses."

"A hundred head of steer is worth four thousand dollars. How many have you lost so far?"

"I'd say five hundred, at least."

"If I get them back for you, that's a recovery of twenty thousand dollars. Won't that be worthwhile?"

"Yes, of course."

"I have a question. So far as I've been able to establish, none of the rustled cattle have been driven out of this general area and sold. What I can't figure out is, what are the rustlers doing with the cattle? They must be held somewhere. Three thousand head would take a rather large valley or a range to keep them on where they have graze and water. Where are all of those cattle?"

Northcliff looked puzzled for a moment. "I say, are you sure about this? If that's true, I simply have no idea where in this range such a large herd of cattle could be secreted away. You and Rusty checked the breaks and found nothing?"

"That's another job I have. If I find the cattle, finding the men who stole them will be simple."

Northcliff ate his meal and finished with coffee. At last he nodded. "All right, I'll give you another week. If you don't turn up something by then, we'll close down your search."

"A week, that should be plenty of time." He stood. "I need to check in with the sheriff. We'll talk again."

Wilderness Wanton

Spur walked out of the restaurant feeling vaguely ill-at-ease. Something didn't play just right with the Englishman, but he wasn't quite sure what. He wasn't going to see the sheriff, he wanted to see Rusty, who had gone out to look over the Box C range yesterday about noon. Evidently he wasn't back yet.

Spur went to his box in the hotel and saw two messages. Both were from Rusty. He was in his room. A few minutes later, Spur knocked on room 208.

"Yeah, who?" Rusty asked from inside.

"McCoy."

The door opened and Spur slid inside. Rusty closed and locked it. When Rusty turned around, Spur was surprised.

"You look dead tired," Spur said.

Rusty dropped on the bed, his head sagging wearily. "That's about the size of it. Got out there along about five o'clock, yesterday, still daylight. First thing I know I got two dimwits shooting rifles at me. I got hid in a little draw in some brush and figured I'd lost them.

"I came riding out at dusk and they was two hundred yards away and raked me with ten shots. I bailed off the animal and she went down dead in her tracks. Then I got back in the draw and hid out until they stopped looking for me. Why the hell they welcome a stranger with a volley of rifle fire out there?"

"Only reason I can think of is that they're hiding something. Maybe we should find out what."

"I'm not wild about going back to the Box C."

259

"Don't blame you. Had any supper?"

"Nope. Trying to get up enough energy to go downstairs. I bet it's been twenty years since I walked that far. I must have been ten miles out of town. Took me two hours of dark to be sure they had stopped looking for me. I built a little campfire and moved back a hundred yards, but nobody came. Then I figured I could get moving toward town."

Spur told him about the chat with Northcliff.

"You said something didn't seem quite right. Was the Englisher nervous, you think?"

"Maybe. Before he was so self-confident. Like he was a prince and we were all his subjects. Like he ruled by divine right."

"Might have been it."

"What do you want for supper? I'll go down to the dining room and bring it up. Room service is my specialty."

"A big steak dinner and some of that new ice cream and a beer."

Half an hour later, Spur brought up his dinner, along with the beer and a bottle of Scotch whiskey.

"Medicine," Spur said. He uncorked it and poured out a third of a glass. Rusty looked at it, took it straight, and in three big gulps it was gone.

"I've got to get you back on your feet. You can sleep the rest of the afternoon until midnight. Then at two A.M. we ride out to the Bar-B and see if we can find any freshly branded animals. You're better reading new brands than I am."

Rusty groaned, then nodded. "Yeah, by then

I'll be ready. I want some new socks, anything still open."

Spur went down to the general store and bought three pairs of heavy cotton socks and a heavier pair of wool footwear. When Spur got back to Rusty's room, the steak and most of the food was gone. Rusty snored softly on the bed.

Rusty and Spur left the livery shortly after one A.M. Saturday morning. Spur bought a horse for Rusty, but got the right to change it after he had a chance to see it in daylight.

They rode north, and Rusty was refreshed and eager. "I got to thinking the only thing them range guards was doing was protecting a batch of fresh brands. Why else they shoot first? That would make Cuthright the big gun in the rustling. The other night we lost those Tabler cattle up in the middle of the Bar-B. They could still have been moved on across the line another ten miles into the Box C range for safekeeping, and for rebranding."

"Starting to make sense," Spur said. "The idea of rustling not for short gain, but for long-range herd development and more steers to sell next spring is starting to make more sense. Takes somebody with a long view of things, a lot of money and a willingness to take a big gamble to pull off something like this."

"Almost any rancher has to be a gambler," Rusty said. "They gamble that the winter won't kill their herd. Gamble that there will be enough grass to fatten the steers for market. Gamble that they can get the market-ready steers driven to the rail pens."

They rode then without talking. Rusty knew the land. They kept off the track into the ranch buildings, angling to the west of them and straight into the best range. Each of the riders carried a kerosene lantern tied to his saddle. Once they came on a good-sized bunch of stock, they would ground-tie their horses and wander among the cattle, checking on fresh brands.

They came on the first bunch when the big dipper was high in the sky, with the pointer stars aimed at the north star. The sky clock told Spur it was about two A.M.

"Let's have a look," Spur said. They left their horses and moved up to the beef. Some of them had lain down, others stood munching on their cuds. Some grazed. They checked the hip brands.

It was five minutes before Spur called softly to Rusty. The old cowhand moved over and looked at the brand in the light of both lanterns.

"Yep, that brand used to be a Bar-L," Rusty said. "See how the bar is a well-healed scar. The top circle and the middle one of the B are both fresh, still scabbed over. It's not a very good job. This steer was rustled from the Bar-L range."

"So Northcliff is the rustler?" Spur asked. "Why would he go to the trouble of hiring me to find the rustlers, if he's the culprit himself?"

"He might not be. That one steer don't prove much. It could have been on the Box C land, got rebranded over there and wandered over here.

You know how cattle mix up on these ranches with adjoining graze."

"Let's keep looking."

In the next hour they found ten more fresh brands. Half of those were blanked out, the old brand blotted out with a flat, solid branding iron. Then a new brand, the Bar-B, had been added in a different spot.

They had found altered brands from three of the ranches, and blanked-out ones that could have been from the other three. The Box C and the S-T were impossible to re-brand into a Bar-B brand.

The two had walked back to their horses and were ready to blow out the lanterns when a rifle shot jolted into the stillness of the night and a round whispered a foot over their heads. They blew out the lanterns, pulled rifles out of their saddles and dove to the side in opposite directions, then rolled another ten feet. Two more rounds came from the north. Then all was quiet.

They jacked rounds into the rifles and waited.

"Don't fire unless we have a target," Spur said. He lay 20 feet away. Just then the rifle fired again and they saw the flash before the sound. Both fired three times into the pinpoint of light from the muzzle blast of the rifle. After their own shots, both rolled away from each other again. This time there was no answering fire.

"Want to go take a look?" Rusty asked.

"Not unless I want to be buzzard bait for breakfast. Let's get mounted and see if we can

get away from here without losing any blood."
Spur looked at his friend. "You hit?"

"Nope, not me. I'm in favor of retreating and
calling it a big victory. We know that too
damn many of the rustled beef have shown
up on the Bar-B range to be just happen-
stance. What the hell are we supposed to do
now?"

"First we get the hell out of here."

They rode at a gallop for a quarter of a mile,
risking gopher holes as they flew over the range.
Then they slowed to a walk and stopped. They
could hear no pursuit. They walked the animals
back into town.

There had been little talk on the way. What
they decided was that they needed more proof.
Catching the rustlers in the act would be the
best way to settle it.

"You said the next rustling could be on Tuesday night," Rusty said.

"Yep, and if the pattern holds, it should happen out at the Box C spread."

"Let's plan on getting out there after dark,"
Rusty said. "I don't want to play target for their
rifles again."

It was nearly five-thirty Saturday morning,
and the first traces of light came over the eastern
horizon as they unsaddled their mounts. It was
a long block and a half to the hotel.

Spur was so tired he could hardly walk. "We're
going to have to quit this night work," Spur said.
Rusty waved and walked up the steps to his
hotel room.

Spur figured that Abby wouldn't be in his

hotel room. He pushed open the door gently, saw the room was empty and slipped in, locked his door and dropped on the bed without even taking off his boots. He went to sleep at once.

Chapter Seventeen

It was a little after nine A.M. Saturday when
Spur felt as much as heard someone pounding
on his hotel room door.

"Open up, McCoy. Come on, wake up. We got
work to do."

Spur managed to sit up and rub some sleep
out of his eyes. He felt washed out, groggy, and
still too tired to move.

"Who the hell is it?" Spur bellowed.

"Sheriff Halverson."

Spur heard the words faintly through the door,
but they were enough to get him erect and moving. He unlocked the panel and swung it open,
then went back to the bed and slumped on it.

The sheriff came in and closed the door. "You
look halfway to dead, McCoy. Out all night with
our wild women again?"

"True, but the females were bovine and we found too damn many fresh brands on steers and cows. I'm starting to get a better idea about this rustling situation."

"You'll have to put that on hold. I talked with your banker friend this morning. Told him about the bank robbery gang in town. He hid most of his cash money in a special spot nobody knows about but him. He also bought three shotguns and sawed off the barrels. He now has five in the bank all loaded and ready to kill people with.

"When he bought the shotguns, Jim over at the General store said there sure had been a run on shotguns. Must be a good crop of pheasants this year. Said he sold three more early that morning."

"Damn. Sounds like Fancy Dan is getting set up again," Spur said. "He always buys shotguns at each town. What are you going to do?"

"Do? Guess. When does Fancy Dan usually hit a bank?"

"In the afternoon. Then he has fewer hours until dark so he can get away from a posse."

"What I want to do is hide three of us in the bank with our own shotguns," Sheriff Halverson said. "When Fancy Dan comes into the bank we'll tell him we have four double aught buck rounds aimed at him and he better lay down his weapons and surrender."

"He won't do that. He'll start shooting."

"He'll be in the open and we'll be behind desks and them wooden file cases."

"A lot of folks going to get killed that way," Spur said. "Why not take him on the street?"

"I got no wanted on him. So I need to catch him in the act. Then if he won't surrender, we can gun him down and be rid of him."

"You're a tough man, Sheriff."

"Don't want some outlaw messing up my town."

Spur's eyes closed and he struggled to get them open. He put one hand down on the bed to steady himself. "When you going to the bank?"

"By noon. We don't want to get there too late."

"Come by at eleven-thirty. I need some more sleep."

Halverson stood and chuckled. "You are about ready to dissolve, aren't you? I know the feeling. I'm planning on taking my best deputy. Only have three. One's on night duty. I'll see you here at eleven-thirty. You want a shotgun?"

Spur shook his head and pointed to his Colt hanging on the bedpost. The sheriff nodded and watched Spur tumble sideways on the bed. The local lawman closed the door softly as he left.

"Come on, E.B.," Jefferson Guthrie said with a touch of disdain in his voice. "You have to push down on a hacksaw to make it cut through that steel barrel. You want me to do it?"

"I can. I had a tough night." He went back to sawing on a shotgun. He was about halfway through. Two other shotguns lay on the bed. Both had been shortened. A box of shells lay nearby.

"I told that towner in the general store I was

going pheasant hunting," J.R. said. "I needed two guns so I could get off four shots. That's why I bought the birdshot shells. Would look damn queer if I said I was hunting pheasants and got double aught buck. Wouldn't be nothing left of the damn bird but tail feathers."

"We got the stuff, now let me tie the cords so they'll hang just right from around your neck. J.R., you like yours higher than I do." It was Folke talking. He was the usual moderator when the three of them got together. "I'll tie the cord on the stock, then you can adjust it the way you want it."

"When we taking down that bank?" E.B. asked between strokes of the hacksaw.

"The bank is open until five on Saturday to accommodate the merchants and the customers," J.R. said. "I checked just this morning. I'm meeting with my eight little helpers and sending them into the stores at exactly three o'clock. There's a big clock standing outside the jewelry store and it chimes on the hour. Won't be no problem knowing when to move in."

"We hit the bank at the same time?" E.B. asked.

"No. We wait until the robbers come out of the stores firing shots, alerting the sheriff and sending him down toward the south end of town. As soon as we see the gunmen run out of their stores, we'll go into the bank. Might be five minutes after three or so."

"Sounds good to me," Folke said. He loaded both barrels of one of the guns, tied the heavy cord so the weapon hung right at his waist and let go of it. It swung to point barrel-down and he nodded.

"What the hell else we do between now and then?" E.B. asked.

"We pack up and get ready to ride. We all need to buy horses."

"We've got horses already," Dianna said. She'd been sitting in a chair by the window. "I still think it's a bad idea to do this bank. We've been in town too long. Somebody might figure out who we are."

"Little chance," J.R. said. He grinned at Dianna and ran the tip of his tongue around his lips. His brothers couldn't see him. Dianna smiled and looked away.

"Yeah, we'll be fine," Folke said. "We haven't robbed a Montana bank. They probably don't even have a wanted poster on us way up here in the sagebrush."

"Up to you," Dianna said. "I'll have my horse half a block north of the bank waiting for you. You'll rein up right at the bank?"

"No, second store north," J.R. said. "There's a saddlemaker there and he has a hitching rail in front of his place. It's a natural place for saddle horses."

Dianna stood. "I'm packed. Bedroll, small carpetbag tied on behind my saddle and a sack of food. Oh, I forgot coffee. I'll go and get some and have them grind it." She went to the door and started out.

J.R. looked up. "The store? I have a couple of things on a list. Could you get them, too?"

She nodded and stepped into the hall.

"Wait just a minute. Not that big a rush. We've got four hours yet." J.R. went to the door and into the hall. Dianna's eyes glowed as she turned to face him. No one was in the hall. Her hand pressed against his crotch, and she reached up and kissed him. His hand fondled her breast.

"Oh, god, J.R.! You promised me you'd do Folke in the bank. You still gonna do it?"

"If it works out. If not then, on the trail. He'll never know what happened."

"God, I can't wait to be with you all the time."

As Folke stepped back his voice came up to normal. "Yes, here's the cash. Remember, don't be nervous." He returned to the room shaking his head. "Women. Never saw what you liked about Dianna."

"She's good to me," Folke said. "In a couple of days she won't be bothering you any, 'cause we'll be gone. We're heading back to Denver. Enough gambling games there that I can move around and not get a bad name."

"How much we gonna take out of that bank?" E.B. asked. "Maybe ten thousand?"

"Doubt that much. Why don't you two go buy horses? We don't want no horse thievery hung on us."

"About time, I guess," Folke said. "You mind the weapons."

"I think I can handle that. My next job is to talk to my eight robbers at two o'clock."

The two brothers left, and a minute later the door burst open and Dianna rushed in. She slammed the door and locked it, then jumped into J.R.'s arms.

"Dianna."

"I didn't think they would ever leave. Come on."

"Right now?"

Dianna fell on the bed, ripped open her bodice and pulled up her skirt. She wore no undergarments.

"I like to be ready," she said.

J.R. laughed softly as he knelt between her pure white thighs.

At the livery barn, E.B. took his time looking over the horses for sale. Folke knew horses better and picked out a roan mare with a strong chest and enough size to carry E.B. well. They saddled her, and E.B. rode her around the pasture for fifteen minutes. When he came back he grinned and said he wanted her.

They paid forty dollars for the horse and another fifteen for saddle and halter and bridle. Then Folke settled up with the stable for his rental horses and bought two more, plus saddles. He got them all for a hundred dollars. The livery man, Old Harry, didn't seem much concerned. He didn't cotton to this pair of strangers and would rather not sell them horses. He decided he didn't want any trouble. Both these men had a hard edge about them which he didn't want to test.

"Thought Dianna said she was all packed," E.B. said as they rode two and led one horse back to the hotel's rear hitching rail.

Folke laughed. "She's a woman, E.B. She gets moody and sometimes lies a lot, like this morning. Hell, she won't be packed up until I do it for her. She's trouble, but she's worth it. She's a fireball in bed, I'll tell you that."

"Better than that whore we both had last night?"

Folke nodded. "Oh, a hell of a lot better than that worn out old whore. You promised me you wouldn't say nothing about that."

E.B. took a long look at his brother. "Don't never hurt to have something dirty I know about you, brother."

"Truth be known, E.B., us three don't get on too good, do we?"

"Not by a hind sight. Now, we best get packed and ready to ride. We gonna save room for all them greenbacks and gold double eagles."

At slightly before two P.M., J.R. Guthrie met with his eight robbers halfway down the fence at the livery. There wasn't a house in sight due to a slight rise on that side of town. J.R. stared at the motley collection of desperadoes. Any one of them would kill him for the fifty dollars he was handing out. As he rode up to them they all mounted and came in a half circle around him.

"Gentlemen, you know why we're here. Do you all know where the big clock is on the front of the jewelry store?" All but one man raised his hand or nodded.

"It's three doors south of the bank. Right next to the saddle shop."

"Oh, yeah, that one," the last man said.

"When that clock strikes three, in about fifty-five minutes, I want each of you to ride to your assigned store, walk inside, rob it, take your cash, and head for the door. Put two rounds into the ceiling of the place. When you get outside, jump on your horse and ride south, out of town and into the next damned county. Everyone understand?"

One man held up his hand. "Why do we ride south?"

"Because when all of you ride in the same direction, the sheriff will think twice about taking on a gang of eight guns. He probably could get no more than three or four for a posse. Stick together until you're well away from town, then go any damn place you want to."

There were no more questions. He handed out the cash, two twenties and a ten dollar greenback to each man, and assigned him a store, restaurant or saloon to rob. He made sure each man knew where his target was.

"Best to mosey in there now and leave your horse as close to your target as possible. Makes for a faster getaway." He watched them a minute. "You're all ready for the trail, I hope. It's thirty miles to the next little town."

They mumbled and nodded.

"All right. I'll be watching you when the clock strikes three. Good hunting."

He turned and rode away. Nobody shot him in the back. He'd seen the questions on their faces, and hostility in two of them. They were the ones who might blow off their anger, but they would never be a real threat.

He was soon out of pistol range and relaxed a little. J.R. rode back to the hotel and tied on his blanket roll and small sack of goods and food. He had sent his big traveling bag on the morning stage with instructions to drop it off in Helena and keep it in the stage office. He gave the driver $20 to see that the bag was taken care of proper. He had all of his cash in a money belt around his waist.

The others were ready. They rode their horses into the alley behind the hotel and slipped the sawed-off scatter guns into the boot usually reserved for a rifle. They fit lower, looked strange, so they covered them with a brown piece of cloth Dianna provided.

At a quarter of three, they rode out of the alley and tied up their horses at the saddle shop. Dianna stopped at the blacksmith on the corner two doors up from the saddlemaker and tied her horse to the rail, then wandered down on the other side of the street from the bank so she could watch what happened.

The three men left their horses and went into the saddlemaker. J.R. came out and leaned against the wall. He saw two of his men lounging next to businesses. There were a lot more saddle horses on the street than usual. A good sign that his eight men were there.

If two or three of them carried out the routine and caused a disturbance, it would be enough of a diversion and should get the sheriff out and riding the other way out of town, chasing the robbers.

Something could always go wrong. J.R. prided himself on evaluating a target, checking it out carefully, then planning everything down to the last detail. So far it had always worked.

275

He heard the first strike of the clock and looked at the men on the street. His brothers came out and pulled the sawed-off shotguns from their mounts.

Both men wore long, loose shirts. The scatter guns vanished under the shirts, and the brothers went down toward the bank. They would go to the shop next door. J.R. would be on this side of it waiting to give the signal. He pulled his shotgun and hid it under his shirt and walked down the street.

By the time the clock had struck its third bong, he saw two men run into stores.

J.R. counted seconds. Fifty-nine seconds later a man rushed out of the general store, put two slugs through the front window, and jumped on his horse. He tore down Main Street at a wild gallop. A few seconds later another man came out of the general store with a rifle and fired once at the robber. There were too many innocent people on the street to risk another shot.

Then it went like falling dominoes. Another robber raced out and fired, then a third and a fourth. By that time a lot of people on the street were yelling. Three men rushed into the sheriff's office, evidently looking for some help.

That was what he'd been waiting for. J.R. heard other shooting down the street, more pounding hooves. He walked toward the bank. His brothers came from the other direction. They went into the money store all at once, their shotguns covering the customers and tellers.

"Nobody move, and nobody gets hurt," J.R. brayed. "Tellers, banker, hands high in the sky.

Way up there. You two gents and the three ladies, lie down on the floor right damn now!"

E.B. vaulted the high counter between the teller cages. He pistolwhipped one teller, who went down.

Folke dashed toward the swinging door at the far side of the bank, darted through it and ran to the vault.

"Hold it right there, Fancy Dan," Spur bellowed. "We've got six shotguns aimed at your gut. Lay down your weapon and go flat on the floor or you're buzzard meat."

J.R. Guthrie turned and fired at the sound of the voice. Two shotguns blasted double aught buck toward him. He screamed, then folded in half and sprawled on the floor next to the two women customers. Great gouts of flesh and blood had splattered on the women and on the white wall of the bank behind them. One woman fainted. The other one sobbed, unable to open her eyes.

Behind the counter, E.B. screamed, fired a shot from his Greener and then aimed it over the counter.

"I've got the bank owner back here. I'm walking out. The muzzle of the shotgun will be under his chin. You so much as twitch and I'll blow his head off."

E.B. pushed Stewart Rawlins ahead of him. The bank president was forced to back up. The shotgun's twin muzzles of death pushed upward under the banker's chin. His eyes were crazy with fear, rolling from side to side, up, down, looking for help. They came through the swinging door and headed for the front entrance.

"Just go easy, nobody else dies," E.B. said. "I want to hear them shotguns and six-guns hit the floor, Mr. Sheriff."

Sounds came as if guns went to the floor. E.B. pushed the banker forward and they stumbled on a customer lying on the floor. E.B. swore and kicked the prone man's shins until he moved aside. E.B. looked at the door. Still 20 feet away.

"Nobody move, nobody say a damn word." He looked at his older brother and nearly broke up. "Oh, God, who shot J.R.? I should kill all of you right now. Fucking bastards! You gunned him down."

Spur watched from behind a solid oak desk and a pair of oak filing cabinets. He held his six-gun with all cylinders filled, waiting his chance. So far the robber hadn't made a mistake. Even a head shot would cause his muscles to spasm and his fingers would fire the shotgun.

Three came in. Where was the third one? Spur looked over as much of the bank as he could see. He hadn't heard anything from the third man, who was tall and thin and wore better clothes than the short one. The third man would go to clean out the safe. Was there a back door out of here? They hadn't come in time to look around. He couldn't see the Sheriff or his other man.

E.B. cut the distance to the front door in half. Someone jolted the door open and ran inside before he knew what happened.

"Flat on the floor," E.B. yelled at the new-comer. "Drop down right now or you're dead. Now!"

E.B. pushed the banker faster, made it to the front door and vanished outside. The heavy door swung shut.

"There's still one of them in here and alive," Spur barked before any of the lawmen moved. "Be damn careful." Spur ran to another desk closer to the front door and drew no fire. He looked over the top of the desk. The safe door was open. Spur couldn't see anyone there.

He took a chance and charged the front door. No shots came. Spur jerked the door open and jumped outside, his six-gun up and ready to fire. A woman held the reins to a horse at the edge of the boardwalk, and E.B. stood beside her. He still had the shotgun under the banker's chin. Spur was still check-mated.

E.B. looked at the woman. "Melody, hardly knew you all fancied-up that way. You got to help me. Bank job went rotten. You got to hold the shotgun here on this banker man, while I mount up. Long as you hold it, the lawmen won't shoot. You'll do that for your old lover man, won't you, pretty Melody?"

Melody stared at him. She remembered the first time he had raped her. She remembered all those times he had done terrible things to her and, damn it, made her like it. She remembered how he had turned her into a whore at fifteen years of age.

"Sure, E.B. I'll hold the shotgun. You just ease

off on the trigger and let me hold it. Any lawmen out of the bank yet?"

"One, big turd with a six-gun. Don't worry, he won't shoot long as you keep that scatter whammer on the banker."

They transferred the shotgun and Melody put her finger on the trigger.

"Don't shoot me, miss," Rawlins said, his voice little more than a whisper. "He tried to rob my bank."

Melody looked at E.B. as he stepped into the saddle. She figured they would try to rob the bank. She knew the clerk at the general store, professionally, and asked him to tell her if some strangers bought two or three shotguns. He got word to her that morning.

So she watched the bank and waited. She had seen the three men drop off their horses and wait around, killing time. Then the robberies down the street came and she had nodded. Just how E.B. had told they had done a bank once before.

Then she saw the three Guthrie brothers walk into the bank. She moved up with E.B.'s horse to have it ready. Whichever one came out first would want it. She might get a chance at E.B.

E.B. eased into the saddle and grabbed the reins.

He looked at the bank, worry etched on his face. "They got J.R. Hey, Melody, sweetheart. You want to come with me?"

"No," Melody said.

E.B. looked down in surprise.

At that exact moment Melody pulled the

trigger on the shotgun. She had moved the barrels away from the banker and aimed them at the rawhider/bank robber/murderer/rapist/child molester E.B. Guthrie.

The twelve .32 caliber rounds in the double aught buck shotgun shell didn't have time to scatter. From two feet away they pounded into the underside of E.B. Guthrie's chin and rammed upward, blowing what was left of his head off his shoulders. The headless torso balanced there a moment, then fell off the horse on the far side.

Melody dropped the sawed-off shotgun and sat down on the boardwalk, where she promptly threw up.

Spur stepped back inside the bank. Nothing had changed. He ran back to his first desk. "Sheriff, you still there?"

"Right, and I don't see or hear anything. What happened outside?"

"Not sure, but I bet you can piece it together. This place have a back door?"

"Damn it!" the sheriff bellowed. "Knew it was too quiet. That third one must be out the back door."

All three of the lawmen ran that way. There was no one in the rest of the bank or in the alley. Spur eyed both directions, saw running bootprints in the dust heading the long way down the alley to the south. South was where the livery stable was.

Spur yelled at the sheriff to go back outside and talk to the pretty girl who had just thrown up on the boardwalk.

"Where you going?"

"The third member of the Fancy Dan gang is down here somewhere. My job is to go find him."

Spur took off at a trot, keeping the running bootprints in sight. Twice he lost them, then found them again. When he came to the end of the business section, he figured the only way the bank robber could have gone was into the livery. He'd want a horse, a fast horse, and he wouldn't care how he got it.

Chapter Eighteen

Spur ran the last 50 yards to the door of the livery. He had his six-gun cocked but no shots came from the open door. He peered into the shadows from the edge of the doorway but saw no one lurking there. Spur stepped into the dim barn and called.

"Harry. Harry, are you here?"

He waited a minute, but there was no response. He went down the closest row of stalls. Most of the horses were in the pasture. In the third stall he found a body on the straw floor.

"Harry?" Spur knelt and turned the man over.

Old Harry groaned, blinked. "The bastard slugged me with a six-gun. Hell, I'd have give him a mount." The horse-dealer sat up and shook his head. "I'm fine, damn you. Don't fuss. He took a saddled horse I had for Mr. Walters. Go get that bastard, I want a chunk of his hide."

"You go see the doctor, hear?"

"Yeah, yeah, I got worse knots on my head from the wife. Now get your horse and ride after him."

"Which way did he go?" Spur asked.

"Not sure. South I think. Less town that way."

Spur pulled in his gelding, threw a blanket and saddle on her, and mounted. "There's also the afternoon stage heading south in an hour. I hope he doesn't try to flag it down."

Spur rode. He saw tracks just outside the livery, but they soon were lost in a jumble of prints on the South Road. As he galloped the first quarter mile, he tried to put himself in the man's shoes. What would he do? He must know about the afternoon stage if he'd been in town as long as his brother. But would he try for it?

The stage driver would know there was a fugitive in the area. Sheriff would surely tell him.

What would the man do? Look for a nearby ranch and eat, steal food and gear and a rifle? Maybe.

He still could try for the stage. Hold it up if he had a rifle by that time. Yes, a nearby ranch was the runner's best bet. Or an outlying house.

The stage road here followed the beginnings of the Missouri river, winding as a small stream moving north here from its headwaters a hundred miles south along the slopes of the Big Belt Mountains.

This Guthrie brother wouldn't be finessing it.
He'd be moving as fast as his horse could take
him. He probably didn't know the country down
this way any better than Spur did. Spur still
figured that he'd be looking for a ranch or a
farm house. He needed a rifle. Spur had seen
the shotgun hanging from a cord around the
robber's neck.

A scatter gun was good in the bank, but not
for long range. With that sawed-off barrel, Spur
wouldn't be afraid of it at 30, maybe 35 yards.
The spread of those double aught buck rounds
at that distance would be at least 30 to 40 feet.

Spur watched the road. Where it was dusty he
made out a single line of hoofprints overlying
everything else. His quarry was still moving
down the road.

He pushed the gelding, rushing her along
across open land when the road curved to stay
with the river. Now and then he checked the
tracks and found them marching ahead.

Where the road followed the river closely,
Spur swing 50 yards to the side into open
country, taking himself out of any possible
ambush.

As he rode along, he consulted his pocket
watch from time to time. If the stage left
on schedule from South Junction, it should
be rolling along here soon. Now and then he
looked behind him.

A half hour later he saw the roil of dust from
the four steel wheels and the 24 shod hooves of
the team of six. He rode to the upwind side of
the road and pulled off to wait. The rig came

along and Spur held up his hand to stop it. The shotgun guard kept him under his gun as the rig came to a halt. When the dust cleared away from the rig, Spur called to the driver.

"You picked up anybody between here and town?"

"Nary a soul. Ain't you that range detective guy? Sure was a shootout in town. From what I hear they had eight stores robbed and a try at the bank. Oh, you was at the bank.

"Old Rawlins shit his pants, you hear that? He stood right there on the boardwalk and when that shotgun went off he dirtied his drawers something fierce. I only got three women passengers. Ain't seen any of them robbers."

Spur rode along the side of the rig and looked in. He tipped his hat to the three women inside and waved at the driver.

"You see any men down the road you use that shotgun to keep them at a safe distance. Get a move on or you'll be late."

The driver whacked the twelve reins down on the horses. The leads dug in their hooves and the other four picked up the idea as the rig rolled on down the road.

Spur watched it go, then moved on. The tracks would be a little harder to see now, but he'd find enough of them.

Two hours out of town he saw smoke coming from a ranch house maybe two miles from the road. He found the tracks of the horseman and followed them closely. Another 100 yards down the trail the tracks turned off the road into the open country, aiming for the ranch.

It was a little after 5:30. He pondered what to do. The bank robber had no more than a 20 minute head start on him, which meant he was just about getting to the ranch house or had galloped much of the way, gambling that he could get a fresh horse there. Did he know that someone was following him?

Spur turned to circle around the house, still a mile away. Soon a kind of haze settled in, making it harder to see. Even if the killer had been watching his back trail, he wouldn't look in this direction. Just before dusk, Spur had ridden even with the house, still a mile north. He turned with the failing light and walked his mount toward the house.

As it grew dark, he picked out two stars and kept them directly over the looming peak against the skyline. That would serve for another 20 minutes.

A short time later, lights flared in the ranch house. Spur galloped on the soft ground for a quarter mile, then slowed to a walk and tied up his mount in some brush at a small feeder creek that chattered down the grade 100 yards from the house.

He moved up on foot toward the buildings. Now he could see a horse standing in the yard near the front door. Its head was down and it still showed flecks of lather on its sides.

Spur lay still in the grass and weeds. Nothing moved around the outside of the structure. The small ranch looked like a one-family operation. Probably no hands. He rose and ran silently to the window that showed light at the front of the house. Over the window ledge he saw a kitchen. A woman worked at a counter and a stove on the far side of the room.

At first he couldn't see anyone else in the room. Then someone spoke from the side, and he saw the legs of a man, and a hat. Spur couldn't catch the meaning of the words. The woman turned from the stove, stared hard at the man, turned back and went on cooking.

He'd holed up here. How could Spur get him out without hurting the ranch family? The only way was to wait. With any luck the man would not stay overnight here. He would want to put as much time between himself and South Junction as he could. Spur retreated 20 yards and lay down in the grass where he could see the front door and the horse.

A few minutes later a man came out of the house with a lantern. He wore jeans and a blue shirt, so Spur knew it wasn't the bank robber. He went to the small barn and brought back a horse, pulled the saddle off the worn-out mare, and saddled the new horse.

The screen banged. Spur eased the Spencer repeating carbine into position on his shoulder. The lantern went out. He couldn't be sure which shape ahead of him 30 yards was the bank robber and which the rancher. The light in the kitchen went out.

Spur heard the creak of leather. Then there was a mumbled exchange, and the horse galloped away into the night. Spur thought of putting seven rounds from the Spencer into the area where the sounds led him, but he never got off a first shot. The shape of the rancher loomed against the moonlit sky and blocked his field of fire.

Spur ran for his horse. He doubted that the rider ahead of him would gallop far. He must know that these Western quarter horses were built for short bursts of speed, but a quarter of a mile gallop would tire them out and reduce them to a walk. Much more than that and the animal could founder and go down.

Spur mounted his horse, pushed the rifle in the boot and rode around the farm house, then worked at a trot toward the stage road. It wasn't hard to find in the moonlight. He had no lantern this time, no way to track the man ahead. He stopped in the soft cooling air of the night and listened. He heard a horse snort far ahead and then blow as if it had just slowed down from a long gallop.

On south.

Spur rode in that direction. He wasn't sure what to do next. He'd ride slowly, letting the fugitive gain on him, but not wanting to run up on him by surprise. He hoped that the man would figure he was far enough from town and find himself a small creek and light a fire and eat some of the food he must have taken from the people back there at the ranch.

Twice in the next hour, Spur came across small streams. He sat beside each for ten minutes, listening, watching. He saw no blossom of a fire, no sound of a horse.

Forward.

It was just before midnight by the star clock

when Spur grinned. He turned slightly and smiled broadly in the darkness.

Smoke. Wood smoke from a campfire. It was like a beacon to a weary seaman hunting port. The smoke tainted the fresh pure Montana air. Out here in the open, Spur could smell a wood fire five miles away if the wind was right. Tonight it was. He rode a little faster now. The wind was coming almost due north. He tracked it for what he figured was a mile, then it faded to his left, quartering the road.

He moved off the track, homing in on the smoke. Twice more he angled to the east. He heard the stream chattering before he saw the brush line.

Spur stopped and tied his kerchief around the muzzle of his gelding. He didn't want any horse talk going on. Horses could often smell one another from a quarter of a mile away and sound off a recognition call or a confrontation whinny. Spur had never been able to figure out which.

He slid off the saddle, took his rifle, tied his mount to a shrub and eased forward. Another 50 yards and he could see the glow of the fire beyond the trees.

Spur moved up like an Indian, sliding forward with a foot when he was sure it would make no noise if he put his weight on it. He had a round in the rifle chamber ready to fire.

At 20 yards he squatted in the darkness, watching the fire area. Twice he saw shadows against the far brush, as if someone had come between it and the fire. He waited. There was no food smell, no coffee. The man must have eaten well at the ranch.

Ten minutes later he crept ahead again. This time he came to the outside edge of the brush and looked through it. He could see the fire, smaller now and burning out. A blanket roll showed at the far side. There was a lump in it leading up to the man's saddle. The horse stood a dozen yards away, quietly munching on some river-produced grass.

Spur checked the area again. The ground around the camp was littered with brittle sticks and dry leaves. The chattering of the stream was quieter here, not enough to cover his approach to the blankets. Were the blankets a trap filled with brush?

Spur knew he could put three rifle rounds into the lump of the blankets, but would that bring quick retaliation by two rounds of double aught buck? Those widely scattering rounds would be an advantage to the shooter here. He could blast at Spur's muzzle flashes with an excellent chance of hitting his target.

Spur shook his head. This bank robber was either extremely lucky in his choice of a campsite or a remarkably good woodsman. Spur frowned, turned and moved back as quietly as he had come. He found his horse and rode back to the stage road. The campsite was over a quarter of a mile from the south road.

Spur went about that far upstream on the little creek, left his horse saddled, and settled down for a cold camp. He took a long drink of water, then another. He kicked around the leaves and grass next to a stately cottonwood to chase out any sleeping rattlesnakes, then stretched out for a small rest.

Years ago he had learned the knack of instructing his mind how long he wanted to sleep. He wasn't sure how it worked, but it did. He simply set up a program that would instruct his brain to bring him awake at a given time. He picked five o'clock. It would still be dark then and give him an advantage. Spur stared for a moment through the broad cottonwood leaves. The cotton-like fluffs of seeds were not yet drifting from the big tree. In some places he had seen them blow across a field and look like a snow storm. He smiled at the thought and then he slept.

Spur came awake easily. He kept his eyes closed and listened. No foreign sounds came to him. He waited, then slowly opened one eye. He saw nothing unusual. He opened the second eye and looked around the rest of his small camp. His horse watched him in the dimness of the pre-dawn.

He sat up, adjusted his feet in his cow-boy boots, put on his hat and went to the stream for a long drink. No breakfast. He could go without food for five days and still function at full power, speed and agility. He wouldn't want to go more than 48 hours without water. He filled the canteen on his saddle and then mounted. Spur rode slowly through the concealing brush downstream toward the stage road, found the spot he wanted and waited.

Wilderness Wanton

From his vantage point, he was hidden from the road, but he could see past some thick maple leaves. He had a clear view of the stage road for three miles south. The stream went almost straight, and he would be able to see a fire if the robber lit one. He guessed that the fugitive would come out of the brush about daylight and angle up to the stage road, hitting it maybe 200 yards out.

Spur didn't like the idea of gunning a man down from an ambush. Bushwhacking wasn't his way of doing things. He'd go for the horse. A pair of rounds through the animal's ribcage would put her down and out of action. The man would be easy to capture on foot.

That was his plan, capture this last living member of the Fancy Dan bank robbery team and take him back to stand trial for murder. Spur guessed that one of the tellers had been killed. Fancy Dan himself had paid the ultimate price, and the third brother had died on his horse in front of the bank. So this bank robber would be charged with murder.

Yes, he would go for the horse. It belonged to the rancher, but he had taken a horse in trade. No worry there.

Spur sat his gelding and waited. Daylight filtered in as long daggers spiking through the inky darkness, turning it into a dull gray. Then, suddenly, it was light.

He watched down the fringes of trees where the creek did a lazy turn to the south. Somewhere down there the robber slept, or awoke and cooked himself breakfast. The wind was at Spur's back so he would smell no smoke or frying bacon.

A half hour after daylight, a horse and rider came through the fringes of trees moving at a walk toward the wagon road. The animal angled for the track, the quickest way to get there.

Spur let him get almost to the road. He figured this was the best spot to shoot. Not over 220 yards. He leveled in with the Spencer, rested it against the tree beside him, and aimed at the barrel of the mount just behind the rider's leg.

He squeezed off the round, jacked the lever down and up in one fluid motion that chambered a new .52 caliber round, found his aim and fired again. No more than two seconds separated his shots. He saw the bay stumble and go down. The second round caught her higher in the back. The rider turned his way, then bailed out of the saddle, hit the ground and took off running for the fringe of trees near the Missouri a hundred yards behind him.

Spur kicked the gelding forward out of the brush into the open land and galloped down the line of trees and brush. He turned into the cover again when he was 30 yards from where the robber had run into the woods. He took the rifle with him and moved forward from tree to tree, working downstream toward the robber.

Spur had no idea if the fugitive would run or stand and fight. He had no information on this brother, not even a name, only some vague references that he was a gambler between his bank holdups. A gambler would be craftier than the others.

Wilderness Wanton

This one would run.

Spur checked the beginnings of the Missouri river. It was at least neck-deep here, maybe more, and 30 feet wide. Not safe to cross in a rush. That pinned the man on this side and probably downstream. But where?

Spur moved out of the brush a moment but saw no one running away from him in the open. He listened. Far downstream he could hear brush moving, branches snapping. Someone ran that way.

He ran for his horse, stepped into the saddle and rode hard downstream until he figured he was past the culprit. Then he slid off the gelding, let him graze and slipped into the 20 foot wide section of brush that bordered the stream.

Somewhere up there was the fugitive. Where? He listened again. Nothing this time. Was he ahead of the man? Had he cut him off? He turned the other way, stepped behind a willow tree and waited. He had learned to wait from the Apaches, the Chiricahua Apaches, the meanest and deadliest of the Indian warrior tribes. They could lie in wait for hours without moving a muscle. They could cover themselves in flat open country with sand until they were invisible, breathing through a hollow stem, and then 50 warriors could rise up out of an "empty" gully and kill an army patrol to a man before they knew they were under attack.

He waited.

A branch cracked upstream. Good. Spur had gone past him, cut him off. Why didn't the outlaw reverse his direction and keep on heading south?

Anger, revenge. He knew what had happened to his older brother in the bank. He must have sensed that the other, smaller brother must have suffered badly as well. Revenge, yes. He wanted a piece of somebody, wanted his pound of flesh.

What would it be, a last-minute charge with both barrels spewing sudden death in the form of the double aught buck?

Spur edged farther behind the tree until its trunk and the lower leafy branches covered him. Again he waited, Apache style, his breathing shallow and quiet so he could hear anything that approached. Something moved to his left. He turned his head slowly. A rabbit bounced into his line of sight, lifted up on its hind feet to look around, then dropped down and nibbled on some green shoots hear the edge of the water.

Upstream another branch snapped and a leaf-laden limb swished back into place after it had been bent forward. Spur's carbine had a round ready to fire. Long ago he had loosened his six-gun, making it ready for a quick draw. He lifted the Spencer and peered past the leaves down the stream bank. A sparse section ahead let him see through for 40 feet upstream.

Nothing.

Then a shape in the shadows moved. Showing in the heavy greens and browns and shadowy umbers, Spur spotted a splash of pinkish white. A face. It moved, and then the face became attached to a body, which took three cautious steps into the thin growth.

Thirty feet away, Spur lifted the Spencer carbine and pushed the short barrel through the branches. He sighted in on the robber's right shoulder. His right hand held the stock of the sawed off scattergun.

"Hold it right there. Not a step, not a twinge."

Folke Guthrie turned into a pillar of steel for just a fraction of a second, then lifted the shotgun. Spur fired. The shotgun bellowed out a roar.

Spur's round dug into Folke's right shoulder, spinning him backwards and to the right. The impact came as he squeezed the trigger, but by the time the hammer fell, the shotgun was aimed at right angles to his original target and blasted into the woodlands.

The force of the heavy bullet slammed Folke to the ground, where he dove and skittered behind a two-foot-thick fallen fir tree log that had young firs growing from its decomposing trunk.

Spur searched the 15 foot length of the log but could not spot the outlaw. The scatter gun lay in plain sight, but the bank robber had vanished. He still had a six-gun in his leather.

Spur darted to the side to look behind the log. As soon as he moved from the tree, a revolver round splattered through the brush a half foot in front of him. He dropped to the ground and, dragging the rifle by the barrel, crawled and scurried for a fir tree six feet ahead.

Once there he peered around the side of the fir bark, but couldn't see along the back of the downed log.

Spur listened, but heard nothing. His Apache

patience wore thin. He had had him. He should have used a heart shot and carried the body back to town. Only that wasn't his style.

For just a second, Spur thought about his horse. No chance that the robber could get to him. The mount was 50 yards on downstream, the robber was moving upstream. What now?

Spur eased away from the fir and darted 15 feet to another conifer about the same size. Now he could see down the length of the rotting log.

No one was there.

Chapter Nineteen

A six-gun blasted close ahead of him. Spur tried to dodge and drop but he knew instinctively that if he heard the explosion of the powder charge it was already too late to try to move. He fell anyway and felt the hot lead slug burn through his thigh and tear out the other side.

Spur controlled a shrill of a scream and rolled away from the sound into deeper brush behind a fir tree.

Two more rounds came as he moved. One nicked his hat, another passed so close over his head he could feel the lead's hot breath. Where was the shooter?

Spur looked at his leg. Bleeding like a gut-shot steer. He pulled a handkerchief from his pocket and pushed it against the backside of his leg. The pain that knifed through him almost made him pass out. A .45 slug goes into flesh with a small blue-black hole and doesn't bleed. When it comes out the lead tears away a chunk of flesh an inch wide and gushes blood.

He pushed the now red bit of cloth harder against the wound. Black spots spun in front of his eyes. He reached his other hand to the ground for support. Bastard was getting away. He must be. Horse. He couldn't slip up on the robber dragging one leg. He used his knife and cut the sleeve off his shirt, slit the tube and tore it into strips, then tied a compress pad on each side of the leg wound front and back. He tied it so tight he winced. He'd need it. The cloth strips ran around his pants leg. It would make it harder to walk. If he could walk.

He crawled to the rear away from the log. Crawled until he figured he was covered by the brush. He grabbed a tree and lifted himself. He still had the Spencer. Good.

For a minute there he wasn't sure if he had it or not. The black spots buzzing in front of his eyes faded a little more now. He got to the edge of the growth and saw his horse 20 yards away.

It looked like a mile. He used the butt of the Spencer Carbine as a crutch. Now he wished he had the longer Spencer rifle.

For five minutes he struggled ahead and at last made it to the horse. He almost fell when he tried to stand on his wounded right leg and lift his left foot into the stirrup. He made it, then had to grab the horse's mane to keep his balance. The big gelding turned and looked at

him, snorted and faced front again. He caught
the saddle horn then and threw his leg over the
back of the mount.

It took him two tries to get his leg all the way
over the broad rump of the quarter horse. The
spots in his vision turned into huge patches of
black, and for a moment it all blocked out but
came back at once.

He pushed the carbine into the boot and rode
upstream. The robber would keep to the brush
for cover.

Spur rode out 40 yards from the growth,
stopped often and listened. The third time he
heard noise in the brush. He fired two rifle shots
into the area.

"Might as well come out of there. You can't
walk all the way to the railroad with that
shoulder wound."

There was no response. Spur fired again and
a six-gun blasted in return. The round kicked up
a puff of dirt ten yards short.

"You've got nowhere to go. I can find a spot
with no cover from the brush and shoot you a
few times. That what you want?"

Two more shots answered but they were wide
and short. Spur checked the saddle bags. Yes, a
box of 30 rounds of the .52 caliber ammunition
for the Spencer. He rode another 20 yards
upstream. The road swung in close to the mighty
Missouri again.

Spur frowned at the brush. What was the
man trying to do? The gentle wind blew in his
face across the stream. By afternoon it would
be a gale.

He looked far down the road, but could see no one coming. When he looked back at the river he sniffed in surprise. Then he saw it, a trail of fire blowing toward him in the dry grass. The rim of flames was 100 feet or more long, starting at the river and blowing directly at him.

Spur kicked the horse in the flanks and rode away from the fire upstream. It took him only a few minutes to outrace the south edge of the fire. There stood the fugitive, a sheaf of dry grass in his hand, lighting more weeds and small brush on fire.

Spur lifted his Spencer and shot the man in the left leg. He went down, screaming. Spur rode toward the fugitive, staying away from the edge of the fire, pinning his target against the river now and the flames behind him.

"You move and I'll kill you," Spur bellowed over the cracking of the flames. Away from the stream the grass became thinner. The fire would soon have no fuel and burn out. Spur rode up the man sitting on the ground.

"Throw your six-gun in the river," Spur barked. "I'm still too far away for you to hit me with it. You're finished. You're the only one of the Fancy Dan brothers left alive, you know that?"

"You kill them both?"

"Neither one of them. You through running?"

"I didn't kill anyone. I ran out of the bank first thing I knew you lawmen were in there." He paused and shook his head.

"I have never killed anybody."

"I'm not the judge. Throw that weapon away

302

and walk toward me. Do it right now. I'm losing patience with you."

Folke Guthrie sighed. He knew when it was time to throw in a losing hand. That time was now. "I tell you I didn't kill anyone. I didn't rob the bank. I didn't do anything illegal and you have no reason to take me to jail."

"Your lawyer and the judge and jury will decide that. Now pitch out that weapon or I'll have to shoot you again."

Folke Guthrie nodded. He took the revolver by the barrel and threw it to the side into the middle of the Missouri river.

"Can you walk?"

"If you let me tie up this rifle wound in my leg."

It took them half the day to get back to South Junction. Folke cut a crutch from a limb and walked back to the ranch house where he had stolen the food at gunpoint.

Spur borrowed a horse and saddle from the rancher and told him he could reclaim them at the livery in town. They rode up to the sheriff's office in South Junction a little after one o'clock on Sunday afternoon. Twenty young boys and a few men trailed behind them as they came to the rail outside the law office. Somebody ran for the sheriff.

Sheriff Halverson took over. The doctor took Spur to his office and worked on his leg. Later he would go to the jail to bandage up the prisoner.

"Want you to get to bed and let that heal for at least a week," the sawbones said. "That round

303

tore up some muscle in there and did some more damage I ain't about to try to fix. I don't want you to get a gimp leg out of this. A week in bed with no walking. You got somebody who can nurse you?"

"He sure does," Abby said from the doorway. "I heard you were back in town. Have a nice ride?"

The medic loaned spur a pair of crutches, and Abby helped him hobble up to her house. She fussed around like a setting hen, putting him to bed, bringing him chicken soup, making him coffee, reporting on events while he was gone.

"So, the young girl blasted the one robber's head off. Seems the bank robber knew her and there's been talk, but who can tell what happened. The sheriff said there were no charges against her. It might have been an accident, and maybe not. But either way the man was a bank robber, a killer, and Sheriff Halverson put it down as the young girl acting in self-defense.

"Soon as she got cleared by the sheriff, the girl caught the north stage. She said she couldn't live in this town after all that had happened.

"Oh, one of the bank tellers got killed. The little guy who lost his head shotgunned him. Then the sheriff and his deputy killed the other robber. So that about wraps up the robbery gang.

"Oh, the sheriff said that this last one called Folke would be charged with bank robbery, assault and battery, and for murder because the bank teller was killed. Be a trial next month when the circuit court judge comes around."

Spur looked up, nodded, thanked her, and a

moment later he was sleepy. Must have been something in the medicine the doctor gave him, he decided, as his eyes drifted closed and he went to sleep.

He remembered waking up once. It was dark out, a lamp burned on the dresser and Abby drowsed in a rocking chair near the bed. She came alert at once.

"Oh, you're awake. Can I get anything for you?"

He asked her for some water, drank a glass and thanked her. Before he could more than touch her shoulder, he was falling asleep again.

The sun was well up Monday morning when Spur awoke again. He smelled bacon frying and the taint of gently burned toast. Abby looked in the bedroom and hurried in when she saw him trying to get up.

"Hey, there. Not so fast. The doctor said a week in bed, remember?"

He dropped back on the pillow. "Yeah, but I figured that would include you beside me."

"I was."

He looked at her, then at the second pillow on the double bed with the dent in it. Spur chuckled. "I guess you know you have a record. There are damn few women I've spent a whole night in bed with, without doing something more exciting than just sleep."

"I like records. Now lay back down and I'll have some breakfast for you in just a few minutes. How do you like your eggs?"

The breakfast was huge, a plate full of grated fresh potatoes fried to a crisp brown, covered with three eggs sunny side up, two pieces of French toast drenched in warm syrup and butter, two pieces of buttered toast and jam, and a pitcher full of hot coffee.

Abby had propped him up for breakfast with three pillows. When he finished eating she took the tray away. Spur rose a little higher so he wasn't leaning against the pillows. He steadied himself and beat back a host of black spots. When his vision cleared, he grinned.

He pulled his feet out from under the covers and looked at his wounded right leg. He lifted it gingerly and flexed it at the knee. Yeah, it hurt, but not like anything he couldn't live with. Spur looked for his pants and couldn't find them. He was naked in the bed.

"Abby, get your pretty little bottom in here," Spur called.

She hurried in, frowning. When she saw him sitting up, she turned the frown into a scowl.

"Absolutely not. The doctor said a week in bed. . . ."

He pointed a finger at her. "My clothes. Either that or I walk downtown naked as a new born babe and buy some new ones."

Abby giggled. "You just might do it." She took a deep breath. "All right, but I better change that dressing first. Doc Partlow gave me some bandages to do it with and some salve. He figured you wouldn't be down for long in spite of his orders."

After she changed the dressing, he pulled on his pants. The wound had started to heal. It wasn't bleeding anymore. That was a good sign.

He was happy the slug had carried all the way through.

Now he could concentrate on the damned rustlers. He knew who was doing it but he didn't have any hard evidence. Those rebranded cattle were circumstantial only. They could have wandered in there from any part of that open range. He had to get something that would stand up in court, if it got that far.

How the hell did he get evidence like that? There was only one way, and Spur knew what it was. He had to get out in the range and catch somebody rustling cattle. Spur wasn't sure if he could ride. He wasn't even sure if he could walk. He started to stand, put weight on his right leg, and yelped in pain. It dropped him back on to the bed.

Maybe not today, maybe tomorrow.

Abby stood in the bedroom door watching him. "You had to try it, didn't you? Give it another day to get used to having a hole punched through those muscles."

"Lady, you have a smart mouth."

Abby grinned, hurried over and kissed his cheek. "I know. Why do you suppose nobody would marry me. Ouch! A girl could cut her lips kissing all those whiskers. Want me to shave you?"

Spur looked up at her and frowned. "I never let a pretty sexy lady get that close to my throat with a straight-edge razor. Some hot water and soap and a mirror and a razor if you have one, and I figure I can scrape the stubble off." He did.

That afternoon, Abby found Rusty and told

him Spur wanted to see him. Rusty stepped into the bedroom and held his hat in his hands, turning it slowly. He looked around at the woman's bedroom and grinned, then relaxed a little.

"You should'a taken me along with you," Rusty said. "I been known to fire a shooting iron a time or two."

"Wish I had. There just wasn't any time. That's done. You hear anything new about the rustling?"

"Not a word."

"Any idea about how we can get some evidence we can take to court on these rustlers?"

"Just one way to do it. I reckon you know about that a'ready."

"Catch them in the act. How do we figure out who is going rustling next?"

"We have two good suspects," Rusty said.

"The Bar-B and the Box C."

"Easy, I take one, you take the other. . . ."

"Not today, maybe tomorrow. Which one you want?"

Rusty looked at Spur. "I can hire a man to help me. You ain't doing any riding for a spell."

"Which one you want?"

"You know the Bar-B land best, and it's closer. I'll take the Box C."

"Way I see it is we watch the home place, wait for a bunch of ten or twelve riders to go out from the corral on a rustling mission just after dark."

"There's a creek with lots of brush a quarter of a mile from the corral at the Bar-B. Perfect spot to wait and watch. If we can't see them on a dark night, we can hear ten riders moving out."

"Take a good sack of cold food along, spend a couple of days at a time, then come in. My schedule said the next raid should come tonight, Monday, but now I don't know what to think."

"I'll be out there tonight."

Spur found his wallet and took out two $20 greenbacks. "Use this for supplies and whatever."

"Too damn much. A fiver will do me fine."

"No, take it. You haven't been paid yet for your work."

"A man gets paid at the end of the month."

"Consider this the end of your first month. You going out tonight?"

"Soon as I can get to the Box C spread. But I'll wait for dark to move in on their land. I don't aim to get shot at again."

Abby brought in three bottles of beer. The small town had an equally small brewery that made beer for local consumption. The bottles were cold, and Abby looked at him and smiled.

"I have my own ice box. Cold air falls so the ice is in the top and I put my milk and butter and cream and beer in the bottom of the box to keep cold."

"Town has an ice house?" Spur asked.

Abby nodded. "We got together and put it up about two years ago. Cut the ice in the winter and somebody brings hay and we mulch it down between layers. It's a big barn-type roof that keeps the cold in. Melts slow in the summer with all that hay around it. We go chip off a chunk when we want it. All the saloons use the ice every day. How is the rustler-hunting going?" Abby asked a minute later.

"Slow," Rusty said. "I'm betting on the Box C. Somehow I don't think our Englishman friend, Northcliff, is smart enough to pull off a long-range operation like this."

"Maybe they're planning on a fall roundup just before snow time and a drive to the railroad when the price will be up on beef because the supply is down."

Rusty nodded. "Possible. Strange damn way to rustle cattle. Be glad when we get to the bottom of this." He stood. His beer was empty. "Miss Abby, I thank you for the brew. Now I best get moving or my boss here will have my hide. I got to go play hide-de-seek with some rustler guys." He waved at Spur and slipped out the door.

Abby smiled and went over and kissed Spur's smooth cheek. "Oh, yes, ever so much nicer. I like Rusty."

"He's a good man. Right now I need him."

"He'll get the job done. You're confined to your bed for the next six days."

"Not likely."

"Don't spoil my fun, I enjoy playing nursemaid to you."

"Do you provide all kinds of services to your patients?"

"Any kind of service that they want." She bent over so her breasts swung down near his face. He reached up and kissed one, then blew hot breath against it through the cloth.

She pulled back. "Almost anytime but right

now. I've got your supper on the stove and I don't want anything to burn. You keep that thought and I'll find some time later on."

"You'll be able to squeeze me in?"

"Oh yes, I certainly hope so." She flashed him a grin and went back to the kitchen. He pushed to a sitting position. He was still dressed. He didn't black out this time. Progress.

Spur swung his legs off the bed and let his bare feet touch the wooden floor. Not bad. Not too bad at all. He eased to a standing position with his weight on his left leg, his hand holding onto the bed's headboard.

So far he felt only the dull ache from his shot right leg. He eased his weight onto it and for a moment a searing pain stabbed through his thigh. Then it was gone. He lifted his brows. Was that all? He applied a little more weight on his right leg and let out a howl of pain and sat down quickly on the bed.

Abby darted into the room.

"What in the world?"

"Just a little experiment. I'm a field agent, not a cooped-up-in-a-lady's-bedchamber agent."

"You're also a gunshot agent and guest in my house, and I won't have you hurting yourself any more."

"Rusty is going out tonight. I should be out tonight. Looks like I can't make it tonight, but tomorrow night for sure. Get me a piece of paper and a pencil, I want to make out a shopping list. I'll need dry, cold food enough for three days."

"To use when you go out and watch the Bar-B?"

"Yes."

"If you go out there, I'm going with you."

Spur laughed and shook his head. "About as much chance of that as a snowstorm in the Sahara." As soon as he said it, Spur wished he hadn't. If he pushed her too much, she might do something unpredictable.

Late Tuesday afternoon, Spur hobbled out of the house with one of the crutches, and with a little help from Abby he mounted his horse. The gelding had been in the livery for two days and was well rested. Spur experimented, moving a little more at a time, and at last he could walk with some semblance of normalcy. Abby had brought up the horse and tied the sack of food behind his saddle. It included four big sandwiches she had made.

"I really think you should have someone go with you," she said, watching him try to get his right leg in a comfortable position. At last he pulled his boot out of the stirrup and let his leg hang along the horse's side.

"I'm fine. Just a little stiff. Now don't worry."

"I'll worry until you're back in town safe and sound and I can change that bandage."

"You changed it an hour ago. It's starting to heal well. Now hush." He reached down and kissed her lips. She murmured and watched him with her eyes open.

"You be careful."

Spur nodded and rode away through town to the north. He had a six-mile ride but wanted to do the last two in the darkness, so he might have a wait somewhere upstream on the feeder creek that watered the Bar-B and emptied into the growing surge of the Missouri river.

Spur was out about an hour from town when he sensed someone behind him. He stopped and turned and saw a rider coming toward him at a steady trot. He waited.

Ten minutes later a small man rode forward, and it wasn't until the horse was 50 feet away that he recognized Abby Buchanan. She wore range clothes, had a gunbelt and filled holster and a smile from ear to ear.

"Hi, cowboy. I heard you needed another hand on your roundup. Told you I was going with you. We're about an hour away from the Bar-B. You going to sit here waiting for dark or move up a little closer before the sun goes down?"

Spur had all sorts of sharp words for her, but he swallowed them. It would be great to have her along. After riding four miles, he was well aware that he would need some help on this spying mission.

"Welcome aboard, sailor. Glad to have you along. That loose-fitting shirt doesn't do a thing for your fine figure."

Abby grinned. "Hey, cowboy, the shirt comes off just real easy. Now, we going to ride, or sit here until the Bar-B guys spot us?"

They rode into the brush along the larger stream and waited.

"You could at least give me a hug," Abby said. They rode close together and he hugged her, kissed her lips gently, and then winced as he twisted his leg.

"Careful, cowboy, we can continue this later

on when we make our camp."

Just at dusk they left the brush and rode the last mile toward the Bar-B ranch buildings. They circled around to come at them from the side where the feeder stream ran. It was dark when they walked their mounts into the brush. Spur moved his gelding across the foot-deep water and looked out the brush on the far side.

He saw the lamp-lit ranch house and two lanterns being carried toward the barn. The bunkhouse door opened and then closed, stabbing a rectangle of yellow light onto the hard-packed ranch yard for a few seconds.

"All looks quiet," Abby said.

"Yeah, but this is Tuesday night, it might not stay that way."

"This was the night you figured they'd strike again?"

Spur shook his head. "No, that was last night, but we didn't hear anything in town, so it didn't happen here or at the Box C. So maybe tonight. It's been six days." They dismounted. Spur swung his right leg over the back of the horse, then kicked his left foot free of the stirrup and slid down the side of the horse so his left foot hit the ground first. When his right leg took some weight he groaned, but cut it off quickly.

Abby waited until he sat down next to a willow tree, then she led the horses into the brush ten feet and tied them. She brought him a bottle of beer from her saddlebags.

"Not exactly cold, but better than nothing. You sit and rest a spell and I'll find a lookout spot and see what's going on at the Bar-B."

Spur conceded. "If they're going out, it should be soon. If they go, they have a lot of work to get done before daylight."

Chapter Twenty

Spur used the crutch and moved up to where Abby lay on a blanket, peering through the darkness at the ranch buildings. She looked through a pair of binoculars.

"Where did you get those?" Spur asked.

"Out of my kit. Oh, originally. A bloke carried a gambling tab he couldn't pay for. I traded his I.O.U. for the glasses. Really quite good. At night they pick up the light and magnify it, too, so you can see better through them than with your eye."

Spur dropped down beside her with a small groan, took the glasses and tried them. They worked. He spotted the light in the bunkhouse, the corral was all quiet, the main house was ablaze with lights in four different windows.

"Nothing is going to happen tonight," Abby said.

"How do you know?"

"I just know. So, since we have the rest of the night, I think it's time I provide some of those other services I offered you under my roof and didn't get a chance to provide."

She had the shirt unbuttoned and let it slide off her shoulders. Abby wore nothing underneath it. She turned Spur over on his back, then knelt over him, letting one breast lower into his mouth.

"Yes, now we're doing you some service." Her hand worked between his legs up to his crotch and found the growing long lump behind his fly. Quickly she undid the buttons and bent his pants back, then pushed through short underwear until she found exactly what she was hunting.

"Oh, my, I think you're ready."

He changed breasts, and she moaned softly. "That feels so fine!" She moved them, coming away from his face and moving her lips down to his crotch. She kissed his full erection and yelped when it jumped in the pale moonlight filtering through the trees.

She kissed it again, then slipped it into her mouth and nibbled at it gently with her teeth.

Spur moaned and his hips thrust slowly forward. "You want a mouthful?" he asked.

"Oh, Lordy. I haven't tried that since the last time with you. Three years ago." She nestled on her side in front of him and her mouth took half; then he began to thrust slowly, evenly, careful not to go too far. He stopped, and a thin wail of anger and pain slipped from his mouth.

"Damn leg," he said.

"Just lay still, I can take care of that little problem." She fussed a minute on the blanket beside him, then slipped off her boots and her jeans and her bloomers until she was naked. She hovered over him a moment, then squatted above his crotch.

"Tonight I'm on top, at least the first time. That way it won't hurt your leg at all." She grinned at him in the moonlight, positioned herself carefully with one foot on each side of his waist, then slowly squatted down.

"Oh damn!" Abby said; then she crooned as his hard flesh penetrated her vagina at that strange angle. She leaned forward to change the pressure, and when he was fully inserted, she lay on his chest, her legs between his spread ones.

"Now that is wild," Abby said. She lay there a minute, then slowly began to move up and down, and her hips danced in a gentle rotation that made Spur yelp in delight.

"Who taught you to do that?" Spur asked, his voice husky and low.

"Nobody. A girl just knows these things, knows how to pleasure the man she's going to marry."

"This isn't the marriage ceremony, you know."

"Close enough for me. Damn but that is wild. I love it this way. It just keeps getting better and better with you, Spur McCoy. Take me back to Denver with you. I'll sell out here in a minute and then we can fuck for six hours every night and I'll be in Denver heaven."

He grinned and wanted to chuckle but the storm was rising. The juices flowed and his breathing came like a steam engine, and his hips pistoned up to meet her downward thrust. It took only ten strokes more and he exploded. He screeched like a she-wolf mating, and brayed again as he drove upward, sending the last of his life-producing fluids deep inside the female.

When he climaxed it set Abby off as well, and they bucked and pounded and rolled and jolted together like a pair of sex-starved rabbits in a carrot patch.

They both were sweating when it ended. She held him tightly, and he clasped his arms around her back, not letting her move.

A weapon fired from the ranch buildings. They both quieted and turned to stare into the darkness and the few lamp lights.

"Six-gun," Spur said. "From inside one of the buildings. Might have been an accident."

"Somebody dropped a weapon practicing a fast draw?" Abby suggested.

They came apart and lay there watching each other and the buildings.

"You were right," Spur said. "They aren't going out tonight. Too late now even if they wanted to."

"Figures," Abby said. "Told you I knew." She slipped her silk bloomers on, then her jeans and her shirt. "You animal, you never even took your pants off."

Spur grinned. "You called the shots, remember? Now, you get some sleep. I'll stand guard tonight and sleep tomorrow. We'll give them one more try tomorrow night. If we get no action, we'll go back to town."

Abby slid over next to him, touching his face, hugging him soundly. "I didn't hurt your leg?"

"No, it's fine."

She pulled back and kissed him, then edged away so she could get his face in focus. "I really liked it just now. It was fantastic. This being out in the woods, bare-assed in the outdoors, kinda makes me go wild. I'd be ready for half a dozen more, but I know your leg must be hurting. I want you to get well quick so we can really roll around outdoors again under the sun or the moon, whichever one."

"It's a date," Spur said. "Let me check the ranch yard out there again through the glasses." He lifted the binoculars and studied the whole area around the buildings.

"All quiet. You snuggle down here and get some sleep. Oh, get the two blankets off my horse, too. Might as well be as comfortable as possible."

She kissed him again, then went to the horse and brought back the blankets and the sack of food. She found an apple and munched on it.

Abby grinned at him in the moonlight. "Sometimes getting fucked real good makes me so hungry I could eat half an apple tree."

"Then you get some sleep."

Tuesday morning came bright and clear. Spur woke Abby early and they made a cold breakfast.

"We can't risk a fire even for coffee this close to the buildings," Spur said. "Some sharp-eyed cowboy might see the traces of smoke coming up through the branches. Water for breakfast today."

They stayed where they were all day. Twice they had to tie the muzzles of their horses so they wouldn't horse talk with riders going by on normal ranch work. No one crossed the creek within 100 yards of their spot, but that seemed terribly close when it happened.

By four o'clock, all was still well. Spur had caught four hours of sleep and felt refreshed. Abby was slowly going crazy. She went without her shirt most of the time, and soon Spur got used to it. Twice he played with her breasts and she was ready to have sex again, but he told her it was too risky. She reluctantly agreed.

Well before dark, they had packed up their blankets and food sack and were ready to ride at any time they needed to.

"Got to be tonight, if the Bar-B is the rustler," Spur said. "I don't see how they can't be the villain in this little drama with all of the rebranded cattle we found in that one small section of their open range."

The dinner bell at the Bar-B ranch rang early that Tuesday. Spur checked his watch. Five P.M. It was early for chow on most ranches. The men ate, then a dozen went to the corral and pulled out horses and groomed them, watered them and then threw on saddles.

"Tonight's the night," Spur said.

By dusk the 12 riders were moving. They left the ranch and rode past the small creek only 50 yards from where Spur and Abby held their mounts's muzzles closed.

Spur saw their direction, mostly east but a little north toward the Bar L, the Logan spread next door.

When it was completely dark, Spur and Abby came out of the brush and followed the riders. They were easy to spot in the moonlight, but Spur could have followed them by the noise they made. They talked and joked. One sang a soft cowboy herding song. The noise-level continued for three miles, then someone gave a command and the chatter stopped.

"Must be on the other ranch property by now and looking for stock," Spur said.

The full moon had come out again, and now they could see the shapes ahead of them. It wasn't a roundup exactly, more like a sweep. The twelve riders spread into a long line with maybe ten yards between them, and they swept all the animals in front of them. When they had enough, the men on the ends turned the critters toward the center until they had a gathered herd.

Then the riders strung out the animals into a trail-drive line, two or three wide, maybe 50 feet long. Then they cut them off in batches of ten and drove them in various directions.

Spur and Abby watched from well back in the gloom in a small gully that left only their heads showing. They followed the last bunch of cattle, 12, Spur decided. They went due west toward the Bar-B with no circling, no back-tracking, straight as a razor for the home range.

Spur saw the fire well before they got there. Six fires actually, each one with branding irons in it. The branding on the other critters had started well before the last group arrived. Three minutes after they hit the area near the fires, the branding on the last twelve was finished and the animals were driven forward, then due north to put them deep into the Bar-B outer range.

Spur and Abby followed the last batch a ways, then they decided they'd seen enough and turned and headed back to town.

They came over a small rise, and 20 feet ahead of them they saw ten riders with drawn rifles. In the moonlight there was no place to go.

"Nice and easy, there, you two," a commanding voice said from the line. "Hands up real high and nobody gets shot dead. You mixed a little too far into matters not your concern."

Cowboys came in from the side and took the rifle and both their handguns.

"Now, we'll ride. I'm sure the boss will be right pleased to find out who you are."

Quite suddenly the moonlight vanished. Someone took the reins of both horses and led them forward. With the missing moonlight came a quick wind and the first spatters of rain. Lightning daggered through the sky, one jagged fork hitting the earth so closely they could smell sulphur.

The rain came down in gushing torrents, soaking them to the skin at once. Some of the cowboys swore. Spur watched the man holding his horses's reins six feet ahead. The man looked back once, then held the reins lightly as he tried to untie a poncho on his saddle.

Spur kicked the gelding in the flanks and he

323

spurted ahead. Spur grabbed the bridle and turned the animal away from his captor. Abby was on the other side. The mount dug in his hind feet and bolted away at right angles to the other horses, jerking his reins out of the cowboy's hand. The man screeched in protest, drew his six-gun and fired blindly into the storm.

The cascading rain blotted out everything ten feet away. All at once Spur was away from the others, groping for the reins. Then he had them and he rode away at the same angle for what he figured was ten minutes, then let the big gelding slow to a walk and blow.

The sudden thunderstorm would be over and gone in ten more minutes. He'd seen these prairie and mountain storms hit and vanish before. He had to be far enough away to stay free, yet close enough to be sure these men were going back to the ranch headquarters.

Spur stopped his mount, curled his good left leg around the animal, and waited out the rain. There was no place to escape it, so he sat there with the gelding's rump to the wind and waited.

Five minutes later the rain stopped as quickly as it had come. Now he could see it flashing over to the east where the prevailing winds pushed it.

He looked around, but could see no one. The moon was not yet out, and a flittering of dark clouds still whispered overhead. He took his directions from the north star and moved at a walk toward the west and the Bar-B ranch buildings.

Wilderness Wanton

He heard them long before he saw them. The dozen cowboys, and a wet and bedraggled Abby, he assumed, were riding at a walk to the east and slightly to the south, evidently aiming at the ranch house. Spur followed them by sound. A half hour later the last clouds whipped away from the moon, and now and again he caught glimpses of the party as it rode forward.

Spur put his big wet gelding into a trot and made up half a mile on the group, then eased down to a walk. Even if someone looked back they would never see him, one rider in the blackness. The dozen ahead were easy to spot, but he couldn't be sure if Abby was one of them or not. He should be able to tell once they reached the ranch.

Spur twisted to ease his right leg. Curiously he hadn't thought of it since they had spotted the branding. His leg must be feeling better, or somehow he had blocked out the pain. He grinned and picked up the pace a little. He didn't want to miss the division of riders once they hit the ranch yard. If Abby was with them, she'd be taken to the ranch house.

Spur rode up through the mists and darkness to a spot where he could see the ranch house, just a minute before the others galloped into the ranch yard. The men turned their horses into the corral and vanished into the bunkhouse. Two men led a third, smaller person up to the kitchen door of the ranch house and went inside. Lights glowed from within.

So, they still had Abby. He had to get her back. She was a witness to a felony, a hanging felony at that. In that house, her life might not be worth a worn out confederate ten-dollar bill.

Spur watched the house. He saw no new lights bloom on this side of the structure. He rode around in the darkness until he could see the front of the house and the far windows facing away from the ranch yard.

Five minutes later, a light glowed in one of the ground-floor windows. It stayed on. A hand pulled down a shade on the window. No new lights showed in the two story ranch house. Abby must be in that lighted room, or they soon would put her in there.

Spur kicked his mount into action and circled the ranch yard in the darkness. When he was behind the barns away from the house, he paused. Yes, that might work. He dismounted and tied the gelding, then moved up slowly toward the smaller barn. His leg hurt a little but seemed better now. Maybe it was the adrenalin pumped into his system. He watched for guards but found none. At the back of the small barn, he listened for animals inside. He couldn't hear any.

One small door opened to the rear. It was not locked. He eased inside and tried to get his eyes accustomed to the blackness. It was darker than anything he could remember. He felt around. Directly in front of him he ran into cut hay. It had dried and been hauled inside. He felt to the side and found more hay.

Spur took a chance and struck a match on the wooden floor. The match flared and he saw at once that the barn was filled with hay all the way to the rafters. He was in a small area that had been emptied.

Spur lit a second match from the first, bent and ignited the dry hay on fire in four spots. Then he ran for the door, walked back to his horse and rode around the buildings in the darkness. He waited on the far side of the house, where he could see both the lit window and the small barn.

Inside the kitchen, Penley Northcliff put down his cup of coffee and stood as the two riders pushed Abby into the room.

"Well, well, well. What did you boys catch out on your little midnight ride?"

"A snooper, Mr. Northcliff," the taller of the two men said. "Caught her watching us doing some late-night branding out on our north range."

"A woman alone?"

"Well, no. She was with some guy, big one, over six feet I'd say."

"Where is he? Did he have an accident on the way here?"

"No sir, he didn't."

"Then bring him in. I want to meet this snooper you caught."

"Can't, Mr. Northcliff. He got away."

Northcliff had been sipping his coffee again. Now he banged the cup down so hard on the wooden table that the fluid spilled out.

"Escaped? He saw you driving the cattle, he saw you branding them, and you let him escape? You know all twelve of you could have just put your necks in a noose, don't you?"

"We had this little thunderstorm move across us. It hit here too. Raining so damn hard we couldn't see each other. He spurred his horse away and we couldn't find him."

"All right, Miss Abigail. Who was your fellow spy tonight?"

"I don't know."

"You know all right, and you'll tell me. I know how to make sweet little ladies like you beg for mercy. Take her into the second bedroom down on the left and tie her hands to the bedstead and put a gag in her mouth. If she doesn't want to talk now, I'll do a few persuasions on her I know about. Don't just stand there, move her."

Northcliff followed them down the hallway, watched them tie her to the bed, then told them to get out. He walked up to the bed and smiled.

"Well, well, well, Abby. Good to see you again. My, you're looking pretty tonight, even though you're not all dried out yet from the rain. We should get these wet clothes off you so you can get dry and warm."

He reached down and fondled her breast. Abby tried to kick him but missed.

"No, no, no," Northcliff said, sitting on the bed beside her, opening the buttons on the shirt, reaching underneath it until his hand closed over one of her breasts.

"Yes, you're breasts are still damp and cold. I know how to get them warmed up. I have just the ticket for you. Always thought you looked too good to be true. By the time I've given you three or four proper English pokings, you'll warm up nicely. Of course we'll have to get rid of those ridiculous pants. Women shouldn't wear pants, you must know that."

He put his hand over her crotch and tried to push her legs apart, but she kept her ankles crossed tightly.

"Well, we'll just have to work on the top first." He unbuttoned the rest of her shirt and spread back the fabric. "Nice. It always amazes me how much a woman's breasts flatten out when she lays on her back. No matter. I'll have you on your hands and knees begging for it one more time before the night is over. We're just starting to get things moving along.

"If I take the gag out will you promise not to scream? I have my reputation to maintain with my men. Will you promise?"

Heavy footsteps came down the hall. Someone burst in the door.

"Fire, Mr. Northcliff! The small barn is on fire, burning like an inferno in July!"

Northcliff scowled, stood and raced out the door behind the messenger.

Spur had seen the flames shoot out a side window on the barn. He waited for the alarm.

Three minutes later a cowboy heading for the outhouse saw the fire and gave the alarm, then fired his six-gun five times in the air. Men poured out of the bunkhouse and the main house. Spur left his horse and ran to the one lighted window on the backside of the ranch house. Curiously his leg didn't hurt at all now.

He could see under the window blind. Abby

lay on the bed, her hands tied to the top of the bedstead, her shirt unbuttoned and pushed to both sides, showing her breasts. He tried the window. Not locked. Quickly he lifted the double hung window up two feet, then crawled through the opening head first and rolled on the floor.

Abby's eyes went wide when she saw the window go up, but she smiled through the gag when she saw Spur. He cut her bindings, untied the gag, and held his finger over his mouth as he led her to the window.

He went out first, his six-gun in hand. No one was there. He figured everyone was fighting the fire. He motioned Abby out and they ran for the horse, Spur limping only slightly. They talked as they moved.

"I'm so happy to see you," Abby blurted.

"Who was at the house, inside?"

"The Englishman, Northcliff."

"He ordered you tied up and held?"

"Yes, he's the boss. He got mad as hell when they said a man got away. They didn't know who you were. They tried to describe you, but it didn't help much. I wouldn't tell them who you were."

"Can you identify any of the men on the rustling job?"

"Sure, two of them positively. I've seen them dozens of times in my saloon."

"Good, a little bit of evidence that will stand up in court, at last."

They rode double, trotting the big strong horse for two miles, then easing off to a walk. It took them another hour and a half to get into South

Junction. By then the north star clock showed that it was after three in the morning.

They went to her house and collapsed on the bed, neither one of them taking off any clothes. They slept.

Chapter Twenty-One

Penley Northcliff waited until no one was watching, then he slipped in the building's back door and went directly to the office he knew well. The man he came to see sat at his desk, his face in shadows, his hands toying with a half-dozen gold double eagle coins that he shuffled back and forth.

Northcliff sat down in the chair next to the desk and wiped sweat off his forehead. He took out a cigar, bit the end off it, then put it back in his pocket unlit. He took a deep breath and stared hard at the shadowed face.

"Yes, you were right. It is hard and it's getting harder. I don't know if I can stand it another week, let alone until spring."

The man behind the desk cleared his throat

and the voice came out with a touch of anger and disdain.

"Northcliff, you're a fraud, a goddamn weak fraud at that. I never should have hired you, just kicked your ass out of the county and taken over the ranch. We've got an agreement, and a contract. You'll do damn well what I tell you to, or you'll be on the stage in leg irons headed for Chicago and a long stay in a good old American prison. Take your choice."

Northcliff set his jaw and scowled at the man behind the desk. "Jail might be better than getting hung for rustling. Last night two people watched us raid the Bar-L and do some rebranding out on our north range. We caught them, but one got away, and then the other one escaped."

"Fools! Damned fools! Who were they?"

"Abby Buchanan, she runs the saloon. Also a man I didn't get to see. From the description he's my detective, Spur McCoy."

A silence stretched out in the room. Then it snapped with a barrage. "You idiot! I told you not to hire a range detective who was too smart. I said get a dumb one we can make a show of using and get suspicion off our backs. Now what the hell have you done? You gonna spoil the whole set-up? I should shoot you right here and claim you were a bank robber."

"He'd still have to prove that any rustling took place. Hard thing to prove if he can't identify any of the riders who took part in the rustling. I fired all twelve of the men and sent them down the road. They each got a month's pay with the agreement that they get out of the county before sundown. They all took off like a shot when I told them they could be hung for rustling."

The man behind the desk nodded. "At least you did one thing right. Now we have to sit tight and hope he doesn't have any hard evidence so he can't make any kind of a move against you."

The man behind the desk took out a ledger and opened it. "Look at this balance sheet. I was just going over your financial situation. It is far from good, Northcliff, you must know that. As of the end of this month I own the Bar-B one hundred percent. You failed to meet any of your loan payments. I own the land, the cattle, the buildings, every damn thing that's out there.

"I should send you packing right now. Only it wouldn't look good. We'll move the sell-off up to fall. Have a roundup just before snow flies. Get the critters to the rail stock pens and get a good price. Will be a little bit more of a risk doing it now rather than waiting until spring, but that can't be helped. You've fucked up the whole scheme of things. We've got to move fast. Now, you get out of town. Get back to my ranch and. . . . No, first go to the saloons and pick up six more hands. Tell them a special job, then sign them on for the season. You'll need them for normal ranch work. Now get the hell out of my sight. I've got to figure out what else to do to salvage some of this damn sticky situation you've mired us in."

334

Wilderness Wanton

* * *

Two blocks down the street and half a block off Main in Abby's house, Spur McCoy and Abby slept until ten o'clock. They got up and had breakfast, then Abby insisted on a bath. Spur helped. He washed her back and her front and then he shaved and said he needed some clean clothes. He went to the hotel and brought back his traveling bag and dressed in fresh range clothes—jeans, blue shirt, a rawhide vest and his six-gun and belt.

"I need to have a long talk with the sheriff."

Abby lounged in the still hot water, soaped her breasts and sat up straight to show them off better. "See anything you like?"

"See lots of things I like, but right now I have to go see the sheriff. You like making love, don't you?"

Abby smiled, crooked her finger at him. "Like it, I love it. Right now, right here if you want to. Twice a day seems about right to me. What do you think?"

"I think you'd kill off a good man in six months." He grinned. "But it would be a great way to go out. Now, rest your sweet tits. I'll be back soon as I can."

"Gonna charge Northcliff with the rustling?"

"Not sure. Since you escaped, I'd bet a double eagle that those rustlers you saw are on their horses right now riding out of the state so fast they'll leave a dozen whirlwinds behind them. Without them, we don't have a case."

"Damn."

"True. See you later."

Spur was halfway to the sheriff's office when he felt something jab him in the back.

"Spur McCoy, that's a .45 six-gun in your back. If you want to live more than about two minutes, you turn into that alley and walk calm like, because my trigger finger is itching and this heavy pistol is about ready to make my hand twist and hurt and I might just fire it accidentally."

Spur turned his head and saw a woman he didn't recognize. "Miss, you must have the wrong man. I don't even know you."

"That's the way we planned it. Straight ahead into the alley. You killed my lover, then you ran my husband out of town and brought him back shot full of holes and facing a hangman's noose."

They were 30 feet into the narrow alley. No one else was there. He felt the pressure ease on his back, and then the weapon pulled away. He spun around, but the woman was six feet away from him, with both hands holding the big .45 revolver pointing directly at his chest.

"So, you were with the Fancy Dan gang. You in on the bank robbery, too?"

"No. They wouldn't let me. I just want to shoot you down and watch you die. Then I'll be able to get on with my life. Folke doesn't have much chance of getting out of the county alive, so I've got to go. First, I want to kill you."

"Miss. . . ."

"My name is Dianna, Dianna Guthrie, if it matters. Folke Guthrie, who you put in jail, is my lawful husband. Now that you know that, goodbye, Mr. McCoy."

She fired.

Dianna wasn't used to the heavy pull on the revolver's trigger. She might never have fired a handgun before. She tugged at the trigger, and the effort threw the aim off. The round hit two feet to Spur's left. He started to rush her, but she thumbed the hammer back and brought the gun up again.

Spur stopped. "Look, Dianna. You weren't involved in the bank robbery, technically. We can ignore that. I won't even report your assault with a deadly weapon against me, and attempted murder. You can walk away from here free and clear. You're a beautiful woman. You'll find another man soon. Why get yourself thrown in jail for something you can't stop? Folke probably will hang, I admit that. But is giving up your life the best way to handle the problem? Being dead isn't any fun, and if you shoot me, somebody is going to track you down and shoot that beautiful body full of holes. Just think, you'll never make love again if you shoot me. You have marvelous breasts. I bet you love to make love, don't you?"

She nodded. "It was so good with J.R. He was a master. The way he played me, it was like I was his violin. We were going to go away after the bank job. Just J.R. and me. Folke would be mad but he would never find us. I loved J.R. so much I just had to be with him. Oh, God, I wish he was here now, caressing me. Petting my titties, making me feel just ever so warm and hot and wanting him." She began to rub her breasts.

"I bet J.R. was a thoughtful lover, you know, warming you up slowly until you were ready. Not rushing things. Undressing you gently, treating you like a lady."

"Uh huh, he did. He was gentle . . . yeah, like a lady. Damn, I wish he was here. The things I'd do to him and he'd do to me. I almost can't stand it."

"I'm here. Tell me what to do." He took a step toward her. She lowered the gun. He stepped closer until he could reach out and touch her breasts. "Beautiful, you have amazing breasts. So firm and tipped up, so youthful."

The gun was at her side. He caressed her breasts. She reached up and undid the buttons on her blouse and flared the sides back to show there was nothing underneath.

"Oh, yes!" she said, her eyes closed now, her head thrown back.

"Beautiful, just marvelous breasts," Spur said, caressing the warm flesh. "So warm, so tingling."

She shrugged and slid the blouse off her shoulders and let it fall to the alley.

"Oh, yes. J.R. Just that way. Fine, so fine, J.R."

Spur reached down with one hand to grab the revolver. She felt him and jumped back, brought both hands to the weapon and fired again. This time the round came closer. He charged her. She turned and ran back up the alley. Spur didn't want to get too close, she still had three rounds. She just might miss far enough to hit him.

He remembered she was bare to the waist. Yes,

chase her out to the street. She looked behind and he pulled out his Colt. He fired in the air and she shivered, watched him a minute, then ran on to the boardwalk. There she stopped next to a store front and looked behind.

A cowboy walking by stopped when he saw her. "Well, lookee here. What we got, a soiled dove turned out of her bunkhouse?"

Dianna looked in the alley behind her, then at the cowboy.

"What in the world are you talking about?" Then she glanced down at her chest and her eyes went wide and she covered her breasts with her folded arms. The six-gun dangled from her right hand.

Four more men stopped to stare at her. Two women came up and shook their heads and walked on by. Dianna scowled. She lifted the six-gun and waved it at them, all the time keeping her breasts covered with her arms.

"You all get out of here. I might shoot. Shoo. Go away."

The men laughed. By then a dozen men and women jammed the boardwalk in a semi-circle around her.

"Hear Noona's got an opening down at her fancy house. That where you going or where you from?" It came from one of the cowboys.

Spur edged into the group. She turned away from him and waved the revolver at a man on the other side. Spur burst through the ring of men and grabbed the six-gun, spun her around and marched her into the hardware store just behind them. The owner's wife saw the situation, grabbed a jacket from a chair, and hurried down the store and wrapped it around Dianna.

"Hold her here while I go get her blouse," Spur said. The store woman agreed. Spur hurried out of the store, waved the curious away, and ran down the alley. Two minutes later he was back with the white blouse. The store woman told Spur to turn around. She got Dianna into the blouse and buttoned up.

"Now, young lady," Spur said. "We've got some talking to do. We can do it at the sheriff's office if you want to, or right here."

She glared at him a minute, then sagged against the woman. She nodded. "Yes, here. Is there anything I can do to help Folke?"

Spur told the woman store owner who Dianna was and what her husband did.

"Honey, you ain't got a prayer. Your man's gonna hang sure as God made little white goats. Best you can do is stand by him if'n you love him. Otherwise, get moving and get a new life somewhere."

Spur watched her. She was maybe 25, pretty and with a curvaceous body. She'd have a new man in a month.

"You have any money?" Spur asked.

"Yes, J.R. gave me some when we packed. Quite a lot."

"My advice is to take it and catch the next stage south and go to Denver or St. Louis. Start a new life."

She nodded. "I ain't got a hotel room." She looked at the woman. "Could I change here, into some stage kind of clothes?" The woman nodded.

"You have a horse ready to ride?"

She said she did.

"Let's go get it. Then you be on that four o'clock stage. I'll keep this shooting iron, if you don't mind."

She didn't object.

Ten minutes later, Spur left Dianna with the store owner, who said her name was Maud. He talked to the sheriff and both agreed about what he'd done with the girl. Then they got to the rustling. They could ride out to the Bar-B with Abby to identify the rustlers, but both figured the men had been sent down the trail last night or first thing this morning.

"Close, but no winning hand," Sheriff Halverson said. "We'll just have to look for a new lead."

"We were so close," Spur said. He went back to Abby's place, and they had a late dinner. Just as they finished, Rusty knocked on the door.

"Heard you been busy, especially down on the boardwalk by the hardware store," Rusty said with a grin.

Spur told Abby about it. She lifted an eyebrow. "I'll talk to you about this later."

"You see anything out at the Box C?" Spur asked Rusty.

"Not much. I spent two or three nights out there, maybe four. I don't remember. All quiet like a Baptist funeral."

Spur shrugged. "I don't know what else we can do. Wait for Northcliff to make a mistake.

I want you to have a good supper and sleep in a bed for a change. We'll talk tomorrow about noon."

Rusty waved and left.

Abby stood there with her fists on her hips, her eyes brimming with fire.

"Now, tell me about this bare-breasted beauty you've been fooling around with on Main street."

Spur laughed. He went into a little more detail about how her blouse came off, and Abby nodded.

"I understand her, poor girl. Lost two men in an hour. Terrible. Then you seduce her in the alley. You are bad, Spur McCoy." Her scowl turned into a grin. "Were her tits as good as mine?"

"Not by half," Spur said, bending and kissing each throbbing orb.

Abby relaxed. "Good. Now I've made arrangements with my barkeep to run the saloon for a month. When this is over I'm going to Denver with you."

"We'll talk about it when this rustling situation is wrapped up."

"Talk, but I'm going."

"We'll talk."

She kissed him. Spur grinned.

"Now I need to go talk to the sheriff again. We can't just sit and wait. We've got to come up with some ideas to force the issue. Maybe we can call for an inspection of all range cattle to find the rustlers. Something like that. We've got to make a move. I'll be back."

Abby caught his hand. "Walk me down to the

342

saloon. I should put in an appearance once in a while."

Spur left Abby at the First Class Saloon and crossed the street to go to the sheriff's office. He passed the alley next to the jewelry store when a shot blasted into the afternoon stillness.

Spur felt a round knock his hat off, and he jolted to the side of the alley. He drew his six-gun and fired twice at a shadow deep in the dimness. No second shot came. He could hear footsteps running away. Spur leaped up and chased the bushwhacker, his Colt at the ready.

He pounded down the alley. When the shadow ahead slanted into the sunshine to go around the last building into the street, Spur fired. The slug jolted into the runner's leg, spinning him sideways before he lunged around the corner.

Spur came up to the last building quietly and looked around the corner. The man lay on the ground 20 feet away, trying to stem a flow of blood from his right leg. One hand held the six-gun.

"Drop it or you're a dead man," Spur bellowed. The gunner fired at the sound, nicking the wood over Spur's head. The government agent fired once. His round spun into the bushwhacker's shoulder, slamming him backward to the ground. The revolver in his right hand jolted away from his grasping fingers.

Spur stood and walked around the corner, his cocked Colt covering the bleeding man in the dust.

A half hour later, Doc Partlow bandaged up

the shooter in the second jail cell. He eyed Spur and grinned.

"With you around, McCoy, my work treating gunshots has jumped by a thousand percent. Just hope you stay around town for a while."

"He won't," Sheriff Halverson said, ushering the sawbones out the door. "He's got more important things to do than provide you with shot-up outlaws to treat."

When the doctor left, Spur and the sheriff continued to question the prisoner. He sat on the wooden bunk that was anchored to the wall with chains.

"You said your name was Marcello, Raymond Marcello?"

The prisoner nodded.

"Who hired you to gun me down?" Spur asked.

"Nobody. I knew you from before. You shot me once in Kansas, but I got away."

"Then you just happened to see me here and decided to get even?" Spur asked.

"Hell yes."

"Hell no," Sheriff Halverson said. "How well do you know Stewart Rawlins?"

"Who?"

"Stewart Rawlins, the president and owner of our local bank."

"Never met the gent."

Sheriff Halverson slapped his thigh in frustration. "Tell you what, Marcello. Right now you're going to stand trial on attempted murder. If convicted you'll get seven to ten years in the territorial prison. It's not a friendly place up there. I'll get your charge reduced to assault and battery, if you'll tell us who hired you and testify in court against that man."

Marcello moved his right leg and groaned in sudden pain. "If you try me and convict me on assault and battery, will I get any jail time?"

Sheriff Halverson nodded. "Probably six months in county jail here and a one hundred dollar fine, or 50 more days jail time if you can't pay."

Marcello frowned, evidently figuring in his head. "Another two months in jail. Hell, sounds better than ten years. I'll have to think it over. Tell you tomorrow."

Spur started to say something, but stopped. The sheriff had a good strategy going. He'd have to try it on other stubborn prisoners. Give them a reduced sentence for cooperating. He'd remember that.

Back in the sheriff's office he looked at Spur. "You all right?"

"Sure, I always feel better after I shoot somebody who's trying to kill me."

"Happened before?"

"Lots of times, twice this week in this lovely little town."

"My guess is this is the last time. You think Rawlins put him up to it?"

Spur nodded. "Absolutely. He's been so disgraced and put down lately and he blames it all on me. Even though we saved his damn bank from getting robbed."

Sheriff Halverson sat back and chuckled.

"Rawlins might as well sell his bank and move out. He'll never live down shitting his pants right there on the boardwalk in front of everyone and just outside his own bank."

"Agreed. Right now I'm sorry we didn't let the Guthries go ahead and rob him. Except for the people in town it would have hurt."

"Now, what about the rustling? We can't just wait for them. That's why you came back, isn't it?"

"Yes. I've been thinking about hiding a posse at both the Box C and the Bar-B. Say we had ten men at each spot and waited for them to go rustling, followed them. When we can testify they were rustling, we attack them with rifles in the act of rustling. We could drop a few, identify the rest, arrest and jail them and have an air-tight case."

"Sounds damn near perfect, only you go to the county fathers and tell them you need $40 a day for those 20 posse members, and you need it for six days. Not a chance in hell you could get the money."

"You can't work with volunteers?"

"Not for something like this. I'd get maybe two men, and those would be worthless no-goods who wouldn't have a rifle and couldn't shoot it if we gave them one."

"Damn."

Some noise in the outer office caught Spur's attention. Somebody shouting. He was halfway to the door when a cowboy burst into the room. He was no more than twenty years old, dusty from a ride, wearing well used range clothes and a hat that had watered more than one thirsty horse.

"Sheriff, you want the rustlers? I can give you the rustlers. Is there a reward? I know who is going to ride out just before dark to rustle cattle and I know exactly where they are going."

Chapter Twenty-Two

Spur eyed the cowboy for a moment. He looked like the real thing.

"What spread do you work for?" Sheriff Halverson asked.

"Used to work for the Box C. Old man Cuthright fired me two hours ago. Me and Jenny, his sixteen-year-old daughter, was kissing behind the barn. She liked it but he didn't. Fired me on the spot. He forgot I know what he's gonna do tonight."

"You telling us that the Box C riders will rustle cattle tonight?"

"Exactly what I'm telling you. I just want to be along to help corral them, especially that old man Cuthright."

"Where will they hit?" Spur asked.

"The Triangle Ranch. Quail owns it. It's the

other side of the Circle L over to the east of the Box C."

"How many men will be doing the rustling?"

"They usually take twelve."

"You know for a fact that riders from the Box C spread have rustled cattle?"

"Yes, sir, sheriff. Especially old Cuthright. He rides along."

"They'll be going just before dark?" Spur asked.

"Right. Count on riding out about six miles and then turning across all the Box C land and hit the boundary between the Box C and the Circle L just at dark. Ride across ten miles of the Circle L and hit the Triangle for a hundred and fifty head or so."

"Can you show us where they'll be when they start rounding up the cattle?" Spur asked.

"Damn right. We best get moving if'n we want to get there in time to catch them red-handed."

Spur checked his watch. "It's a little after three o'clock. It'll take us two hours to ride to the Circle L. We'll notify them what we're doing, then ride through their land and wait for the rustlers to come across and follow them."

"Sounds good to me," Sheriff Halverson said. "I'll round up a posse. We need at least ten more good men. I can hire them at $2 a day."

"I'll go get Rusty. He'll want to be in on this. Let's meet at the livery so we don't let the whole town know what we're doing."

"Meet you at the livery in a half hour," Sheriff Halverson said. "Should be time to get everyone there. Dub Crawford, you can get a fresh horse

down there for the return ride. You best get
yourself something to eat if you want to. Just
don't be late."

The young rider laughed. "Hey, I'd give three
months pay to see the look on old man
Cuthright's face when we close in on him."

They rode out at a quarter to four. Thirteen
men, all with rifles, pistols and ropes. They
moved south out of town, then turned east
at an easy canter for the Circle L ranch, the
Lathrup spread.

A mile out of town, they let the horses walk
for a mile, then lifted them into a canter again.
The canter was a more natural pace for most
quarter horses. They could maintain that speed,
about six miles an hour, for long distances. Spur
knew they didn't want the animals worn out by
the time they sighted the rustlers, so they kept
the pace mostly to a walk.

Spur rode beside Dub Crawford, the cowboy
who had brought the news. The sheriff had
told him that even if he'd done some rustling
with the Box C riders, he would be granted
immunity from all charges, because he was
coming forward to inform the sheriff about
known lawbreakers.

Dub grinned. "Damn glad I can't be pros-
ecuted. Hell, most of the guys out here doing
the rustling are just following orders. I guess
they know the risk they're running, but it's just
a job and they need a job. I sure did. Course I'm
out of work now."

They came to the Circle L outfit a little before
five o'clock. Spur and the sheriff talked with Len

Lathrup and told him what the plan was.

"So that damn Cuthright has been stealing my cattle all along," Lathrup growled. "Might have known it. I want to send along at least six men with rifles to help you. Hell, I want to go along myself. My outfit is about eight miles wide up where I'd guess they'll be crossing. Up there is where most of the Triangle stock is. Take us an hour and a half to get up to that area. There's a patch of brush and timber up there we can wait in and see just where Cuthright and his men come across."

Spur nodded. "We'll have some scouts out on each side to watch and listen for the rustlers. Then we'll send out three or four men to follow them with contact riders in between and our main body moving up. That way we won't make so much noise that we scare them off."

"Sounds like a military operation," Sheriff Halverson said.

"As long as it works," Spur said.

The cook at the Circle L had charged into high gear as soon as he saw the 13 men ride in. He had supper ready for them quickly, and they rode away from the ranch a little after five-thirty. They would be in position slightly before dusk at seven and then wait for the rustlers. Spur talked to each man, warned him about not talking, not making any noise, and especially not smoking.

"The glow of a cigarette can be seen for a quarter of a mile at night," Spur told them. "The smoke from one cigarette can be smelled for a mile if the wind is right."

They arrived slightly before seven in the patch

of woods. It was a long finger valley that came down from the foothills. There were no real breaks here, just a few gentle valleys that were grazed. In several spots the timber from the higher slopes had seeded down well into the broad valley.

In these firs and a few hardwoods and some brush, the 20 men sat on the ground and waited. Spur was a quarter of a mile south of the edge of the woods, and Rusty was about that far on south beyond Spur. They would catch the first sound of the dozen oncoming men.

Spur had Dub Crawford along with him. They sat their horses and waited as the darkness closed around them. They were in some brush where a small feeder stream drifted down from the mountain above and couldn't be seen by anyone more than 20 feet away. It was dark now.

"They get four or five miles into the Circle L land by the time it's this dark, then they have only another four miles to where we are."

"What if they cut through a mile below us?" Spur asked.

"They won't. They know where the most cattle are, the most steers especially. That's what they want most. Better for a quick sale. They scouted this area yesterday. They'll come through here near us, or maybe a quarter of a mile below Rusty."

They waited.

The full moon which had helped Spur before was waning, but now it was covered with a thin sheet of clouds that blocked most of the reflected light.

They continued to wait. Spur couldn't tell how much time had passed since darkness had fallen. He didn't want to strike a match to find out what his pocket watch said.

They waited again. The clouds blew away for a moment and Spur could read his watch in the bright moonlight. Almost eight o'clock.

Spur caught the sound of a horse wickering, then another. Now the soft sound of hooves came across the open country. Spur and Dub strained their ears. Both pointed in the same direction. The riders were between them and Rusty. They sat stone still.

The clouds whipped over the moon again and the darkness seemed to close in like the top of a casket. They heard a few words, one low chuckle, than a sharp command and silence. A few minutes later they could hear the group pass them by and continue on to the west. Spur whispered to Dub.

"Walk your mount back to the woods and bring the rest of the men at a fast walk. I'll be on the point and have Rusty between us. Get to where you can see him and string the others out behind. I'm riding to find Rusty."

As if to save him the trouble, Rusty rode straight for them, coming out of the murky night. He pointed west, and he and Spur moved that way, their mounts at a walk. Dub rode for the main party.

They moved a little faster until they could hear the rustlers ahead. Then Rusty lagged behind until he could just barely see Spur, and soon Dub came up behind with the others 30 yards behind him. They rode that way for another hour, then Spur stopped. The men all came together.

"They're rounding up a herd right in front of us," Spur said. "When's the best time to move in and capture them?"

"After they start driving the cattle away from this spot," Rusty said. "Before they split the herd up into tens and twelves. Then we can prove they were rustling. After they break up into small groups, we'll lose most of the rustlers."

It happened that way. They waited half an hour and spread out on both sides of the trail back. When they heard the herd coming with the cowboys on either side, Spur gave the signal with a six-gun shot and the men opened up, each firing one round into the air.

"Rustlers from the Box C ranch," Spur bellowed into the sudden silence after the shots. "You're surrounded by forty rifles. Lift your hands and ride slowly this way, or you'll all be massacred by my riflemen. Give up now or die."

Six of the men rode forward. Six others faded into the night on their horses and were not found.

Four hours later, Spur, Lathrup, the sheriff and the rest of the posse rode into town with the prisoners. Cuthright, the owner of the Box C ranch, wasn't one of those captured.

Spur talked with the prisoners one at a time. He threatened to hang each one, and most broke down and wept and pleaded. He got from them the names of all 12 of the rustlers, and the fact that Cuthright was along. By morning, Spur had an airtight case against the rustlers and some more interesting information.

They had rousted the district attorney out of bed when they got to town after midnight. By morning they had charged all twelve rustlers and Cuthright, and Spur had figured out their strategy.

Sheriff Halverson agreed to the plan and sent riders to all seven of the ranches, telling them they were being ordered by the sheriff to come to a meeting of all the ranchers in the valley. They would meet at one o'clock in the First Class Saloon.

Spur reminded the sheriff to send that special guard out that they had talked about, then he went to the hotel for a five-hour nap.

Spur had on clean clothes when he walked into the First Class Saloon at a quarter to one. Most of the ranchers were there. Northcliff paced the far end of the room, a glass of whiskey in his hand. On his trips past a back table he refilled his glass from a bottle.

Only Cuthright was missing. He slipped in the door promptly at one o'clock. Spur smiled when he saw the rancher wore a six-gun. He wondered if the man could use it. Sheriff Halverson called the meeting to order.

"Wanted you all to come here today so I can tell you that we have solved the problem of the rash of rustling that's been going on now for nearly three months. Our district attorney is here as well in case there is any need for him to level charges. Now, I'd like to turn the session over to Spur McCoy, who has been helping me on this problem."

Spur went to the front of the saloon. Half a dozen drinkers sat at tables around the sides of the room fascinated by what they heard.

"Men, this rustling has been most peculiar. I've chased rustlers for fifteen years and I've never seen anything like this. The cattle were vanishing off ranches, but none were being driven to market. The railroad reported no shipments except the usual small herds from ranches in this area.

"This made me curious. An estimated three-thousand five-hundred head of steers, brood cows and young animals have been rustled. Where did they go?

"At last we figured out where they went. Nowhere. All the rustled cattle are today right here in the valley, mostly in the back ranges. None have been sold. Most of them have been rebranded, and they were to have a spring date with the cattle pens down on the railroad.

"No reason to hide the cattle. Just use a running iron and change the brands that could be changed, and blank out the others and rebrand. By spring nobody would know the difference.

"Right now, we have six of the rustlers in jail. They have talked and talked and talked. Last night we broke up a rustling raid on the Triangle Ranch carried out by twelve riders from the Box C ranch. Included among the twelve outlaws was the so called owner of the Box C, Mr. Cuthright.

"Don't go anywhere, Cuthright. We have a

warrant for your arrest. Just sit still. But surprise, there wasn't just one set of rustlers, there were two in this grand scheme. The other rustling outfit was the Bar-B, belonging to Penley Northcliff. Don't you move either, Northcliff.

"It worked out well. These two ranches rustled cattle near their own boundaries, drove them into the home range, either the Box C or the Bar-B, rebranded them, and mixed them in with the rest of that ranch's herd. What could be simpler?

"Next week, we'll have a county-wide roundup, gather the stock in the Bar-B and the Box C, and cut out every animal that has a fresh brand on it. Not a tough job."

"You can't do that," Northcliff shouted. "You don't have the authority."

"Oh, but I do, gentlemen. I'm not really a range detective. I'm a member of the United States Secret Service sent here by the government to iron out this situation. I have jurisdiction and authority and the cooperation of the county law officers. We'll want a sworn statement from each of the innocent ranchers in the valley testifying to the best of his knowledge the number and type of cattle he has had rustled. The rustling reports by the Box C and the Bar-B were fabricated to help throw off suspicion.

"After cutting out the fresh brands, the cattle will be distributed as nearly as possible to the spreads that lost them. It won't be one hundred percent right, but we'll get them back as close as possible to the same number of steers, yearlings, brood cows, and so on."

Spur motioned to Rusty, who went to the back door of the saloon and brought in a man. He had his head down and shuffled along in a foul mood.

"Ranchers, I'd like to present the power and brains and money behind all this rustling scheme. He's Stewart Rawlins, your friendly local banker. Rawlins foreclosed on the Box C almost a year ago, and has been running it himself with Cuthright as his manager ever since. The Bar-B fell to a similar fate, and has only recently been fully foreclosed on by the bank. Rawlins came up with the plan of home-ranging the stolen cattle and then forced his two managers to carry out the plan."

Rawlins jumped up, a derringer in his hand. He held it against the head of one of the drinkers at a table near him.

"Enough of this. Nobody draw or this man dies. You hear me? I've got nothing to lose. You try for me and he's a dead man." Rawlins edged toward the back door, holding the cowboy in front of him and the two-shot derringer against his skull. As he pushed open the back door, two men stepped inside and nodded at Rawlins. Both carried shotguns.

"Anybody move in here for ten minutes, these men will shoot you dead. Be smart and stay right where you are." Rawlins pushed the cowboy shield to the floor and darted out the back door into the alley.

When the ten minutes were up, the two shotgunners backed out the rear door and vanished into the alley. Spur went out the front door to where he had tied his gelding that noon. The sheriff and two deputies had collared Northcliff and Cuthright and led them off to jail.

Spur checked the rifle in the boot and his loaded .45. He walked his big gelding down to the first cross-street and rode down to the alley that went behind the First Class Saloon. Across the street, Rusty came up from where he leaned against the wall of the hardware store.

"He's riding a bay mare and headed out Third Street there, going due east out into the prairie. Want some help?"

Spur shook his head. "Nope. Shouldn't be much of a job. He'll probably run the horse to death and stand there wondering what happened."

After half a block, Spur picked up the hoofprints. The animal was galloping. The rear shoes threw up a shower of dust from the back and left deeper prints on the front.

Third Street was only two blocks long, at right angles to the river road. At that point it ran into the wild country that was mostly gently rolling high plateau, angling down gradually to the east a hundred miles to the start of the Great Plains. Out in the open country, the tracks were easier to follow. They gradually turned to the southeast, and then south.

By this time Spur was three miles from town. The banker's capture by Rusty had been his first clue that the jailed cowboys had told the whole story of the rustling, including his part in it. He had had no chance to plan an escape. Now where was he going?

It was by then about three o'clock. The banker might figure he could stop the southbound stage and buy a ticket to ride. Spur picked up the pace a little, and by the time he crossed the South River road, it was nearing four o'clock. The stage would be along in a half hour.

The stage road shadowed the beginnings of the Mighty Missouri, and here and there the track ran into patches of woodlands near the river. It was toward one of these that Spur saw the tracks aiming.

Spur stopped 50 yards out and sent three rifle shots into the patch of woods. He waited but there was no immediate response. A moment later a rifle snarled from the woods and Spur's gelding leaped forward, screaming in pain. Spur controlled the animal, then rode hard for the edge of the woods 20 yards away. A second rifle shot came but missed him and the horse.

Inside the woods, Spur began another slow move forward. Then he changed his mind and ran ahead, making as much noise as he could. He had the Spencer rifle in his left hand and the six-gun in his right.

When he figured he was 20 yards from the spot where the banker had fired, he stopped. Now he began his slow move forward without a sound. He hoped he could panic the banker and make him show himself.

Five minutes later, Spur could see part of the area where he figured Rawlins must be. At first he spotted nothing, then something moved and he saw a horse munching on small greenery.

Spur found a fist-sized rock in the mulch at his feet and threw it high so it would come down in the brush ten yards ahead. When it landed, it made a clatter through the leaves and trees and branches.

The rifle snarled again, and this time Spur saw the small puff of white smoke from the black powder. Spur aimed slightly to the left of the smoke and a foot off the ground and fired the rifle. A scream billowed out before the sound of the shot had faded.

"Damnation! You shot me, you bastard. You shot me!"

"What did you expect? A slap on the wrist for rusting thirty-five hundred head of cattle?"

"McCoy?"

"Yeah."

"Don't let them hang me. I couldn't stand that."

"The judge and a jury of your peers will decide that."

"Everyone in town hates me. I couldn't get a fair trial here."

"That'll be up to the judge. Throw out the rifle and your hideout and any other weapons you have. Where are you hit?"

"My right arm. Bleeding like a stuck sow."

"Throw out the weapons. Then we'll get you patched up." Spur held his breath. A moment later he saw a rifle tossed away from the brush, then a six-gun and the small derringer.

Two hours later, Spur rode into town with Stewart Rawlins on the horse he had stolen

from the alley. The five innocent ranch owners
had been meeting with the sheriff to plan the
roundup on the other two ranches. Each had
reported his losses to the sheriff when they
happened, and now they totaled up the number
of steers and brood cows and heifers lost. Sheriff
Halverson came out with a big smile.

"I best call Doc Partlow again. Let's hope this
is the last time we'll need him in the jail for a
while."

Spur asked the sheriff if his jail was full, and
the lawman said he figured this would bring him
as full as he could get. He shook Spur's hand and
hurried away with the prisoner.

Spur took the gelding back to the livery, then
used some ointment on the bullet wound on the
animal's rump. It was only a crease and would
heal in a few days.

When he was on his way to the First Class
Saloon, the door to the newspaper office opened
and Opal came out. She motioned to him. Spur
went over and stopped beside her.

"Yes, Miss Davis? Is your first edition ready
to go to press?"

She smiled. "Not quite, Mr. McCoy. Could
you come into the office? I want to show you
something."

He stared at her and she blushed.

"No, no. Not what I showed you before. Now
be nice. Not that. Come on."

Spur grinned and followed her into the office.
She had a proof sheet of the front page of the
first issue. He looked at the inch-high headline
across the top of the front page.

Federal Lawman Solves Rustling.

"I had a lot of help," said Spur.

"Yes, now don't be so modest. Sheriff Halverson never would have done it without you. Why didn't you tell me you were a Secret Service agent?"

"You didn't ask. Anyway, it worked out better this way. Northcliff never would have let me anywhere near this town if he had known who I really was."

"It makes a fine story. I talked to the sheriff for two hours."

"Good. Now how is the important part of your life coming along?"

"What?" Her brows went up, and the touch of a blush showed at her throat. "Oh, well, better. I . . . I . . . Oh, damn. There is a young man here in town I really like. I hope he likes me. He's the son of the people who run the general store. He says he'll take over the store in two more years. He's twenty-four and a real gentleman."

"Has he kissed you yet?"

"Oh, my, no. He has held my hand, though. And I sat beside him at church on Sunday."

Spur grinned. "Opal, I'd say you have made a good start. My best advice?"

"Oh, yes, please."

"Keep all of your clothes on until you get that wedding ring on your finger. It's best that way."

Her blush rushed up from her chest and stained her neck and cheeks. She covered her face with her hands.

"Oh, my, such talk." She grinned. "I understand. It was just wonderful what you did for me, what you didn't do, when I . . . when I did undress a bit. I thank you again."

"My best wishes." He reached over and kissed her cheek. She caught his face and turned it and kissed his lips lightly.

"The next man I kiss will be my husband to be."

Spur waved and went out the door.

At the First Class Saloon, he found Abby pacing the space in front of the bar. She looked up, her face filled with a frown.

"Heard you were back in town."

"Yep."

"Heard you brought back the ringleader, Rawlins."

"Yep."

"Heard your job here is about over and you'll be going back to Denver soon."

"Yep. You have any paper and pen? I need to write a telegram to my boss in Washington DC."

Spur wrote the short message. *Rustlers and bank robbers here wrapped up. Heading back to Denver in two days.* He signed it Spur McCoy and addressed it to the telegraph office at the nearest town, enclosing a five dollar bill to pay for the message. He and Abby walked the letter to the stage depot. It would be in the driver's pocket on the four o'clock stage.

They changed drivers there and Spur gave the new one a five dollar bill to be sure to take the letter directly to the telegraph office as soon as he hit Helena. He promised. Five dollars was two days pay for him.

Abby insisted they go back to her house. Spur said first he wanted to collect the remains of his belongings at the hotel and pay his bill. He promised to meet her at her place in half an hour.

When he walked in the door at Abby's house, he could smell a cherry pie baking in the oven. It was his favorite kind of pie but he didn't remember saying so.

He pulled a chair up in the kitchen and sat down watching her.

"Getting in practice. I figure in Denver I'll make a cherry pie every three days just to keep you happy."

"Denver?"

"Yes. When you leave, I leave. I'm going to Denver with you. I've never been on a train. Is it true that they have beds on some of the cars?"

"Yes, Pullman cars they call them. They're seats during the day and at night swing down and make into beds."

Abby grinned. "You ever . . . you ever made love in one of them Pullman beds?"

"A time or two."

"Promise me we can?"

"I can't take you back to Denver."

"You're not taking me, I'm going in spite of you. I have some vacation due to me. A holiday. I want to be in Denver so you can show me the wicked big city."

Spur nodded. "No way I can stop you from going to Denver."

Abby grinned. "Soon as the pie is done, we have a date down along the river. I know a spot

365

down there that's private and you can see just
for miles but nobody can see you and I want
to make love in the sunshine. Bet you've done
that, too."

"True," he said. Spur reached up and kissed
her soft lips, just a barely touching kind that
sent lightning sparking between their lips. "How
soon will that damned pie be out of the oven?"
Spur asked.

Later, in the little woodsy glen near the
Missouri headwaters, he watched the pretty
girl beside him. It had been fine and would
be again. He kissed her gently, then wondered
what else was happening in the country? He'd
been out of touch for almost two weeks. What
would his next assignment be?

Abby purred beside him. Yes, he'd show her
around Denver. A month would be about right.
He might be gone on another assignment before
then. It would be interesting.

"Spur McCoy, you stop thinking about your
damned business and pay a little attention
to me."

Spur grinned and lowered his lips toward her
enticing, naked body. "I can do that," he said.